CASTRO'S LAST MOJITO!

BRIAN LLOYD FRENCH

*****

RAI Books

Toronto

WHAT READERS ARE SAYING ABOUT "CASTRO'S LAST MOJITO"

Carsten Stroud, New York Times Best-selling Author of Niceville:

I Loved This Book...This book is not only a powerful read, it's also a perfect shot to the side of the head for all those blissfully unaware folks who go off to Cuba every year for some sun and surf and come back chirping about "how happy and smiley all those Cubans are!" This guy knows Cuba the way Hemingway knew it. Compelling and raw and gutsy.

D. Spilman: *I finished the book in a frenzy - very nice read - the website is even better. What a great way to sustain topical interest. A tight and twisting plot......with the action kind of like a roller coaster ride......peppered with historical references; people, places, events, well lubricated with rum and Cohiba-smoking and that irrepressible vitality that endears Cuba and it's people to our imagination and hearts long after any economic relevance........for me on a par with the lure of Tango and Buenos Aires. Plays nicely with other books I've read about Cuba; notably "Cuba and the Night" and "Havana Nocturne".*

Andrea Whyte: *This is not really my usual type of book but I must say I did enjoy it. It's more actiony and man things than I usually read, but it was a good quick read. I liked the descriptions of places and people in Cuba. I can recommend this.*

El Rajo: *An excellent read. A real time insight into modern day Cuba. Only the canucks go to Cuba for vacation and this author has for sure spent some time there. Good description of the culture, music, food, dance, politics, women, night life and rum. Also a sad commentary on the deterioration of this once beautiful island. A good suspense novel with a super twist at the end.*

Z. Mark: *If you are interested in Cuba and like a good mystery then this book is for you. I read it in one sitting and thoroughly enjoyed it. Mr. French has managed to inject important history lessons without making them burdensome, as well as educating those of us from the US on some interesting points from our friendly neighbor to the North: Canada! (anyone who has attended public school will get the reference!) It is clear the author has a love for Cuba and the Cuban people! The plot is interesting and the story flows....do get this book. A fun read!*

John A. Peterson: *Just a great book for summer reading and anytime, held my interest throughout. I would recommend this book to everyone that has an interest in Cuba Part true and part fiction, A well written book.*

DEDICATIONS

"Mojito" is dedicated to Kate for her eternal love for me and her everlasting beauty and kindness, to Yoani Sanchez for her remarkable bravery and to all Cubans who strive to create a better future for themselves.

ACKNOWLEDGMENTS

The author wishes to thank those who have supported his work on this and other projects:

Drummer Don Gibbons for helping the author understand a little more about Cuban rhythms. Looney for being an early and encouraging reader.

Late Tom Trafford at TRHS and Drs. Bob Cockburn and Roger Ploude at UNB. Bill Marshall of Toronto International Film Festival fame.

Manuel H., "PipoPiano" Perigo, Damian Marrero, Gilberto, Zelde, Ariochi and Lafitta, Silvio Canto, Jr. and my other Cuban friends and the many Cubans whose life experiences added the pimento and realism that I've tried to reveal in Mojito!

BLF
Toronto 2016

www.mojitonovel.com

Viñales Valley

Pinar del Rio

1

MIKE MCCAUL had come to Cancun to kill. He got off his company's Airbus 310 at Cancun airport and cleared what passes for security there. He stopped into his office, told his company's local manager to keep up the good work and got a limo to the company's destination hotel on the Cancun strip.

When McCaul arrived at the hotel he went up to his reserved room without checking in; executive privilege. He put on a pair of thin black leather gloves he had in his back pocket. His key card worked and so did his combination to the safe and he opened it. He took out a Sig Sauer 9 mm automatic, a Ka-Bar Bowie knife, a balaclava and a black Adidas athletic bag. He put his tools in the gym bag.

Also inside the safe were night vision goggles, camo paint tubes, a GPS navigator, an LED light, a car key fob, about four ounces of putty wrapped in plastic, a squeeze bottle of soap and a few other wired gadgets and goodies. McCaul pocketed the light, GPS unit and key fob and put the rest in the bag.

He entered the bathroom, washed his face and looked in the mirror. He'd been told that he looked like Kiefer Sutherland, but Mike had met the actor at a party one time and noticed that the guy was a lot smaller and that his hair was more blond. Plus, McCaul really did what Kiefer only pretended to.

McCaul put all his civilian stuff in his almost empty carry on and went down the elevator to the lobby and out to a dark back corner of the parking lot. There was a black Jeep Wrangler. He pressed the unlock button on the key fob, got in and started it up.

He turned on the GPS unit and clicked the link for saved directions, then on the link for his assignment. The unit was on loan from a friendly super power and had a magnification about a thousand times better than anything that Google Earth users had wet dreams about. And the map, satellite views and thermal imaging were displayed in real time from a specially tasked satellite that had been rented for a few hours at considerable cost to McCaul's client. They didn't care about cost. It was part of their package. So was McCaul if he didn't get home. Both were provided for in the fee.

Following the GPS instructions McCaul drove south to Rte 180 and then about an hour inland. He pulled off the highway onto a side road and drove about twenty klicks. For the last five he reduced his speed and turned the fog lamps on and the headlights off.

He looked for and found a narrow path and followed it about a hundred meters into the jungle. He drove the 4x4 into the bush, checked to make sure the interior lights were off, got out and used the Bowie knife to cut foliage and hide the jeep.

He turned on the small LED light, pulled out the gym bag and emptied the contents on the tailgate. He stripped and put on black cargo pants and a black long sleeved shirt and the balaclava and then camoed anything left on his body that might reflect light.

He filled his cargo pant pockets with the remaining contents of his tool kit and got his bearings and quietly closed and locked the Jeep door.

He let the GPS unit guide him to his destination that showed on the unit as being about five klicks over fairly rough terrain. It took him a half hour in a comfortable dogtrot to get where he was going and another half hour of careful and silent prowling before he was discovered and in trouble.

He'd tripped a motion detector, discovering the beam a second after he'd passed through it.

He jumped into a dried up creek and waited. His intell had told McCaul there would be six of them looking for trespassers and assassins.

He had a knife and sidearm. They probably had Mac-10s, the awful portable preference of that type of fiend whom McCaul was sent to harm. They were coming. He waited. He put on his night vision and the world turned green.

The first one moved like a moose. He passed within three feet of McCaul, deaf and blind to his peril, and was dead in two seconds by Ka-Bar; dying while blood was still gushing from his throat. Not even one of the geckos in the audience noticed.

The second was to his left and called what McCaul supposed was the decedent's name.

McCaul grunted with a Spanish accent and hid behind a tree. In ten seconds the second target was down and done. Then there was a buzz, and foliage all around him was torn by a swarm of bees. They had silenced Mac-10s. 'Great', McCaul thought: 'fifteen rounds a second'. Their weapons were noise suppressed. But the shooter had it on full automatic; which was good: it tagged him as an amateur; he would empty the mag faster than he could replace it.

McCaul ate ground and waited for the magazines to empty. There was no noticeable movement from the bad guys.

McCaul backed up, still belly down, about twenty meters until he had a field of vision. He waited. There was a movement to his left and he adjusted his night vision. There were two. No more than five feet apart. Geniuses. Not. McCaul killed them both with two quick taps. The recoil of his silenced sidearm was loud enough to be heard in the quiet night and he sensed movement to the right of their position. He became a ghost and silently moved behind some foliage and hunted.

The targets had a hacienda about a hundred meters away, McCaul knew their path of retreat and he was a lot less in a panic than they were. He circled around; got behind them, and ruined their day with two twenty-meter shots that combined took less than a second.

If the intelligence that cost his firm's clients fifty k was accurate, there were two more left: Sylvio and Sergio Navarro. They were thirty-year-old twins that passed on to turistas about a quarter of all the drugs sold in the Riviera Maya. He had a map of their estate and of the hacienda that included all the security codes. They should have paid their cleaning staff more and treated them better.

When McCaul came within sight of their place, he had memories of Al Pacino's palace in Scarface. It was pristine white marble, the size of a significant public library and there were twin red Carreras parked in the front driveway. He knew there was a servants' passage and he knew how to get there and get in. If they had an inkling that he was coming for them, it was likely that they had one less janitor.

McCaul put a dollar's worth of C-4 with a timer on the mansion's front gate, set the fuse and moved twenty meters to his right around a corner toward the servants' entrance and waited a few seconds. The explosion tossed the steel gate fifty feet in the air and rubble even higher. The twins likely thought the marines had invaded.

He put in the security code and was inside, not just the compound, but inside the structure itself.

He waited. After the explosion and the rubble finished falling, it had become deathly quiet.

He slowly and silently moved through the dark kitchen, avoiding all the brick-a-brac and copper pans and pots hanging from the ceiling, and into a cathedral ceilinged dining area. Through the other side, past an interior waterfall, a snooker table the size of a yacht and a massive marble statue of the Virgin, the main door stood open. He hid behind the statue and waited.

The twins rushed back to their sanctuary and carefully backed inside their front door. They each held one of the deadly Ingram machine pistols. McCaul shot them both, getting one of them in the forehead as he reacted to the first shot. He strolled over and made sure with two more taps.

He opened a fridge next to their hot tub and took a bottle of Dom Perignon champagne from a stack to keep him company for his return trip. His dogtrot back went faster than before. Back at the jeep, he cleaned up and scrubbed his camoed body parts off with a special cleanser, changed into civvies and drove back to his hotel. He finished the bottle of Dom en route and tossed the empty bottle into the ditch.

He left all his goodies in the blacked out rear of the SUV and locked the doors and dropped the key fob in a dumpster surrounded by rats the size of cats. He was back in his room and hotel bed by midnight. He could sleep well before his mid-morning flight back to his home in Havana.

* Santa Clara, Cuba *

"Se ha caido Fidel!"

Fidel has fallen!

Kate stood and shoved her way closer to the stage. She had been preparing to leave when it happened. She was really just here for footage and background, not expecting anything of any interest to anyone to happen in Santa Clara, Cuba.

This was Kate's first big international assignment for CNN after leaving Canada's leading TV news network to become a bigger fish in a bigger pond. And she was a catch for the network: a gorgeous brunette, a digger, relentless and a counter to CNN's bevy of blondes with southern accents.

Santa Clara had been the site of the penultimate battle of the Revolucion. Che had bulldozed a rail line that derailed a train full of Batista's soldiers, armed for bear, who were commanded to make a last stand against the Castro insurgents. Depending on whom an interested party talked to, either the nationalists had surrendered and been murdered or Che's men had killed all 400 in a firefight using rifles and Molotov cocktails. Remains of a train and a bulldozer from the conflict were within sight of the plaza where Fidel was speaking.

Fidel had spoken for over an hour; huffing and puffing and pausing for dramatic effect; jabbing his index finger into the air to emphasize his points. Finally, and at long last, even for his many acolytes among the thirty thousand people present, Fidel ended. He strode strongly and confidently forward to personally touch a selection of safe and trusted supporters.

Looking over the heads of those in the front row he had failed to see a short step ahead of him and fallen flat on his face. Shaken, he was surrounded by his supporters, helped to a chair and spoke to the crowd to assure them he was okay and could still talk. Fidel can always talk.

Kate had her digital camera and used her reporter's determination and elbows to get closer to the action. She videoed the event and the aftermath on her portable. Her clip, along with her own commentary, appeared on CNN that evening.

In response to her report a U.S. State Department spokesman said, "We heard that Castro fell. I guess you'd have to check with the Cubans to find out what's broken about Mr. Castro. We, obviously, have expressed our views about what's broken in Cuba.

"The situation in Cuba is of our primary concern. The situation of Mr. Castro is of little concern to us, but, unfortunately, of enormous importance to the people of Cuba, who have suffered very long under his rule. And we think that the kind of rule that Cuba has had should be ended."

But the entire empire of security services within the United States government had a great deal of concern about this event. And they began acting the way they always do; to protect their interests.

2

AS ALWAYS there was a big line up at Customs at Jose Marti Airport when McCaul got back to La Habana and he renewed his relationship with Cuba's first line of defense.

McCaul had been in Cancun for less than a day doing a job that almost no one else could do, or at least would confess to. He often pretended to be a travel agent to do such things.

He only had a carry-on so had only to clear Customs and didn't have to wait for Marti Airport's often thieving gang of baggage handlers to do their thing with his luggage.

The International Terminal 3 at Jose Marti Airport in Havana was up to the standards of almost any in North America and was a gift from the Government of Canada. Since the days of Pierre Trudeau Canucks had picked up the slack from the American embargo to provide Cubans goodies that their own fragile economy never could. Canadians were their largest trading partners with a lot of this from their tourists enjoying the island's beaches.

McCaul descended the escalator into the customs room and its dozen Cuban customs officers, each in a little bulletproof booth. There was at least an hour's worth of people in each line, smoking, talking with strangers and commiserating with family. Some looked a little worried.

For whatever reason, the Customs guards seemed to take about twenty minutes with each person to examine their Turista Card or credentials, compare pictures in the passport to its owner, take a picture and provide an official stamp. McCaul assumed that maybe they're paid by the hour and not the piece.

But with McCaul's work visa granted as the Cuba-based employee for Globalair he got through with a lot less hassle than a tourist or returning resident would.

He exited the terminal and the impact of exhaust fumes on the senses was throttling; the day was humid enough to almost liquefy the sooty pollution.

A security type of some kind waved McCaul up to a grinning, fiftyish little cab driver and an equally middle-aged Toyota. He opened the trunk; McCaul dropped his bag within and climbed in the back and instructed the driver to take him to his apartment off of 23rd Avenue - La Rampa - not far from the old Havana Hilton, the legendary ice cream park and Meyer Lansky's old Capri Hotel.

The smoke and fumes were gritty and the air seemed as if it was saturated with coal dust. Looking at the cars, it would not have surprised McCaul to learn they were, indeed, all fuelled by anthracite.

The driver was highly adept at missing other vehicles and most of the potholes while maintaining 120 kph and smoking a huge Churchill. He tuned his radio to a Miami station playing "The Miami Sound Machine" and exhibited typical Havana cabbie friendliness by giving Mike a non-stop and detailed travelogue about every point of interest they passed.

Soon after leaving Havana's airport, and passing by a Viva la Revolucion sign, McCaul re-entered the third world: huge acreages of farmland randomly overgrown or tangled. There were mushrooms in the fields picking something green. At least they looked like mushrooms, but they were farm workers in gigantic straw hats. They passed ramshackle concrete block huts; some scarred by burn marks or falling in on their foundations. Off on one side stood a huge stadium for soccer or baseball, completely enwrapped by creepers and various other foliage.

They sped down the Avenida de la Indepencia and drove between the stately rows of palm trees that lined both sides of the impressive roadway and passed by the Plaza de la Revolucion, Fidel and Raul's office building and the Jose Marti Tower. Mike could see the famous Che metal sculpture on the side of the Interior Ministry adjoining the square.

McCaul had decided to move to Cuba a little over a year before after a busted romance and a couple of close shaves in civilization. It was more convenient for him to get around the Caribbean countries than Toronto. Plus, he liked the place immensely and didn't have a lot of friends left back home.

He had kept his place in Toronto, though; in the city's exclusive near-downtown neighbourhood of Rosedale. It had been the coach house of the adjoining mansion but was a luxurious Tudor in its own right. It had three bedrooms, a pool and a generous back yard that ended in a ravine where foxes, rabbits and hated raccoons played.

In Havana, he'd been tempted to live in the oldest part of the city, Habana Vieja, but its grime and its hustlers, hookers and drunken turistas had made him look a little further a field. Miramar was too much like Miami, Centro was rough and tumble, so he had chosen Vedado.

Vedado was a slightly upscale neighbourhood in Havana populated mostly with relatively wealthy Cuban bureaucrats and officials. It's home to the Castros' headquarters, the biggest collection of hospitals in the city and the university.

There were a few creature comforts in McCaul's neighbourhood along with the university; one was the ice cream. They don't have a lot in Cuba, but the cigars and sugar are world class and he normally partook in at least one Cohiba and one ice cream cone a day. His apartment was only a block away from Havana's famous ice cream park, the Coppelia, which was across the street from Fidel's first headquarters at the Havana Hilton, but McCaul thought that was a coincidence.

They pulled up to his century old apartment building. McCaul got his bag and paid with a U.S. twenty, walked up to the second floor and knocked to see if Janisleydis, his housekeeper was in. This was her day to work. She opened the door.

"Señor McCaul, you are back! Let me take your bag."

Mike said hi and followed her into his perfectly scrubbed and shining flat.

Every time he walked into his place he speculated as to who might have lived here before. Its ten-foot high front door, twelve-foot high tin ceilings and cornice moldings, white marble tiled floors and stained glass windows were stunning. He thought a previous resident must have been at least a Mafia capo, if not a consigliere, and had been at least eight feet tall.

The furnishings came with the place and were acceptable if not ostentatious. One of the things McCaul had added was an ultra silent generator with a solar panel for the many times that Fidel's power monopoly failed. He had a flat screen TV, a DVD player and a portable Bose stereo but seldom used any of them.

Janisleydis also came with his place. Actually it was her place; it had been assigned to her family for her father's loyalty in serving in Angola. Her parents had passed on, but had passed on to their daughter an apartment that got her a $1,000 monthly rental from Mike. This made her very wealthy in a country where entire families were expected to exist for a month on ten bucks.

Of course, she couldn't spend the money or look rich. But she lived with her cousin nearby who was the local CDR rep so she got away with it. The Committee for the Defense of the Revolution was the Marxist equivalent of a Neighbourhood Watch but watched the residents to make sure they're being perfect little socialists, not to discourage strangers or intruders. A real neighbourhood watch would be pretty useless in Cuba; nobody had much of anything worth stealing.

McCaul thanked her for doing such a beautiful job. "Oh, muchas gracias, Señor. I be back next week." She nodded and left him to himself.

McCaul got a pay cheque every two weeks from a charter air travel company called Globalair to be their Vice-President of Security for the Caribbean region. Supposedly his job was to make sure that his company's passengers got back home to tell their lurid stories of Caribbean delights.

But that was a false front. He got his real income for doing special projects for a company called Flanders. Just Flanders; no Inc. or LLC at the end because it doesn't pay taxes or even officially exist. The company would never be found with a Google search. A guy named Jud Webster owned both the airline and Flanders, though the latter was a well-kept secret and Jud was invisible as it was in his ownership.

Webster had been in Britain's Special Air Service in the sixties and seventies and made his bones fighting the IRA and in the Suez and the Congo. After he left the service he'd been a free agent mercenary until he had made a big score in Lesotho. McCaul suspected that it had been in diamonds and that he was easily worth more than a hundred million.

Webster had started Flanders in the nineties, after settling in Canada, by recruiting a number of ruffians with whom he'd taken down or propped up governments in various places. Now he had close to a hundred operatives doing what McCaul did; whatever had to be done for discrete clients that could generate a whole pile of money.

Jud was good at his work and no amount of research could ever find his connection to the "security contracting" company he owned, nor what it really did. It was in no government's interest to have him found out; so none had ever looked too hard, or ever would. The company had never done any work for the Canadian government, though. It was too close to home and too fragile in its security to protect state secrets of its own.

The travel company was also a great benefit to Flanders as a goodly share of all the troublemakers in the world were at vacation destinations full time or at least occasionally. They were well guarded, but relaxed, and so were their keepers. For Webster and McCaul there's something almost poetic about taking down evildoers when they're enjoying paradise.

Webster had guys in Iraq, Syria and Afstan and almost every other global hotspot doing VIP security and black ops. Much of what they did was outside of someone's law. But no one who shouldn't know ever knew they did it.

McCaul had a bottle of dark Havana Club in the kitchen cupboard and poured a healthy measure into a heavy crystal glass, cut and squeezed half a lime into it and added some ice cubes. He turned on his laptop and checked his email.

McCaul had one of the few privately owned wireless internet hookups in Cuba. It was a gift from a friend of Webster that owned a few resorts on the island, was a close friend of Fidel's and also owned the services of a couple of Fidel's security big shots. There was a hidden ultra-encrypted dish on McCaul's roof among the ubiquitous tangle of wires and rabbit ears that seem to occupy every rooftop in Havana. McCaul also got satellite TV, but mostly only used it to watch NHL playoff games when the Montreal Canadiens were still competing.

He deleted all the get rich quick and genitalia enlargement spam and was left with a few Google Alerts on global hotspots and one email from Webster. He opened it. It asked him to call when he arrived back.

He loaded up Skype and clicked Webster's link.

"Webster residence." It was Clarence Wong, Webster's chief cook, bottle washer, valet and chauffeur.

"Hi Clarence, I'm back in Havana, is Jud there?"

"He is, just a moment, Mike."

"McCaul, there you are." Mike heard him exhale and cough. He was onto one of his favourite Hoyo de Monterreys early. "How went the trip, Mike?"

"The clients will be satisfied, Jud. The twins won't do no bad no more. What's up?"

"I received a call from Earl Inglewood yesterday to propose a project for us."

Inglewood was a drinking buddy of Webster's as well as Canada's Minister of Defense.

"Are you on a secure line?"

"Encrypted Skype, I suspect that Raul has bigger lines to tap than mine. The Canadian Government?"

"They still remember you in Ottawa, Mike, you can run, but you can't hide."

He was referring to a less than rosy view McCaul has on working for the Canadian Government. After six years with Canada's Airborne Regiment he joined the Royal Canadian Mounted Police. He'd been promoted rapidly and got put on their Intelligence team.

While providing security for Chinese delegates to an Asia Pacific Conference in Vancouver, Mike had discovered that a couple of the delegates had applied considerable leverage to keep Canadian officials from examining industrial espionage by their ex-pats against Canadian tech companies.

All evidence made it appear likely that one of the delegates would be using diplomatic privilege to take some high-tech prototypes back to China to be reverse engineered. But some Canadian elected officials had been naughty during junkets to Thailand and the Asians had pictures. So all efforts were taken to make sure no efforts were taken to arrest the thieves or stop the thievery.

McCaul and his direct superior had wanted the thieves arrested while in Canada. The politicians didn't. He had caused a heck of a snowstorm.

It had resulted in the RCMP being directed to shut down the investigation, McCaul had been shut up, demoted and back-officed doing paperwork and pressured to leave with threats of dishonour heaped upon him. Even though all parties conspiring to ruin his career knew full well that he was innocent and was among the horsemen's top agents. But his reputation was ruined and all his cronies started avoiding him like the clap.

He'd gotten demoted from field work and disgraced for doing the right thing, and hadn't lasted a month at a desk before Jud had found a place for him. Mike had met Jud through his daughter, Elaine, to whom Mike had been engaged for a time. Webster and McCaul had always gotten along better than she and Mike.

The years with Flanders since had been often exhilarating to Mike and a time or two a little scary, which was good.

"So what does Earl want, Jud?", Mike asked skeptically. Helping out the Feds in their hour of need wasn't on his bucket list.

Webster said, "Well, what I know is that it's a special project to help out our friends in D.C. and it takes place down your way. I think they want some recon work done before they get too far along with their current discussions to kiss and make up with Raul.

And I think our PM wants to bask in the glow of the President's friendship. Their leader is way more popular up here than our own is."

Mike said, "I've got no prob talking to him."

"Good. Can I link him in?"

"Sure."

Mike heard him call to Clarence. "Clarence, will you come and hook up this damn phone to Earl for me." There was some rustling and noises and finally a voice at the other end.

"This is the Minister's office." Clarence introduced himself and a second later Mike heard, "Inglewood."

Jud took control, "Earl, it's Webster and I have McCaul on the other line."

"Well, Mike McCaul, it's been a long time."

"Yes, Minister, it has been that." He liked Earl but thought he was sometimes a little too charming.

"So, Mike, how ya like living behind what's left of the Iron Curtain?"

"Love it so far, Earl. Mostly hot and sunny. What have ya got in mind?"

"Mike. Foggy Bottom's putting a lot of pressure on Foreign Affairs to pick up our military commitment to Syria or to do some of their dirty work elsewhere if we don't. The second's more popular politically for us because we can hide it under official secrets. We're picking Cuba."

"Keep talking, Earl. What do I have to do?"

"It's real simple. The POTUS and his Company want to know who's running the place. Fidel seems to be alive, and it's doubtful that he works 7/24, but they want to know if he's still pulling any levers. Also, whether Raul is straight about normalizing things or just playing games.

"They also suspect that Raul might be hosting some real nasty anti-American sorts in return for oil and cash."

McCaul broke in. "ISIS?"

"Or their cousins.

"If the Castros are playing footsie with the Arab nasties, there's a problem. At best this won't work with the POTUS's desire to be friends and at worst they might cry havoc and unleash the dogs.

"At the very least, they want more comfort in the Cuban situation before they take any steps to reconstruct the relationship."

"So you want me to be your Man in Havana? Why me?"

"First off, you're on the scene. The assignment calls for someone who has the trade craft, can move around Cuba freely and knowledgeably, and can ask the right questions to the right people. You'd also need to do a lot of snooping around while looking like a travel agent. With your Airborne and RCMP experience, you're the only guy we got who can do this. And be totally off the record."

"Sounds good so far. What's in it for me?"

"Well, Mike, that depends on what you might ask for?"

"Hmmmm. Earl, you know that I've got a little issue with this. Your predecessor really gave me a hard time. You know I don't get invited to Mountie reunions any more."

"Yes, Mike, that's a travesty. How about a written apology for your demotion, as well as a letter of commendation that will go on your service file. I'm also delegated to, say, offer some additional concessions or incentives if you ask. Fair enough?"

"How about this. You pay a normal fee to my employer."

Inglewood said, "No problem."

"I'd also like a bonus of some considerable amount, say $100,000, paid to the Rosedale AIDS Hospice and presented by the Prime Minister himself on the day I start."

"Well, I can ask, I don't think he's ever been in one before. Is that it?"

Mike sensed that Inglewood thought he was getting off easy. It came to McCaul that finally he had leverage and could get his rep repaired, play a "get out of jail free" card with the guys he'd worked with in the past who had ignored him since the Asian Conference slander. A media release on his adventures wasn't an option, but a public award from the government who had impugned him would be. Something that would cause no one to ever question his integrity with the government and past history again.

McCaul said, "Well, how about one of those Orders of Canada, Earl?" He took a good long drink and tilted his head back to wait for an answer.

Inglewood chuckled. "I suppose that could be a possibility, upon successful mission completion and absolute secrecy." Inglewood said.

"I can't control success or all the secret tellers. I think I should get it in any case," McCaul said.

"Okay, I knew you'd be stubborn. Done. Our staff officer in charge of this assignment will meet you tomorrow in Havana at 1600 hours at the

16

Telegrafo to start things rolling. His name is Lucien LaRue, he's a sergeant in JTF2. You know them..."

"Yup. They make Delta Force look like girl scouts. I got to play with some of their guys in Airborne", McCaul said. "Works for me."

"You got it. I'm hanging up to confirm things. Thanks, Mike."

Jud said, "Thanks to you, Earl." Earl hung up.

Jud spoke, "you good on this, Mike?"

"Now... I'm good."

3

MCCAUL OPENED THE FRENCH DOORS to his balcony and once again enjoyed his view of the Malecon between the Havana's high rise TV Centre and the Hotel Nacional. The clouds were starting to be blown away by a gentle off shore wind and it promised to be another glorious and ridiculously humid Havana day.

His relocation to Havana had been personal.

A couple of years ago he had a love affair break up. He'd been seeing a woman for over a year and after a lifetime of solitary confinement, he had thought that this was it. Around her he felt less serious and liked himself more.

Kate McKee had been a TV reporter who made men all across Canada stand up and pay attention every night at ten o'clock. To Mike, she was stunning, but she was also animated, incredibly fun, persnickety, took no prisoners and suffered no fools. And she was a terrific foil to his always taciturn self.

But she had chosen career over him. Even with promises that things wouldn't change between them, she had moved on to bigger and higher incomed things and got a job in Atlanta with CNN and mostly left him behind. And he hadn't seen her since, except on CNN. She was gorgeous and he missed her terribly.

McCaul had wanted a new start. None of Flanders' employees kept a residence in a civilized place that had active intelligence agencies that might be forced to spill the beans by government enquiries. So along with this, as well as being asea and heartbroken, he decided to leave town.

In his travels with Globalair and Flanders the city that had always appealed more to him than others was Havana. At least in the non-hurricane months. He lived in the Cuban city, but still went back to Toronto every few months.

Havana is a city of survivors.

Some Cubans had made it through the hard times working as mercenaries for the USSR in their attempts to spread Marxism to the world's poorest places.

Older residents had lived before the revolution and survived Batista and the mafia and managed to somehow still be around. Many still remember the times, and Fidel, fondly.

The young survive by not knowing that others lived any better than they do, except from their wide-eyed survey of tourists and occasional radio reception from Miami.

All, except for the socialist elite, still survive from the most racist and meanest police state in the hemisphere, a lack of reliable electricity, a paucity of clean water and a diet of rice and root vegetables. They were also funny, friendly, generous and Mike loved the music. To date he hadn't touched any of the spectacular beauties that abound.

He was still dressed in his travel clothes, which was no way to walk around in the city, and walking around the city was one more reason he had moved here.

He pulled off his linen suit and pulled on a pair of shorts, a Montreal Canadiens tee shirt and a pair of feather light Puma runners. He stuffed a small wad of Convertible Cuban Pesos in his pocket, left and locked up. He trotted downstairs and started jogging down La Rampa toward the Caribbean. In a couple of minutes he was dodging old Chevys, rattletrap Ladas, cyclo-taxis and the Audis of government officials to cross the Malecon and continue running along the sea wall.

McCaul passed the Maine Memorial, which celebrated the explosion of the US warship that started the Spanish American War. He ran by kids diving, old men fishing and lovers hugging. He ran harder as he neared the old city and sprinted up Colon until he got to the Revolutionary Museum. He glanced at Fidel's means of return to Cuba: the small fishing boat, "Granma", that he had commandeered from an American tourist, and the tanks and airplanes that had supposedly made Cuba free.

And McCaul entered old Havana, walking up the city's famous Prado, Paseo de Marti, to Parque Central.

The Parque Central is a great place to enjoy a bench and cigar, play some dominoes, or argue about baseball. Beneath the ubiquitous Jose Marti statue there was a large group of animated fans, some with bats in hand, noisily discussing the state of the Latin American Baseball League as Mike crossed the park.

On the other side of the park was the Museum of Fine Arts, a stunning classically designed structure, across from a magnificent new luxury hotel to house the hordes of American tourists that had been anticipated but had never arrived.

Every second step McCaul had a young black guy ask him if he wanted chicas, langostas or cigars.

He passed the Floridita Bar, supposedly the favourite haunt of Ernest Hemingway. There were a couple of bearded Hemingway look-alikes wandering around aimlessly, most in khaki cargo shorts, some getting their pictures taken in the famous watering hole next to a bronze statue of Papa.

One step onto Calle Obispo, and again it was obvious to McCaul that it was a very special place. Sloping gently downhill with more potholes than gravel or cobblestone, the 30 foot wide pedestrian-only mall was awash with people: late middle-aged couples looking for photo subjects, sidewalk fixers, sidewalk hustlers, cigar sellers, 80 year old paper boys, children playing tin can soccer. Music blaring, people dancing, sweating people leaning into holes-in-the-wall buying ice cream. People strolling down the byway licking their ice cream with rapturous expressions, laughing all the way, smoke trailing behind from cigars in their free hands. Middle aged Hemingway doppelgangers smoking fat cigars and speaking in English, Italian and German.

Buildings on either side of the alley that lifted spirits: many, many generations old; people leaning over balconies festooned with plants, yelling at compañeros across the street, and being laughed at back.

Many dogs, none of a consistent genealogical heritage, yapping, snarling, wrestling and jumping on anything that seemed the least bit edible. Old women, obviously weak from age and lack of food, quietly holding out their hands, looking for even a gram of charity.

Cars parked along each side street. The ubiquitous Havana jalopies, some in much better condition than others, like they had just rolled off the showroom floor after their buyer had seen a "see the USA in your Chevrolet" television ad. Some others lurching along, like every breath of exhaust might be their last. Cubanos in various stages of conducting mechanical work on their beloved cars, some leaning into engine compartments, others just visible as disembodied legs sticking out from underneath.

McCaul came to his favorite bar, Casa del Escabeche. It's a little place on a dilapidated corner with brown wooden doweled walls, and a smiling little doorman named Kepo who welcomed him in. Its name was revealed in a neon sign on the wall. It had a great little takeout window that served fried rice that was likely the worst looking, but best tasting, that McCaul has ever eaten.

The bar was perhaps 20 steps wide by 10 deep, with a burgundy wooden bar directly in front of the entrance. The bar paralleled the back wall, from the front right of the room toward the back.

The place was quiet in the early afternoon, with the only inmates being the bartender and a husky mulatto guy in the corner at a table seeming to hold court over a duo of male admirers. It looked strange to McCaul, because the group members all looked Cuban; usually locals were forbidden from CUC bars without a turista with a wallet.

"Señor, have a chair, put a load down." His English was good, but not good enough to realize what he'd just said.

"Hola, I'm Mike."

"Sit down, Señor, I'm Aries. My friend, Manuel, he want to buy you a drink." He nodded toward the guy in the corner.

The mulatto guy said, "Senor, have the Ron siete anos. No ice. On me."

Mike said, "Aries, do pour." And he poured a solid three fingers of the viscous dark rum without ice.

McCaul sipped, it was good, very sweet and powerful. He toasted and nodded to the buyer of his drink.

"Siete anos, Señor. You are Canadian, of course."

McCaul nodded.

"Are you here casing the joint?"

Aries had seen some American movies, circa 1960, probably starring Joe Friday.

"No, Aries. I'm just a travel agent."

The bartender leaned over close to McCaul, "I think you are more than that, Señor." He whispered, "I want to help you, Mister Mike."

He reminded Mike of Peter Lorre in Casablanca. "I hear you're not here to help Fidel, but to help Cubanos, Señor."

"That's not really true, Aries. I'm just here on business; but if I was, how could you ever help me?" McCaul sipped his rum and glanced over Mike's shoulder toward the corner table and nodded slightly.

"I know things and people, Señor."

McCaul heard a slight ruckus behind him and noticed the corner table meeting was wrapping up with hugs and smiles.

The big mulatto guy from the meeting sat down next to Mike, offered his hand and smiled. McCaul remembered seeing him around.

Mike set the rum on the bar and shook. "Manuel, Mike McCaul."

The hombre was dressed in an obviously expensive black linen suit with black leather sandals and a black linen tee shirt. His hair had been carefully short cut in a style common in any North American city. He bore little resemblance to a typical Cuba in his dress and apparent confidence. He could be on Bay Street in Toronto. In the summer.

"I know your name, Señor." His English was only slightly accented.

"How do you know my name?"

"Señor, if the secret police know your name, then I know your name." He raised his class of amber rum in a toast, "Viva la Cosa Nostra."

McCaul clinked his glass, another adventure.

"What's your game, Manuel," Mike asked.

"Beisbol. But I try to live well. I'm a hard worker." McCaul noticed a three-inch scar along the left side of Manuel's neck.

"I'd like to work with you."

"You want to get into the tourism business?"

"Señor McCaul, Duarte's secret policia have a file on you that I was told about. Many of his people keep two jobs. One job is with me and I pay much better." He took a drink of his rum.

"They say you are a former spy and probably working for Los Americanos. But they are not sure so will just keep an eye on you. I was told about you by a mutual friend."

McCaul thought, 'So much for our security program'. He took a longer drink.

Manuel looked around and whispered, "I am a new revolutionary. I am what you might call a banker. My grandfather was a business partner of Meyer's from America who left in the plane with Presidente Batista when Fidel succeeded in his coup." He pronounced it "coop".

"My grandmother and father were left behind and my grandfather was assassinated in America later after he was deported. But I have done quite well here."

'I have met the Cuban Michael Corleone', McCaul thought.

"Mi amigo has a car outside if you would honour me by sharing a meal."

McCaul thinks, 'why not? I've got a couple of hours to kill' and nodded, "Sure."

4

IT WAS STARTING TO GET DARK as Mike's new friend guided him back along Obispo toward the Parque Centrale and opened the rear door of a like new Corolla station wagon in front of the Floridita.

McCaul got in the back and Manuel in the front passenger seat then turned around toward Mike. "This is my car, Señor. I buy it from a nurse named Petronia for five thousand CUCs. She earned the right to buy a car from Fidel by him selling her services to African revolutionaries for many years, but she wished cash more than transportation. Fidel has always sold his people to the highest bidders and so will his brother."

Manuel tooted the horn. "My friend Abelardo drives the auto as a taxi for both of us. It is better to have a car to make money than to have the convenience."

A thin white guy dressed in tight red bell bottoms, a white golf shirt and aviator sunglasses, despite the dusk, appeared from among the smokers and got in the driver's side. He turned and offered his well-manicured hand to McCaul and he shook it.

"Abelardo."

"Mike."

"Bienvenido, Señor". He turned the key and launched his CD player at mind numbing decibels with Barry White using his basso for a loud love tribute to his babe at the time.

Abelardo waited for a couple of Panataxis and pedicabs to pass by and rocketed around the Parque, changing gears as slickly as an F1 racer and driving almost as quickly. After making the circle Manuel yelled to the driver in Spanish and Abelardo pulled into a side street and slammed on the brakes and pulled to a stop with the engine running.

In a second, a man in uniform appeared from a doorway and passed a bulky burlap bag to Manuel who plunked it on the floor. Abelardo stepped on the gas and pulled away in another second.

McCaul thought it might be a head from its size and heft, but Manuel turns around to assure him. "Don't worry, it's not a head, Mike." He had read McCaul's mind. "It's a can of petro. The policia drain their tanks and sell it to me."

McCaul chuckled. What a place.

Manuel said, "Let's go eat."

Abelardo continued showing his F1 skills and in a few minutes and a thousand bumps in the road later they pulled down a dark and narrow street and slammed to another stop in front of a well-lit passageway.

They got out and entered and Mike wondered for the hundredth time how tall the old Spaniards had been; there was another twelve foot high doorway. They entered and Manuel pointed out a mural of a face on the wall within the Cuban flag. "Comandante Camilo Cienfuegos, Señor. A great hero."

McCaul had read about him. Camilo had been a brother in arms of Fidel and Ernesto Guevara. Competent while Che was erratic... Calm, while Che had been emotional. Successful in war, while reports on Che's military leadership record were mixed.

McCaul knew that Camilo had risen from the streets of Havana to becoming a young exile from Fulgencio Batista in New York City. He had joined Fidel in the Sierra Maestra and risen from an undisciplined fighter to a brilliant captain of the point platoon, the most critical position in an attack. He had received a battlefield promotion to Comandante and led a seven hundred-man force of the Rebel Army. Camilo had furiously attacked government troops in Camagüey and Las Villas and was in charge of the victorious forces in Havana when the city was captured.

The group were on the ground floor of a magnificent atrium gone to seed. There was a stunning cracked and broken marble staircase with a beautifully carved statue of a woman sans head and arms. On the wall across from the statue was a transcript of a Fidel speech; a metaphor for this puzzling island; decaying beauty next to tired propaganda.

McCaul followed Manuel up the stairs. "This is the famous La Guarida paladar, Mike. All the movie stars and politicians dine here when in La Habana."

Mike had heard of the place but never been.

The courtyard was filled with clotheslined apparel and there was a cacophony of sounds at all levels of this ancient high rise; music, laughter, parents yelling at children, children yelling at each other. They climbed stairs.

Finally, at the third floor, Manuel knocked on a door, it was opened and they entered and Manuel was welcomed with a hug by a light skinned beauty and some small talk. He introduced her to McCaul as Marta and Mike managed an "Hola, Señorita."

She hustled them through a lightly populated dining room with a hodge-podge of table and chair sets and walls with bookshelves and paintings and placed them on a tiny balcony with barely enough room for a small table and two chairs. They sat and overlooked the dark street bustling below. A Spanish guy wearing a white tank top undershirt studied them from a balcony across the alley.

"We can talk here. This is where celebrities sit who don't wish to be bothered by commoners."

In a second, Marta brought them a bottle of bubbling water and a red wine. "I have ordered in advance for us; I hope that is okay," Manuel said.

McCaul said, "Of course, it seems you know your way around here."

"Si. I come often." He poured for both of them and Mike took a sip of the wine. It wasn't half bad. Mike looked at the bottle; a tempranillo following Cuba's Spanish roots, from country west of Habana.

"We can talk here, Senior McCaul."

McCaul said, "I don't have a lot to talk about. I just keep an eye on our airports for the company I work for."

Their waiter arrived with fresh rolls and a chopped salad.

The salad, flavoured with some simple vegetable oil and red wine vinegar, was delicious. Its tomatoes didn't resemble the nasty, mostly green, medallions seen at private restaurants and there was more greenery than cabbage. The bread was fresh and warm.

Manuel took a drink of wine. "I am working with people wishing to toss Fidel and his old monsters into the Gulf. They need things, I get them things," he said.

"What's in it for you?"

He said, "Well, my grandfather was in gambling and I expect that American gamblers will be more generous than Cuban burócratos."

Marta brought their appetizers; a plate of shrimp dribbled with a pepper sauce.

She said, "Camerones Piquante, Señor." The sauce had very little heat but lingered on Mike's lips pleasantly like a kiss from his lost love, Kate. Marta placed another bottle of the wine to replace the one that Manuel and he had swallowed thirstily.

After McCaul scrubbed his plate with a bit of bread, a bus person cleared the table and Marta arrived with the main course; chicken grilled with a honey sauce, a side dish of gratin potatoes and some real, almost live, broccoli. Mike dove in with both utensils. It was perfect; the pollo sweet and crispy, the spuds alive with flavour and the broccoli crunchy and fresh.

McCaul had lived mostly on faux pizza and bad fried rice since he had lived in Havana and this was a revelation. It was as good a meal as he had ever eaten.

Manuel shared his life story with McCaul. How his grandfather had left without notice and how his father and grandmother had looked for days trying to find his body or at least find out what happened. They were forced to live as beggars in a small apartment in Centro, his grandmother not able to receive any support from any official because of her husband's history with the American gangsters.

He told how his father was refused entrance into schools and how Manuel had helped support the family, even as a small child, by hustling for anything of value. He told Mike how cruel the Russians were, how they treated all Cubans as slaves while they impregnated as many women as they could.

How finally, when Manuel was a teenager, his mother's brother had visited from Miami and left them money to live on. Cash had continued to arrive and the family no longer risked starvation. But Manuel was still refused entry to university, so he had gained a masters of trade; he became able to get almost anything for almost anybody. Now even highly placed officials depended on him to get them the luxuries they were not officially allowed to have. So they did him favours and he ran no risk of being arrested.

Marta arrived with two Café Americanos, two biscottis and a snifter of brandy. McCaul was quiet having heard Manuel's story. It would win a Pulitzer. He wondered how many thousands of similar ones could be told across the city.

"So Mike, consider me as a resource for you. If you need something, just tell Aries and you will receive."

"Manuel, I appreciate your offer, but I don't know how I could take advantage of it. I'm sure that the secret police think every gringo living here is a spy of some sort. But I'm only here for the sunshine and low taxes."

He chuckled and placed his napkin on the table and he rose. "Whatever you say, Señor. But I will keep eyes on you and help if you are troubled."

McCaul said, " Sure. We don't have to pay?", and joined him standing.

Manuel chuckled. "Señor, they have to get their cognac and broccoli from somewhere."

Mike followed Manuel out. Marta was joined by a well-dressed middle-aged man. McCaul shook his hand while Manuel hugged Marta and then they reversed positions and left.

Abelardo was waiting in the car, surrounded by children. Manuel gave them each a peso note and the duo got in the car and returned to La Floridita and a gaggle of Hemingways, while being serenaded in the loudest possible way by Barry White.

5

HADRIAN FELIX, HARRY TO HIS FEW FRIENDS, walked from his airport taxi drop off point to the front doors of the Hotel Nacional. He glanced briefly at a couple of attractive women walking in bikinis toward the hotel pool from the front door. They were blonde and blue-eyed and looked Norwegian or Swedish, which was in direct opposition to his dark complexion, however he did share their blue eyes. They checked him out. He was fairly tall and very thin, the result of years of long distance running and a need in his business to stay more fit than those out to capture or kill him.

As always, the first thing that he had done when he landed in Cuba was to buy a package of cigars at the airport and he had enjoyed a Siglo VI on the cab ride to his hotel.

Most often, when Felix visited Cuba, and he had done this dozens of times, he had worked from the U.S. Interests Section offices on the Malecon. The old facility in the Swiss Embassy had been upgraded and renamed as an Embassy of their own which tended to attract the odd protester and dozens among the thousands of new American tourists who had misplaced their passports or were shocked that their Amex cards wouldn't work.

This time, however, he was on his own, none of the Embassy staff knew he was in Havana. Anything he did on this trip was without the specific knowledge of any superior in the CIA, though the overall strategy came all the way from the very top.

With the bosses intent to be best friends with Castros, there could be no chance that they would find out about the CIA meddling in Cuban affairs.

The Company had buffers from command to delivery built throughout their hierarchy. For an assignment of this importance, one of those buffers had been declared dead and was buried with full honours, although really he took early retirement and now lived like Marlon Brando on an island in Oceania with a bevy of young women and men to entertain him.

If anything bad happened there would be no way to trace Hadrian's mission back to its real sponsors. The company had learned this technique a generation before from watching a mafia movie and it had worked perfectly since.

Officially, Felix was off duty, fishing in Alaska and out of touch. Officially, if he were captured, he would be declared a rogue and illegal and would receive no diplomatic protection.

That was the way he liked it.

Hadrian's father had been a legend in the Company's Latin American Bureau. He had done anything that had to be done, south of the USA, except for Mexico. That was someone else's turf and had fallen mostly under the DEA.

His father had installed and removed a half dozen puppet dictators, tortured drug kingpins and funded revolutions. Rumours were that he had been in Cuba in the 60's and followed Che to Bolivia and was in on the Cuban rock star's demise.

Felix had been with his Dad before he had disappeared in the first Haiti action in the 90s and had personally been 2-I-C in the attempted coup of Chavez in Venezuela and the removal of Aristide from Haiti in 2004.

While the outcomes of these adventures hadn't been the greatest, Felix was still rewarded for controlling the events and minimizing political damage. His greatest successes had never been made public, but there were new leadership regimes in three Spanish-speaking countries that owed him, and his superiors, for their jobs.

In Cuba, his work was mostly done, short of seeing things through to the end and completing a few follow-ups.

He checked in and had his bags sent to his room and proceeded to the Churchill Bar, until he came to his senses, went to his room and changed into swim trunks, put his android phone in a fanny-pack and went to the pool. There was Sweden to conquer and occupy. Plus he had a meeting.

He took the short cut to the pool through the lobby and sat next to the cabana bar. A waiter came over and took his order, a Habana Speciale with no rum. Felix had many vices, alcohol was not one.

While checking his email on his smart phone he kept an eye on the subjects sitting on the edge of the pool and dangling their feet in the water. They were bookends; both three or four inches under his six feet, both with hair sculpted in the same long and wavy style with a Veronica Lake curl. One with a blue bikini to show off her eyes, the other with a yellow one to show off her hair. Neither with either a burn or a tan; they were new arrivals as well.

Hadrian looked around for his meeting subject. The guy was five minutes late. A minute later a skinny guy looking less sunburned than burned out came into the pool from the driveway entrance.

He sat down next to Felix and waved to the waiter and ordered a Mojito in almost perfect Spanish. He was in his sixties and looked every day of it. He said, "You buyin'?"

Felix shrugged knowing that he could afford it better than the guy could.

33

Felix said, "You're late".

The guy said, "I had to walk here. I'm a little short."

Felix replied, "I guess maybe you should work a little harder for us, then."

The guy was a lost soul, driven to move to Cuba because it was about the only place he could afford and yet offer him a lifestyle he enjoyed; he was a fanatic about Cuban music.

The guy responded in a Buffalo accent, "Pal, I don't get invited to Fidel's cocktail parties."

"Ya gotta try harder and dress nicer then. What ya got for me?"

The guy lit a cheap Cuban cigarette. "Nothing much. I guess I see fewer green suits around. The grays seem to be giving the locals more hassle. Kids got more cash, they all got phones and dress better than before."

He finished his Mojito and waved for another one. "I'm a drummer not a spook, Hadrian."

"Call me Felix. Okay. I got something for ya. It's worth a nickel, I'll advance ya half."

"What is it?"

"You're gonna count cars going into the Castro's HQ for a week. Note the times of day, type of car and number of passengers. You'll need to drop off your report in an envelope at the Embassy by the end of next week."

"Felix, that's a little scary for me. You know what they did to the Danish kid who was snooping around there."

"You got a choice? You want some cash? You'll do it."

"Okay. Where's my cash."

Felix gave the guy an envelope and he left without saying goodbye.

After the guy left the poolside, Felix took a drink of his pineapple juice, replaced his phone in his fanny pack and walked to the diving board. He had gotten his degree at Texas A&M with the help of a diving scholarship and he proved it. He bounced several times on the board, soared high above the water and executed a perfect swan dive. He swam underwater the full length of the pool and back, climbed back on the board and did a perfect inward pike, finishing it at the very bottom of the pool.

He came to the surface and noticed the girls had moved over to the poolside bar and were watching him. He paid them no attention from his position at the board and swam over. He ordered a fresh drink and said hello.

- # -

The guy left Hadrian Felix and the Hotel Nacional behind and took the walk east down the Malecon, past the stallion rampant statue monument to Antonio Maceo and toward a little café across from the high rise Ameijeiras Brothers hospital.

The hospital was named after three brothers who had died in the early days of the revolution. It became famous in a documentary made by a rotund American filmmaker to embarrass his government. It's served best as evidence of how the Castro's use their health care for propaganda than as a hospital; it had sanitary issues.

The café on Padre Varela was one of the few that would encourage gringos to buy food with local pesos, not CUCs, and Don Hughes was a regular. The food was perfunctory, but his service was always good because he would always leave a 1 CUC tip. For this he was allowed to enter and leave through the back so as not to attract the attention of any policia that might be parked in front of the hospital.

Don also liked it because it was almost next door to the Casa de la Trova, a little venue for old time musicians to play traditional music. Every now and again they would allow Hughes to fill in as a drummer and feel like he belonged in Cuba, although he knew he could never live up to those who had been born and bred in the sounds of the place.

The third reason he liked it was Marisol. She was the thirty-something daughter of the managers who kept him company and offered him a more comforting bed than his other that he rented in a small apartment with an old soldier.

As Hughes almost always did, he ordered the fish; it was always fresh and cheap. As he always did, he ordered a Mojito; a libation that if he counted, would have been his fourth of a dozen or more that he would drink during the day.

Holding it out of sight under the table, he looked into the envelope that Felix had given him. Inside was a fair stack of 10 CUC bills and he carefully removed two, then folded and placed the envelope in his right sock.

This assignment worried him. Very few of the trivial assignments he received from his handler had any risk. This one would require him to try and not be seen in a place fifty yards from the Interior Ministry and police barracks. It was where a young Danish student had been murdered simply for being there. He didn't have a wardrobe of various costumes or fake beards, but he would need to try and disguise himself.

He'd also need to invent some reasons for him to be in the Plaza de la Revolucion for entire days. He thought he might try and act as a Spanish photographer in one persona and maybe as a professor from an American university sympathetic to the Castros and Cuba as another. Maybe he'd act as a reporter for an American newspaper who was opposed to the belligerent Miami ex-pats. In his year and a half living in Cuba he had put together some credentials as a professor and a journalist and even had copies of articles in his name that the CIA had arranged to have published in the Miami Herald.

He thought he might try and surreptitiously take pictures of each car that pulled up to the security hut and entrance to the HQ. That would save him trying to make notes and might be safer.

He finished his lunch and wandered down to the Casa de Trova to see if they would let him sit in for a matinee performance.

6

EVEN LUCIEN LARUE recognized himself as being particular. Over two decades in uniform had made him this way. Even on civvy street, his shoes were always polished and his clothing always neat as a pin. In Bosnia and Afstan he was often the butt of jokes for the properness of his attire, and this was in a group who spit and polished themselves and their clothes and gear every day. But he had been this way since he was a boy when he hadn't had very much and had to make the things he did have last as long as possible.

Today he was wearing a blue Montreal Canadiens tee shirt, immaculate white Dockers and white runners.

LaRue had always been the first one up in the morning in every military unit in which he had served. Getting up at seven in Havana made him an early riser but he felt lazy and a little dull from the extra hour and a half in bed.

He was staying at the Telegrafo, a remodeled hotel from the 1800's located on the Prado at Parque Central. He'd come down to Havana a few days before to get acclimated and get his Spanish up to scratch. But he wasn't a stranger to the place; he visited Cuba at least a few times a year. This time, though, he was on assignment.

He never rode an elevator when he could walk, so he exited his third floor room and took the staircase down into the bar and walked through the restaurant onto the Prado. He liked Havana in the morning the best; the hustlers and hookers were otherwise occupied and he could have an espresso and not be bothered. Usually.

He stopped in Francesa's pastry shop, walked up to the cashier and got a triple espresso to keep him company. On his way out an old guy was selling Granma newspapers. These were propaganda rags that provided income for retirees from the military unable to sell their bodies or cigars. The paper man offered him an English version, but LaRue wanted Spanish to bone up.

The old vet apologized and told LaRue he'd be back in a moment and left him in quick time. He returned and traded a Spanish version with LaRue for a 5 CUC bill.

LaRue thought how hard Cubans worked to serve gringo turistas. A single convertible peso, a CUC, received from delivering a service, was two or three days of a family's cash flow from the Castros. LaRue thought that people in Canada and America often lose such a tiny amount of cash under their car seats every day.

LaRue was still at a Sergeant's pay grade out of choice, but with his seniority and all his living expenses covered off he was financially comfortable. He was also meticulous in his money management, so he was wealthy by most people's standards.

He returned to the cashier and got another triple espresso in a paper cup.

One of the new gadgets in his professional toolkit was a Blackberry and he checked it and read an email that confirmed that he had a meeting with his new assignment contact, a guy named McCaul, the next day at sixteen hundred. This gave him some time to meet with his local contacts and prepare. He wondered what this McCaul was like; whether he was just another goon who killed for money or if he had the ability to actually empathize and feel things. Appreciate the values of Cubanos, not just the architecture and women.

He sipped his espresso and wandered across the Parque Central and down the hill and angled his direction southerly toward the old convent of San Francisco of Assisi and the old plaza. He took his time and enjoyed all the noises of the old city coming to life.

There was any number of jalopies being coaxed into igniting. Delivery truck drivers were arguing about who had the right of way on a narrow street and dogs were snarling and wrestling over a piece of edible trash.

He passed by a young black girl, maybe fifteen, nicely but barely dressed in clothes designed to attract gringo attention. She looked troubled and her eyes had the dead look of a child without hope; it likely being sucked away during a night spent being abused by a perverted gringo.

He motioned to her and she shied away, but he repeated it and she approached him cautiously.

"Little one. Do not waste your life this way. Do you go to school?" She shrugged.

"I will pay you to go to school. Understand?" She gave another shrug.

"Here is viente CUCs. Go home and clean yourself off and stay away from people who want to use you and harm you." She snatched the bill and started to walk away.

"Niña!" She turned back toward him. "If you are here in one week at this time, and you go to school every day, I will give you another one. But I will want to look at your homework."

The girl shrugged, but this time with a hopeful, not doubtful expression.

"You can trust me, Niña. Ask around about me. My name is Cien. I will be here next week and be very disappointed if you are not. You promise?"

"Si. I will try."

"You promise?"

She nodded and ran down an alley.

LaRue continued on and arrived at the old plaza. It was huge, denoting the significance of Habana when the Conquistadors were robbing gold from the Aztecs and Incans while their priests pursued souls. The square surrounded a huge fountain and was surrounded by immaculately restored buildings from a time in Habana long gone.

He looked for and saw a stout, gray haired hombre sitting on a bench near the fountain feeding pigeons with bits of dried corn. He wandered over to him through a flock of tourists taking pictures of everything in eyesight.

"Hermano, you're treating the birds better than the Castros treat people."

LaRue's new conversation partner looked up and smiled and spoke in Spanish. "Amigo, the pigeons don't demand human rights."

LaRue chuckled and joined the man on the bench.

"How are you, Brother Frank?"

"I am relaxed, I came here early for no other reason than the sun was shining and I could not sleep. I stayed in the convent and few things interest me less than nuns." Both men laughed.

LaRue had a box of cigarillos and offered one to the Roman Catholic churchman who shook his head while LaRue lit his and said, "What's our situation?"

LaRue handed him an envelope.

"Cien, you are a hero."

"Amigo, I'm just paying alms for my guilt."

"You are still a hero."

"Maybe a little one."

Francisco carefully closed his bag of corn and leaned forward. "Your father was a great man, Cien."

41

"So they tell me."

LaRue noticed a tourist pointing a camera coming their way and he and Francisco rose.

LaRue said, "I will see you in a few days, amigo. Adios."

"Hasta la vista, amigo."

They walked away before the tourist had a chance to snap.

7

MCCAUL WOKE UP A LITTLE WEARY after a day of hunting and killing followed by an afternoon and evening of dining and drinking. Abelardo had dropped McCaul off at his place and he'd slept like the dead until after nine.

Yesterday had been a little bit disconcerting for McCaul. First off, having a bartender suspicious of him; secondly, the local mafia chieftain offering to help him out when even McCaul didn't know what he might be up to and worse, that the secret police had him on their watch list.

The last one was, of course, the most worrying. If McCaul appeared to do something a little out of the ordinary, then one of the million police and spies in Havana might take notice.

Havana doesn't really have one million people and one million police, although that's what locals say. But there were big penalties for not reporting something that can be possibly anti-revolutionary, every corner has a member of the National Revolutionary Police and every street a citizen spy in the Committee for the Defense of the Revolution.

Actually, there might be more than a million cops in the place.

McCaul thought his mission was threatening to get out of control before it ever even started.

McCaul checked his email and found a confirmation that he'd be meeting Lucien LaRue at four pm at the Telegrafo bar. On-line he read the story of the two drug lords murdered near Cancun; the Mexican authorities said it was almost certainly the actions of a rival drug gang. Bueno.

He put on a fresh tee shirt and shorts and his Pumas and did his tough isometric exercise program for about twenty minutes followed by a hundred quick sit-ups and fifty push-ups.

He ran down the stairs, stretched, and started trotting up the hill toward the university.

He passed students of every colour. The University invites students from everywhere, especially paying students from capitalist countries they can re-educate. They also offer scholarships to students from developing countries, filling the gap made by the re-tasking of Patrice Lumumba University in Moscow.

After a block he picked up speed and in a couple of minutes was through the University gates and running up the hundred or so steps to its entrance.

At the top he did some Rocky Balboa shadow boxing, fifty more push-ups and then bunny-hopped back down the steps to the bottom again.

And that was enough. He was bushed and spewing sweat the way he liked to.

He walked back down to La Rampa and the Coppelia Ice Cream Park.

Habañeros have very few distractions that were not by definition healthy. Yes they smoke like chimneys; mostly a cigarette brand called Popular that cost pennies a package or cigars rolled by a friend or relative or some borrowed from the local factory. But otherwise, booze was too expensive to abuse and drugs were way too expensive to even consider.

A family of four might, if lucky, get rations for eight ounces of beef or pork a month and maybe three eggs. They have to make a little protein go a long way.

So Cubans, overall, were among the healthiest people in the hemisphere. Seeing a portly one is possibly a lucky charm.

But they loved their ice cream and the lineup around the block at the Coppelia, even in the morning, proved it.

But with all the equality enforced in Fidel's Cuba some, those with real currency, were more equal than others.

A few years before Fidel stopped allowing use of the U.S. Dollar and started using a scrip he called the Cuban Convertible Peso. Everyone else calls them CUCs. It allowed him to take an extra 10% off the top when Americans visit and change their money.

At the Coppelia, as at many places on the island, CUC payers don't stand in line.

Time was more valuable to McCaul than to the Cubans, so he went in the CUC non-line to pay about fifteen times more than locals and got himself a heart stopping Sundae with real banana, real pineapple and two scoops of real vanilla ice cream with real chocolate sauce.

It took him all the way home to finish it, and he smiled all the way.

McCaul had a couple of hours before he met his new partner in intrigue. He showered and selected clothes that a typical innocent tourist would wear at the Telegrafo.

So he put on walking sandals, a pair of navy linen pants and a pink Tommy Hilfiger polo shirt.

The Telegrafo was a fair hike after a hard workout and he walked up to Neptuno and went east. Neptuno runs on a straight line all the way from the University to Habana Vieja, the original settlement. The street goes from McCaul's part of the city, Vedado, which is middle class, and through Centro, which is filled with crowded apartments occupied mainly by almost no income families.

There is hardly a three-foot stretch of Neptuno that doesn't have a pothole and the sidewalks were mostly three feet wide and filled with dog leavings, so it's not the best of places to stroll. Its buildings mostly look like they're bombed out, but the damage is just from age and a lack of interest or funds to do repairs.

McCaul arrived a little bit early to meet up with LaRue so he strolled over to the Gran Teatro to see what was on the performance agenda. The National Ballet; never been there and never done that. Never would.

He stopped into the pastry cafe next to the Telegrafo and had a chocolate croissant and a double espresso. The service as always was slow, but the wait was worth it...

McCaul had grown up on Toronto's mean streets trying hard to get into trouble as often as he could and sometimes succeeding.

His father had been a tough old shanty-bog Irishman who, when he landed in Canada, had been sent to a work gang in Northern Ontario. He had saved enough to buy a little house in Toronto's slum of Parkdale, brought his family over from Kerry and started a kitchen cabinetry business.

McCaul and his three older sisters had eaten well, but they didn't have much in the way of luxury or adventure. McCaul's marks were good enough to go to college, but the family bank account wasn't. McCaul knew that his father expected him to take over his business but had known that he would have birthed a calf if he had been forced to do so.

So one spring McCaul had taken a streetcar downtown, visited the Canadian Forces Recruiting Office and signed up for adventure and maybe a chance to wear a fancy uniform and spend nights drinking exotic potions on foreign islands.

And while he had his share of adventure in a number of hotspots, his high school marks were noticed and he'd been sent to the Royal Military College and gotten a Bachelors of Science and ended up a lieutenant.

He and his regiments used to train a lot with Delta Force and British commandos and they were transformed from skinny teens to tough and mean bastards.

He looked across to the Parque and admired the huge Royal Palms swaying gently in the breeze. As always the broad street between the park and him, the Prado, was busy with all forms of human transportation that doesn't fly. Football helmets zipped past rickshaws trying to avoid rattletraps, hansom cabs and taxis.

McCaul finished up and walked next door and went through the front doors of the Telegrafo.

The Hotel Telegrafo is a reconstruction masterpiece.

Lower wall surfaces of light native wood and upper walls of reddish toned wooden paneling surround the hotel's light marble lobby floor. A couple of distinguished columns adjoin quite grand entrances to a magnificent main dining room and to a beautiful atrium bar with a mosaic wall. Fidel had established a development company called Habanaguanex to funnel money into redeveloping the old part of Habana and a big wad of cash had gone into the Telegrafo.

He walked through the lobby and into the bar. His counterpart was already seated, assuming that the dark complexioned military type wearing a cream coloured sports jacket sitting at a table wasn't a Castro spy.

He nodded and McCaul nodded back, walked over and introduced himself. He rose and offered his hand, "Lucien LaRue".

McCaul said, "This place is pretty small, I think we should probably go somewhere less public."

He said, "I agree."

LaRue gave a five CUC note to the bartender for an untouched beer and let McCaul lead the way out into the street.

Probably the largest tourist hotel nearby is the Parque Central, so they risked their necks crossing the street, walked across the park talking about LaRue's flight, got to the Parque and went up to the roof and took a seat near the pool. McCaul ordered them a couple of mojitos, which arrived while they were still exchanging pleasantries.

LaRue was sharply dressed in a light beige suit and appeared to be taller than his height, which was a few inches short of six feet. He had spare, monkish dark hair and really reminded McCaul of somebody.

Trudeau! He really looked like a young Pierre Trudeau; very stylish, intelligent looking and calm.

He said, "You live here, Mr. McCaul?"

"I moved last year, it's far from prying eyes and the weather's really good when it's not really, really bad."

"Cheap?"

"Yeah, but there's not very much to spend money on, so I trek back to Toronto once a month to fill up on goodies and basics."

"You're JTF2?"

LaRue said, "Oui. In New Brunswick, when I grew up, you joined the railroad, the Royal Bank, or the Army. The army sounded like more fun. I enjoy exciting things, so I started with Airborne."

The Canadian Airborne Regiment had been among the most honoured, and finally, most dishonoured of Canadian fighting units. It was also McCaul's old regiment.

The duo's predecessors at Airborne had been heroes at Normandy, but while McCaul had been posted to his home base in Trenton, near Toronto, the regiment had been disgraced and disbanded for highly publicized and embarrassing activities by a few members in Somalia.

"Many of our top Airborne members that were not court martialled were recruited to join the Joint Task Force, which I have served in since."

"I was Airborne when I was a kid," McCaul told him. "Did six years and got into intell with the Mounties' Emergency Response Team."

"Where did you serve?"

"I did one junket to Bosnia with the Patricias. Got into and outta the Medak Pocket."

"Then we are brothers, I was there too." Lucien said.

McCaul chuckled, "You were probably the French guy who bossed me around."

LaRue laughed, "Likely. I was a bossy ass-hole back then."

McCaul laughed out loud. "So was I amigo, so was I."

LaRue laughed back and asked, "How much do you know about Cuba, Mr. McCaul?"

"Just what a gringo who's been here a year would know. Which is mostly what the Castros want us to know, which isn't much. How about you?"

LaRue took a drink of his mojito. "I have been coming here quite often for many years, so I've gotten to know the place quite well."

McCaul asked, "Have the people been spoiled by socialism? Is their health care and crime rates as great as the propaganda says they are?"

LaRue said, "I know many Cubans, Señor, but I don't know any fat ones at all. They don't eat, drink or do drugs because they haven't any money. I suppose that contributes to their life spans. They don't die in car accidents because no one has cars and no one can afford to waste petrol by driving fast and burning it quickly.

"As far as crime, Cuba's a police state. There's at least one para-military on every street corner. So we're safe. The entire Cuban security apparatus, including their neighbourhood spies, are there to protect Cuba from Cubans, not to be a significant factor in Bay of Pigs Two. But to be honest, there is a lot of violent crime between Cubans, usually over girlfriends or sisters.

"Health care is good if you have money to pay for it."

McCaul nodded while he muddled the mint in his drink. "So, Sergeant LaRue, tell me what we're going to be doing."

LaRue spoke without an accent, softly and without any hesitation.

"Mr. McCaul, we have reliable intelligence that the Cuban leadership is offering Cuba as a safe haven for terrorist activities to be conducted against our friends in return for substantial sums of money and petro. This is despite the Castros indicating their interest in pursuing better relations with the USA.

"Our goal will be to confirm or deny the truth of this intelligence, and, if true, collect damning evidence that can be presented to the Security Council of the United Nations and the world media. This might allow a further conclusion to be made by the USA relative to this risk."

McCaul asked, "How do we do it?"

LaRue responded, "Our covers will be as employees of Globalair, we'll be examining security concerns and visit remote areas in the West and Southeast provinces of Cuba and in the city of Havana.

"We'll conduct casual interviews with officials in the Cuban leadership structure, as well as undertake whatever intelligence gathering activities we can."

McCaul said, "What's our exit strategy?"

"Hopefully, we'll leave peacefully on one of Globalair's charters. In the event of distress, we would need to commandeer a speedboat and get to international waters."

"You swim?" McCaul asked.

"Part of the job."

McCaul looked at his watch and it was almost five. "On whose authority is this being conducted? I don't want to get into a pissing contest between Fidel, the Prime Minister and the President."

"The P.M. has authorized this action, but has required that his leadership be provided with plausible deniability. In the event you're discovered and arrested, the Government of Canada will offer diplomatic support for your release as long as you keep this authorization confidential.

"I expect I will be jailed as a spy. But the Government of Canada will not acknowledge any role in our undertakings."

That frightened McCaul a little. He had personal experience that the Canadian government tended to ignore the needs of its citizens in the interests of maintaining friendships with pals from abroad.

But he hadn't really expected any more protection. In his profession this was standard operating procedure.

McCaul pushed back in his chair to indicate there was no more to say and LaRue did the same.

"Are you checked in, Sergeant?"

"Call me LaRue, Mr. McCaul. That's what my brothers in JTF2 call me. And yes I am. I also confirmed an adjoining room for you in the event that we need to be in the same place for overnights or you need a room for meetings." He passed McCaul a key card. "303."

"Cool. Call me McCaul or Mike. Interested in wandering around Havana a little bit?"

"Oh, very much. I enjoy wandering the city."

They elevatored down to the lobby and McCaul started them toward his usual place. Now that it was getting close to dusk Mike thought they might be able to find some music.

Walking past the Floridita, McCaul's thoughts were confirmed; he heard deep, emotional rhythms hard to find anywhere but here. Gentle and passionate, deep and emotional. Bolero. They arrived at Casa del Escabeche.

8

CUBA HAS A MUSICAL HERITAGE at least as great as any other culture: guaguancó, pulsing rumba, bluesy guajira, lilting son, longing bolero dripping with sexual tension.

McCaul knew the song, but had never heard it sung with such longing.

He had not, though, seen the singer before and McCaul knew talent when he heard it; the singer, or sonero, was Hispanic, brightly dressed and fairly stout, with long, glistening and tightly ringleted hair. His baritone, surrounded by deep sounds of percussion and strings, filled the small bar. "Besame Mucho" - a Bolero tune McCaul had heard, but never before like this.

The band finished the bolero and started an enthusiastic salsa song.

Couples quickly occupied what space there was between the bar and the band. Singles dancing Sambas, others were just swaying to the strong rhythms.

LaRue and McCaul shuffled by the dancers and band and bellied up to the bar.

McCaul had asked one time what escabeche meant and he had been told that it was pickled fish and there were quite a few pickled people in the bar: dancing, a few translating, some singing, laughing, talking, asking for mojitos, shouting mojito. Arms around the shoulders of strangers.

Plainly dressed Habañeros with other Habañeros; better-dressed Americans, Canadians and Euros trying to find a common tongue; a party girl making her charming moves on an unsuspecting turista. Helping him feel handsome. Maybe not for money, but at least for a generous party and a love companion for a few minutes, hours or days.

McCaul noticed a couple enthused with the music, dancing near the corner of the bar. The man was fairly tall and very slim, coal black, with a straw fedora and a wide smile. His dance partner had her back to Mike. She was a foot shorter, with thick brunette hair in a blunt cut, her modest hips held in a pair of tight pants swaying well to the rhythm. When the couple turned in profile, Mike smiled in disbelief.

It was Kate McKee; McCaul's lost love who had chosen fame and fortune over him.

Mike turned to Aries, "Dos mojitos, por favor," and turned back to watch Kate dance.

Acting dumb, LaRue asked, "What's a mojito?"

"Have one, you'll like it," McCaul replied. Mojitos have become the national drink of Cuba, surpassing Cuba Libres and Daiquiris. It is a seductive blend of limejuice, club soda, crushed mint leaves, sugar and Habana Club rum. A lot of rum in the better ones, usually a little less once the bartender notices a gleam in your eye.

Kate and her dance partner swung around just as the drinks arrived. She noticed Mike and laughingly waved. Her partner smiled just as brightly. The drinks arrived, LaRue paid, and Kate pointed her partner to join the two Canadians.

Mike barely was able to take a sip of the wicked mixture before Kate swung him around and gave him a complete body hug.

"McCaul, what the hell are you doing here!" She reached up to give him a kiss on the cheek and snatched her own mojito from the bar for a generous drink.

"McCaul, this is Eduardo."

McCaul shook hands with her friend who smiled widely and shook vigorously. "Hello, Eduardo." His smile was effusive and Mike felt his own grin stretch.

McCaul almost shouted over the music, "I live here now. When you left I didn't have any reason to stay in Toronto. What about you?"

Kate said, "I'm still with CNN. They've got me down here doing a special on Fidel and Raul. I've missed you, I tried to call you a few times when I was in Toronto, but your office said you were out of the country and couldn't be contacted."

"Mike, how about the ballet?"

"I don't dance."

"You big silly. I mean do you wanna go with me tonight? I've got tickets."

"Sure, sounds like fun," McCaul said, but didn't really mean it. There were a lot more pleasing things that might be done with Kate in the dark, but he thought in this special case, he might compromise.

Meanwhile, LaRue and Eduardo were gabbing away in Spanish. Mike had been hanging around Spanish speaking Caribbean countries long enough to speak it a little and understand a little more. But not well enough to hear and interpret on the fly.

Kate pulled him away from the bar to try and keep up to a lively salsa tune and to his surprise his feet seemed to end up in the right places and they finished the song laughing and holding hands.

The music stopped, and the band put down their tools. Eduardo rushed over to the singer and brought him over to meet his new friends. "McCaul, esto es Miguel Damian Marerro." Damian reached out his hand and McCaul shook it. "This is my piano player, Oswaldo Perigo." Oswaldo smiled broadly and gave McCaul a hug, making the Canadian smile.

McCaul said in bad Spanish: "Hola, Damian, Cómo sean usted? Hágalo como un mojito." The singer nodded and Mike ordered up another round for their group and the band.

LaRue got up and offered regrets, it was after 6 pm and he said he wanted to unpack and get settled. He left and Kate reached up to speak in Mike's ear over the hubbub.

"Mike, let's get going. I know a great paladare just around the corner we can eat at after the show."

McCaul turned around and offered Damian his hand. The sonero said, "Amigo, jugamos todas las noches en la Bar Monserrate."

Mike's weak Spanish allowed him to know that Damian played nights at a nearby bar. McCaul smiled and said, "Gracias, Damian. Tarde."

Mike turned and got a hug and back slap from Eduardo, a couple of handshakes from the other band members and he and Kate left.

They walked back up Obispo toward the Parque. The street was still hopping and busy and they strolled along while getting caught up on their love and work lives. Both of their love lives turned out to be mutually pathetic, which made him happy.

She was so very lovely to Mike: a mane of thick brunette hair, full lips, wide brown eyes, and a perfect light brown tan. She had on a pair of navy cargo pants and white sneakers, with a striped white shirt and looked and talked like a college girl.

"So let me tell ya about the Cuban Ballet, Mike. It's run by the only living prima ballerina assoluta, Alicia Alonso. She's almost ninety, blind as a bat, danced with Balachine in the 30's and was a global star before she came back to Cuba. She was the original Giselle."

"Umhumm." Mike had no idea, whomsoever, Giselle was and whatsoever Kate was talking about but was thrilled she was.

55

There were bereted and grey uniformed police officers two to a block, speaking into their walkie-talkies and interviewing residents, especially those in the company of turistas. The country, really Fidel, is terrified that his subjects might learn something about open society that he didn't want them to know.

They walked back past the Museum and by the Marti statue in the Parque. Mike was becoming very comfortable in saying "no gracias" to the dozen or so young men offering cigars, taxis or other treats. They came to San Rafael and the Gran Teatro.

There was a relatively small crowd of patrons outside of the Teatro in line for the performance of the Ballet Nacional de Cuba. The two were running late.

"The Cuba form of dance combines their athleticism with Russian traditional form. Their male dancers jump higher than anyone else and their ballerinas are about the most beautiful and lithe." Kate would know. McCaul wouldn't.

He looked forward to seeing the litheness.

The foyer of the Teatro was tired and not unlike that of Massey Hall and the Royal Alex back in Toronto. Kate had tickets in the orchestra and he followed her toward their seats. Once they entered the main auditorium he was surprised that the seats were new: plush red velveteen. When he sat, the narrowness of the area between rows made his knees almost touch his chest, but he thought that this would let him more comfortably rest his head when he fell asleep.

The music started, then the lights came up, a duo walked out and McCaul was totally captivated for almost two hours.

After the duo (Kate told him it was a pas de deux), there was a group of ten or so couples, then a collage of dance excellence that just left him stunned.

The athleticism by both the male and female dancers was shocking; Mike could barely imagine how much discipline and training had gone into developing their individual abilities. He could only imagine the pain of the training the dancers must suffer just to get and keep their jobs. When it was over Mike clapped the loudest of anyone, he thought.

When the dance troupe had left the stage, another round of applause started and Kate pointed him toward the balcony.

"Look, Mike, its Alonso herself." The legend was wrapped in crimson with a turban and looked like a movie star from long ago; Gloria Swanson as Norma Desmond. McCaul wondered how tough the old woman must be to be able to demand so much from her dancers. He suspected that, even in her blindness, she could likely sense if one of her dancers missed a step by a centimeter. And that the dancers knew this and were terrified to feel her wrath.

On the way out, McCaul concluded that there was something to this dance thing that he had never ever even imagined. 'If this was what dance is,' he thought, 'I think that I'll attend every chance I get'.

Mike was gushing steadily when they left the ballet, and gushing was something he seldom did. He felt like a kid who had just attended his first NHL game.

Kate looked at McCaul sideways and slyly. "Sure, Mike, it was great. But I'm hungry."

She pulled him toward the right and down along the adjoining pedestrian only street.

McCaul had read once that San Rafael had been Cuba's main shopping street. Both sides of the street were lined with faded window signs of used-to-be American department stores and boutiques: Woolworths, Westinghouse and Sunbeam among others.

There were dozens of couples strolling hand in hand down the broad street, not window shopping as would have been the case fifty years ago, but engrossed in themselves.

For a change not one couple they passed was a north-south combination of intimate employee and employer that McCaul often saw and frowned upon. All were locals and it was a nice change for him.

A couple of blocks down the street Kate led him through a yellow door and up a steep narrow staircase to a locked gate. He noticed on the other side of the gate a picture of Celine Dion, of all people, and a photo of a well-restored red Chevy Impala book-ended by two smiling Cubanos. She rang a bell.

"This place is awesome." She rang the bell again and whispered. "It's owned by a couple of gay guys, so you know the food will be great."

A couple of seconds later a thin Cuban girl with a huge halo of ringlets around her Madonna face opened the gate and led them in. As they were being seated, a fairly substantial Spanish guy, one of the men in the picture, came toward them smiling and offering his greetings to Kate.

"Hola, mi nombre es Montana. Dé la bienvenida a mi casa." McCaul offered his thanks and they shook hands. "Wadju like today. We hab bery fresco langosta y camerones. Sound good?"

"It sounds wonderful," said Kate and they were led into one of the dining rooms. The apartment was immaculate with high ceilings and beautiful finishes.

McCaul knew that after Russia withdrew their economic support for Cuba in the mid 90's, Castro had to come up with an immediate solution to generate new sources of foreign currency. So he had begun to license restaurants and lodgings in private homes, called paladares. The license fees were very high, however, and McCaul suspected from the high security that this one was of the unlicensed variety. There was likely a higher price to pay for this modest attempt at earning a buck if Montana ever was caught, or if he didn't pay off a few cops and CDR reps.

The little dining room they were led to had two tables for four with mismatched chairs and plastic Disneyworld placemats. Their lovely server came in and inquired about their drink preferences.

"Dos cervesas, por favor."

They sat down and she brought them two green bottles of Cristal. They poured the crisp lager into juice glasses, clinked glasses, and drank thirstily.

"Quite a place," McCaul said.

"Isn't it? Boyd and I got brought here by a couple of amateur tour guides the other day. The lobster tails are massive! God, it's great to see you. I've really, really been lonely."

McCaul wondered why she hadn't called him, but was even more disappointed that she had been just down the street, while he was pining and killing people to survive without her.

"So why are you guys down here anyway and who's Boyd?"

"I did call you, by the way!!! But you were never in and I was always on the move.

"Fidel's sicker than anyone knows, even with his latest problems and Raul is worse than his brother and a better liar. The succession plan can't work, Raul's successor is older than he is. Heaven knows how the vacuum might be filled. Somehow, some way young black Cubans will have to be heard from. So we're down to at least prepare for the change, if not cover it when it happens."

"You know something, Kate? I've been down here over a year and I know almost nothing about the politics, except what I hear in bars."

He asked, "So what do you know about Raul?"

"He's probably gay and they say he goes out in the countryside looking for cute young boys for fun. Cubans call him China Lady because he likes to make himself up like a girl and he is really quite effeminate. I've seen pictures. That's probably why Fidel has persecuted the gays here so much."

"And who's that guy who's the head of the Assembly down here?"

"Señor Ricardo Accardo." She pronounced it with an attempt at an extreme Spanish accent. It came across with extreme sensuality.

"A puppet. There is never a word from his mouth that hasn't come out of Fidel and Raul's. Way too weak to win a transition fight.

"Cuba is run by octogenerian Spanish men that were with Fidel in the beginning. You won't find a black or anyone under sixty-five doing anything important. He had a couple of young guys around fifty that seemed to like the idea of someday taking his job and they've disappeared."

The server brought in a huge bowl of spiced shrimps and a plate of chunky deep-fried taro potatoes and ketchup. They each scraped some of both on their plates and tasted. Both dishes were delicious.

McCaul asked, "Isn't there anybody on his councils or in his army that's looking to take over?"

"Cubans don't say 'when Fidel dies'. They say 'if Fidel dies' and Fidel thinks the same. No one in his right mind would dare to indicate an interest in leadership. Fidel is vicious with potential rivals and he's crowned Raul as heir. He's got a couple of guys who he might move up if Raul dies first, and there's supposed to be a couple of groups up in the mountains, but I don't know that they could muster a real threat. There are a few opposition parties, but they're not real; mostly just dreamers."

"What about out of country?"

"A couple of wannabe Jose Marti's living in Miami, but none that are young enough and well enough known. Besides, they're pretty much as loco as Fidel. There's was talk about Fidel inviting the President from Venezuela to take over, because he was providing his oil but they're worse off than Cuba. The biggest rumour is that Fidel's getting money from the China and the Persian Gulf, and they'll have a say on who's next."

The server arrived with four huge lobster tails, a plate of sickly looking tomatoes and cucumbers, a big plate of rice and black beans, and a small bowl of pimento sauce. They ordered another round of Cristals, refilled their plates and sliced into their lobster that discouraged his ability to converse intelligently for a few minutes.

"Mike, it's so great to see you. I really, really regret that I couldn't get to spend time with you when I got the new job. The U.S. networks pay a great dollar but expect to own you mind, body and soul."

McCaul smiled and looked sheepish, slightly revealing the heartbreak that he had felt and the happiness he felt now.

"Kate, there has not been a day go by that I have not missed you intensely."

She reached across, under the table, and put her hand on his knee. She gently squeezed and smoldered. He felt himself rise a little bit to the wanted attention.

They paused and smiled at each other.

He broke the trance they were in when he asked, "Can you explain one thing to me? How they can still call it a revolution after almost fifty years?"

"I've talked to a lot of old folks about the old days. And they say the revolution pretty much died when Che started jailing college kids and shooting professors after they took over. Since then it's been just like any other tin-pot dictatorship banana republic. But the Castros do a fantastic job stifling opposition."

Mike asked, "Don't they have great healthcare?"

"Compared to what? Everybody I talk to down here can't get an aspirin tablet and they have separate facilities for tourists and VIPs. They sell the services of their nurses and doctors to other countries for hard cash."

"What if Fidel were to die?" He asked.

"The Pentagon is all set for that, Mike. They've already notified marinas along the Florida Straits so that fuel won't be sold if the beard goes and that there'll be a blockade preventing any loco ex-pat cruiser jockey from going back to claim their ancestral lands. The Yanks want total calm if Fidel goes."

The server came around to clean up the empty serving dishes and their empty bottles. Two fresh Cristals were in her hands.

"Kate, What exactly are you doing down here? And who's Boyd?"

"Boyd's my cameraman. I want to win a Pulitzer. The Castro story, when it ends, will be one of the biggest in modern news history. I want to be the person who is remembered for reporting it. There are a lot of people down here who hide their hatred of Castro and are looking for chances for the stories to get out.

"Down here, most people haven't seen CNN, but they know it exists, and for them I'm their best chance at creating change. For me, I want to be the one that does."

"Kate, are you nuts? If all this stuff is true and they suspect you know this stuff, all the press credentials in the world won't save your butt."

"Darling, this is what I do. And if I do it, and get hurt, que sera sera."

Mike had forgotten, Kate was a beautiful, fun and sensuous woman, but was an alligator in her work and took no prisoners.

She shoved her chair back. "Let's go for a walk and try and find a club."

McCaul moved his chair back and the scraping sound brought in the server with the bill. Kate put two twenties and a ten on the table, they rose, the server accompanied them to the gate and let them out and they walked down the narrow stairs into the streets.

San Rafael was busy with music and smiling animated people; basic Havana without tourists. Kate led them away from the lights and further into the dark toward Centro. A block down the street they turned right and strolled a couple of blocks down a dim alley.

McCaul stopped her and turned her around, she looked deeply in his eyes; he felt her quivering slightly in the cool breeze off the sea. He bent slightly forward and she stood on her toes and he gave her the deepest kiss he ever have. The first kiss since he had last seen her. And she kissed him back with just as much tension and desire.

They held each other and he whispered in her ear.

"Kate, you have to be really, really careful with your speculations."

She dropped to her heels.

She whispered back, "Come on, Mike. Would you stop doing your job just because it was a little bit scary sometimes? And besides, what are you doing down here? I don't think Jud Webster gives one horse's patoot about airline security in Cuba. What's your secret?"

Mike knew she didn't know his real job. But she was a world-class snoop. Before he answered he looked around. The revelers were inside. There was barely a trace of humanity in the streets, although the sounds of stereos and televisions could be heard coming from open doors.

"Kate, that's not relevant. I'm prepared to deal with stuff that might get thrown my way. These are very, very serious people down here, and they will bury you alive and tell your family, employer and government they're still looking for you under every stone."

"Mike, I got CNN on my side. They wouldn't dare."

"I just don't want you getting into so tight a mess that you can't be pulled out."

"Give it up, Mike. I've got my teeth in a hot story and I'm not about to let go just for the sake of what some banana republic commie flake might try to do."

They turned right again, back toward the hotel, and heard the pleasant hum of music ahead. A block more and they came to a lean-to of a disco, maybe room for a hundred people, with a corrugated plastic roof and a stand up bar at the back. The band was playing "Chan Chan", a lively song about old friends remembering time spent together admiring a woman's buttocks on the beach. Now that's Cuba.

There was a doorman who welcomed them to "Buena Vista Social Club".

Of course, this was a clever ruse to capitalize on the success of the movie and album from a decade before. The real Buena Vista Social Club had burned down almost a lifetime ago. But, it seemed more and more to McCaul, Cuba was a collection of clever ruses.

But ruse or not, this place was hopping. A lively combo with two gorgeous conga-playing vocalists in feathery costumes possibly rescued from the Tropicana in the fifties, a couple of guitarists and two trumpet players.

The place was simple, white resin plastic tables and chairs, but the joy of the music and the energy of the happy and likely horny patrons made entrance mandatory.

Mike paid the doorman ten dollars and they entered. They sat at one of the few open tables long enough to order two drinks before Kate pulled Mike up to dance.

McCaul tried to stop thinking to allow his feet to do their stuff, and again, they seemed to always land in the right place. He thought that either this music was remarkably easy to dance to, or mojitos somehow endowed their imbibers with natural rhythm. Dancing juice.

And Mike really enjoyed dancing with Kate and wondered if maybe it was her magic that was transposing its rhythm to his feet. Regardless of the reason, after the band's extended mix version of Chan Chan, they ended up in each other's arms, laughing and smiling. She gave him a big hug for a small woman and reached up to kiss his cheek.

This rendezvous was not the least bit unpleasant for Mike. She made him warm up all over.

When they got back to their table, their mojitos were just being delivered. Mike paid and they had a very short life.

Kate took a long drink, jumped up and said, "Let's go!" She pulled Mike to his feet. He surrendered to her will.

They walked the block to the hotel chatting about the music and remembering the dinner, and previous times together in Toronto. Her arm in his, they laughed and snuggled all the way.

"Mike, do you remember the first time we met?"

"Only about every other day."

"Really?"

"Yup."

"You were so cute."

"I'm never cute, Kate. Maybe hunky, but not cute."

"Oh, you were cute and thank God you rescued me from that Claude guy."

"I'm just kind of glad that I pulled over into an alley."

She snuggled closer, "And I'm glad you played your music so loud."

After they entered the hotel elevator they had a crucial decision to make. Both of them were here to work not play. But the urge to play was tremendous.

She whispered in his ear, "You give me goose bumps. But they oughta call them good bumps."

He surrendered to her again and allowed her to guide him to her room.

9

THE PHONE RANG just as Mike was starting to wake up. Before he reached over to pick it up he felt a little emptiness from leaving Kate to return home in the middle of the night.

"Mike, rise and shine." It was Webster as jolly as usual.

"I'm all arose and all ashine, Chief, what's up?"

"I just wanted to call and let you know Manny Gant has offered you the use of his helicopter down there. He's up here for the next month and I saw him at the club last night. He figures he'd rather have it used than let his mechanic and pilot get lazy."

Emmanuel Gant was principal owner of a dozen high-end hotels in Canada and six resort properties in Cuba as well as some other islands. He was a close friend of Webster as well as the Prime Ministers of both Canada and Cuba.

"Well, that's great, Chief. Thank you. I was wondering how we were going to get around, it's a lot bigger place than it looks on the map."

"I thought the same thing, Mike, so when I saw Manny last night I politely asked if it might be made available for a good cause, and he's happy to help."

Mike suspected that Webster had played his Order of Canada card to get fellow Order Member Gant, a difficult character, to agree to support the 'good cause'.

"Manny said he'd call his Cuban people first thing this morning, and it should be ready for you by ten o'clock. Meanwhile, Mrs. Hollis arranged for you to visit our destination resort and office in Cayo Coco this afternoon. The helicopter will be a big help, I think. The pilot's name is Ronaldo. You should ask him to take you to the Kristal Laguna resort. He knows the place.

"What's happening down there, Mike?"

"Not much yet, Boss. Just did a little tour of the nightspots last night. Did hear some scary rumours that might confirm our suspicions. Pretty much what Inglewood talked about. The scary thing is the source; Kate McKee's on top of the story which means who knows how the word will get out. But it's sure to get out."

"Well, you look after yourself, Mike. The Castros are old, but they still have all their teeth. Speaking of which, Manny's chopper is at the domestic Terminal 1 and his friendship with Fidel means you can travel anywhere on the island without any worries of interference."

Just before McCaul was about to sign off, he thought he better see what Webster knew about the pilot. Did they want Gant, and even worse Fidel, to know what they were about? Sure as shootin' Fidel would want to know what Gant was up to and would have a mole inside of his organization.

"Chief, can you do me a big favour in the next couple of minutes?"

"Of course, Mike. What can I do?"

"Can you call Manny Gant and find out exactly how trustworthy his flight and ground crew are?" McCaul thought, 'Gant's no patsy. He would have a complete dossier on everyone around him'.

"Already done. You're all right, Mike. Ronaldo and his brother the mechanic are, shall I say, close relatives of Manny's. He has been travelling there for thirty years, you know."

So Manny Gant had developed more than resorts in Cuba.

"Okkkaay. I'll let you know how I make out tomorrow."

He said, "Thanks, Mike," and hung up and so did McCaul.

McCaul got up, stretched and did his morning calisthenics. He showered - the water was hot, strong and seemed pure - and he shaved while enjoying the flow.

As he was towelling off his cell phone rang again. It was LaRue.

"LaRue! You're up early."

"Well, I just thought we should get off to a fast start, Michael."

"Let me get dressed, and get over there. We've got a chopper we can use that'll be ready at 10 o'clock." In a minute McCaul finished towelling, pulled on some clothes, ruffled his hair dry, and became a striking symbol of Canadian manhood.

He filled his pocket with CUCs, went out to the street, found a Panataxi at the corner and was whisked to the Telegrafo.

LaRue was in the lobby, dressed in light cargo pants, a dark green short-sleeved shirt, a dark windbreaker and hiking boots. He and McCaul went through the bar and into the dining room.

Kate and Sasquatch were seated at a table near the sidewall and she waved at the two Canadians to join them. "Mike, this is Boyd, my cameraman." She looked to McCaul like she had just visited a spa and had a full night's sleep, not spent a few hours enjoying heated passion.

Boyd was hairy and about six foot six and maybe on his thin days went three hundred pounds. McCaul shook Boyd's catcher's mitt of a hand and they all went up to the buffet table. Kate waved at the waiter to bring coffee and he poured small cups and left the pot while the group got their grub. The buffet looked to McCaul more Golden Griddle than Marriott.

Boyd picked out about six pounds of fatty bacon that met his selection criteria.

Kate said, "So what's on your agenda today, Mike?"

"Well, the good news is we got ourselves a chopper to ferry us around. LaRue and I are heading out to Cayo Coco for the day. Can we drop you somewhere?" Mike had a sip of coffee; it was good and very strong but lukewarm.

"Oh, Mike, that would be wonderful. We've been trying to find a way to get to Gitmo. You know it can take fifteen hours to go by land."

McCaul moved his bacon around on the plate and tried to find a non-fatty morsel. He couldn't.

"Gitmo is only about four hundred miles out of our way." McCaul offered a deal: "Why don't you guys drop us in Cayo Coco instead and take the chopper and we'll come back on our flight tonight?"

The waiter brought what McCaul thought might be papaya or mango juice and he had a drink. It was as cloying as both mango and papaya usually were and he set it back down.

"That would be perfect."

Kate tapped the top of Mike's right hand, left it there, and gave him her look: smoldering and sensual and promising even more unimaginable delights than those they had shared only a few hours before. He wanted to melt and agree to every whim of her slightest fancy. Then he remembered she used that same look to get millions of men to watch CNN every night. And that remembrance changed his urge to succumb not one bit.

"Mike, can we meet you out front in fifteen?"

"Yup."

She and Boyd left to get their stuff. She seemed to float to the door while Boyd followed behind with jolly green giant strides.

Mike stood up in his usual slightly clumsy way. LaRue rose much more elegantly. McCaul wondered if LaRue made footprints when he walked in the sand; he was very stealthy.

The two met Kate and Boyd outside a few minutes later and jumped in one of the mini-van Panataxis. McCaul told the driver their destination, got in the front seat and turned toward the back as far as he could to face the other passengers.

Mike didn't mind looking backwards, away from their destination, it was more than a little frightening to look straight ahead. This driver, like the one he had coming from the airport, seemed to be in training for the Cuban auto grand slalom demolition.

"So what are you going to do in Gitmo, Kate?"

"Oh, you know, just following up some ideas, getting some stock footage, that kind of stuff."

"Please tell me you're not going to do anything scary." Mike already knew the answer, but had to ask anyway.

"I'm a reporter, Mike. Stories don't come to me, I gotta go get them."

When they arrived at Marti Airport, they ended up in the old terminal. Old meant old. Not as ancient as Havana's eighteenth Century cathedrals, but definitely the equivalent in the aviation world.

The cabbie seemed to be disappointed he didn't get a chance to deliver a travelogue to earn his five-dollar tip.

They scooted into the terminal and, since they were obviously the only non-Cubans in the building, were quickly recognized by Gant's pilot and he came forward to meet them. He was mulatto, mostly black, and small, maybe 5'5" and 120 pounds.

"Señor McCaul, si? Mi nombre es Ronaldo. I am pilot of Señor Emmanuel."

He shook all their hands enthusiastically and McCaul wondered if they were going to get an aerial tour guide report on Cuban culture and architecture.

They passed through the terminal's basic security to enter the airfield. Gant's bright orange chopper was about fifty yards onto the tarmac, and already running. It was a fairly new Sikorsky S-92, a customized chopper that could probably seat twenty people. Gant was nothing if not ostentatious.

Ronaldo was smiling from ear to ear. "I hope you like my Seekorsky, Señor. It is my baybee. I love it and wash it all over every day. It can fly almost 1,000 kilometers, Señor."

McCaul knew from his Airborne days that the Sikorsky called for a two-man flight crew, but Ronaldo as a true Cuban, seemed fully confident to be able to manage on his own. Redundancy is not common in any factor of Cuban existence.

Mike helped Kate into the aircraft and Boyd boarded next, carrying his mini-cam like a brief case. Somehow, LaRue was already sitting in the co-pilot seat, which left McCaul in the back; he figured that Lucien must have wanted a bird's eye view of the terrain.

The chopper might have been built to hold twenty passengers, but its narrow interior was fitted-out for a half dozen: it had two comfortable leather sofas, a full wet bar, a plasma TV and DVD player and Mike was sure many other unseen amenities.

Gant was famous for having a way with ladies and a hot tub would not have surprised Mike.

Boyd promptly grabbed one of the larger love seats and was soon snoring, barely under the decibel levels of the rotors.

Once they got off the ground Lucien invited Kate to join the pilot up front and came back and sat down across from McCaul.

"So, Mike, we haven't talked much, have we?" McCaul lounged back in a love seat and cracked a bottle of Perrier. He passed one to LaRue who did the same.

LaRue said, "This is an exciting mission."

"Yup."

"What do you think about Cuba and the Castros?"

"I like it, not so crazy about them. Seems to me it's about time for them to go."

"Mike, you think it's a good idea to allow Kate to be around? Should we trust a TV reporter?"

"I wouldn't trust her with sensitive information for a second, Lucien. I've known Kate for a while, and she is a very good reporter. Which means that she is a very bad security risk. I'm more worried about her getting in a jam with no one to depend on but us."

McCaul paused, sensing there was something else. "What's really on your mind, LaRue?"

"Well, Mike, I've great sympathy for Cuban people. I wouldn't participate in anything that would see them worse off than they already are."

"Why so sensitive?"

"Amigo, there's something I have to tell you. My mother's name was Marguerita. She left Cuba a few years after the revolution and joined my father in Canada who had escaped Fidel a while before. He changed his last name to that of an old man he lived with in Canada before she emigrated.

"I'm a full-blooded Cubano, buddy. That's the reason I was so anxious to be a part of this thing."

McCaul was only a little bit shocked: LaRue's Spanish wasn't learned by cassette or in a government sponsored course, it was too natural.

"My mother and father worked very hard to raise me. He was an educated man who had been a close comrade to Fidel. But he could not be around the murders that Fidel and Che committed after the success of the revolution. So he escaped and moved to Canada and worked in the woods and that's how I came to be raised in Miramichi and the reason that I joined the army."

"Do you still have family in Cuba?"

"Yes. My mother came from somewhere in the mountains in Pinar del Rio. I'm not so sure where. I know I have three aunts and a cousin there; they still exchange letters with my mother who is very old now."

McCaul took a long slug of Perrier and thought for a moment. "Is there something you should tell me, LaRue?"

He stood up to get another cold drink then sat and leaned back with his hands behind his head for a deep breath, before leaning forward toward Mike with his forearms on his knees.

He looked McCaul straight in the eyes. "Mike, my mother has spent a lifetime without her family and she asked me to try and find her sisters. She wants to know they're okay, and see if we can help them. We're not rich, but we're millionaires compared to them."

This put a different spin on things. McCaul wondered whom he could depend on and whom he needed to worry about. Would LaRue's mission be complementary to his, or would it cause a conflict. Was there a chance that he might be discovered by the Cuban intelligence service doing his own stuff and screw up the main mission? Where was his heart in the assignment, and worse, would it affect his actions? McCaul needed to know.

"I need you to be there when the mission needs you. That's what I need. So. Will you be there?"

LaRue said, "I hope I can get away from our mission for a day or so to try and find my aunts. I will try and make sure that nothing that I do interrupts or interferes with our mission.

"Will this be okay, or would you like me to resign?"

McCaul thought he had few enough friends in Cuba, and none that could do what LaRue could. To him, half a LaRue was better than none.

"Okay with me," McCaul replied. "Can you let me know a little bit in advance when you have other places to be and other things to do?"

"I will do that, Mike. I would like to visit Pinar del Rio tomorrow for the day if I can."

"That will be okay, Lucien. But when I need you, I need you."

"Done."

There was a rustle in the front and soon Kate joined them.

"It's so beautiful, Mike, you don't know what you're missing back here. I can't wait to fly over the mountains on the way to Gitmo."

From Ronaldo came the standard invitation in Spanish to secure the group for landing. Everyone took seats and a few minutes later they gently settled to earth. They emerged to find that they weren't at an airport at all, rather at a Heli-Pad adjacent to a gorgeous new hotel adjoining the beach.

Kate gave them both air kisses and LaRue and McCaul disembarked Gant's flying palace for the beach. They were at the NH Krystal Laguna, previously El Senador: a luxury hotel originally built by a bunch of NHL Hall of Famers.

Ronaldo made sure they were clear and rose slowly but then rocketed rapidly back toward the mainland.

LaRue and McCaul wandered toward the main building taking in the almost boring eternally perfect sunny day, the crystal blue water in the lagoons surrounding much of the property and the white sand below a stretch of gently waving palms.

They stopped in at the front desk and asked for the general manager and were escorted to her office. Serge Savard and his fellow Montreal

Canadiens had pulled out all the stops in the place and LaRue thought the finishings were up to any hotel he'd ever visited.

McCaul had read about how they had needed to pull out, though. The joint venture with the Castros had basically seen the Canadians provide the millions of dollars of investment and operating costs while the Castros took the profit. So they sold out to a Spanish hotel chain and returned to Montreal licking their wounds.

They met with the resort General Manager and her head of security. They guided them through the gorgeous main building, meandered around the stilted suites and even took a look at the kitchen. The hour or two dragged by, but they kept their smiles, and managed to go through the new security protocols with the key staff.

McCaul waited for something to happen. Why had Webster arranged for them to come here?

After a late lunch of fish and salad they got up to take a taxi to the airport for the security review there. As they were about to get in an old rattletrap taxi a fellow gringo motioned to them. They stopped.

"You guys got a couple of minutes?"

McCaul answered, "Why?"

"Because you need to."

That made McCaul and LaRue pay attention and they closed the taxi doors. This guy was obviously the reason for their visit to Cayo Coco.

Their interrupter was a little over average height, reed thin, mid-forties, and dressed in a navy woven Guayabera shirt over khakis and beige sandal shoes. He had jet-black hair and frigid blue eyes.

"I'm Hadrian Felix." He was obviously American. McCaul guessed Texas. "I'm your local cousin. My friends call me Harry. You can call me Felix." Obviously a rude, pompous American.

"The Company?"

"Um humm."

"I figured you guys would be kicking around here somewhere. I'm McCaul and this is LaRue."

"I know that. How about having a cigar?"

They followed him back into the hotel and past the bar to the patio and to a corner table.

Felix passed around stubby Cohiba Robustos. They were accepted and lit. The waiter came over and took their orders for mojitos. They puffed and looked each other over.

McCaul said, "I guess our meeting here today wasn't random."

"Nope. State set it up with your people yesterday. First off, we really appreciate your help on this. I'm even down here on a Canuck passport," he said in between puffs.

"I'll pass on your satisfaction to the Jefe Maximo," Mike said. "So why you?"

"I'm illegal here - been working as the top Cuban Intell analysis in Langley for almost twenty years. But I got no official status. If I get caught doing anything that the Cubans don't like, then I'm probably their guest for a while and a propaganda superstar.

"But I can assure you, if I'm here, then it means this is really important."

Their drinks arrived.

"Between me and my Dad, we've been hanging out at the Cuba desk for almost fifty years. Sort of made our careers from Cuba. My Dad even got thrown in jail by Che way back when."

He took a sip of his drink.

A small musical group was setting up near the bar and a lot of other patrons moved over to be close to the action. The group had its standard black bongo player, a mulatto guy with a tres guitar and a Spanish sonero with his maracas, a guiro and clave sticks. They started up with "El Cuarto de Tula", about a girl so hot her room caught on fire.

Felix didn't sound Canadian. In Kitchener-Waterloo, his accent would ever only be heard on a TV show. He was a very adept smoker and looked very serious. He could never be mistaken as a Canadian by anyone who had ever seen one of them. McCaul thought that the CIA might do better recruiting in the Midwest if they want to have their people walk freely in the streets of communist capitals as Canadians.

"Cuba's entering a dangerous place for us." He took a drag and exhaled, "Fidel might not think he'll ever die, but he will."

"And no good can come from it. Raul is trying to control things but won't be around for long. So who knows what will come next. The most obvious options are bad. Venezuela we could have dealt with but the Chinese will be a very big problem. And there's some even more scary possibilities."

McCaul asked, "Like what?"

"Think Al Qaeda. Think the druggies from Mexico or Colombia. If he goes, then there's nothing to stop Cuba from getting one hell of a lot worse." He shoved his cigar back in his mouth like a Vegas gambler raking in a pot.

"You guys can't do some sort of deal with anyone in country?"

"We don't see it. Realistically, it took us fifteen years to do a free trade deal with you guys, and we mostly like each other. Can you imagine how long it'll take to get a treaty with sworn enemies? Especially when we got a million ex-pats in Florida from here who want to return and get their haciendas back.

"That dog just won't hunt."

McCaul had mostly been chewing on his cigar, but he gave it a long draw and a long exhale. They were in the middle of trying to seal the biggest geo-political fault line that had existed in the Americas since the conquistadors came to visit.

Mike coughed.

The band was doing "Chan Chan." Again. Again.

Felix spoke, "Let's get down to business. We've arranged with your people to get you a meet with the Beard; maybe Raul, too. We want you to give us a full appraisal of their mental and physical condition. We need some idea of what Fidel's time frame is. When he goes down, who knows what will happen. It's his personality that has kept this place together."

McCaul nodded and LaRue stayed quietly intense.

The singer decided it was time to descend on their table with his maracas to persuade them to tip or buy a CD. He moved in on Felix.

Felix looked at him and said coldly, "Fuck off" and the singer sheepishly retraced his steps.

"We wanna know how he reacts with Raul; see if he seems dismissive. Ask him about security for tourists outside of the cities and towns."

"Anything else?"

"We hear there's some rebels in the northwest. If you get a chance to hook up with them, do it and keep us informed. We wanna know if they're Cuban or not."

McCaul said, "And you have some transmitter or electronic stress detector that you want me to glue to his beard or something, right?"

"No, but that would be nice if you could manage it. We just need a first hand report from someone we trust.

"Anyway, you guys have some things to do, so I'll leave you to them. I got fifteen to get to the airport and on a plane back to Havana. That should get my heart rate up to where I like it. I'm in the Nacional if you need me. I'm registered as Steve Harper, eh." He got up, left a US twenty, stubbed his cigar out and left.

LaRue and McCaul finished their drinks, bought a CD from the insulted sonero and caught a cab to the airport.

They met with Globalair's local agent in the terminal to do a look around. It didn't involve very much; the terminal was tinier than Regina's. Its simplicity makes it secure enough. Besides, McCaul and LaRue weren't really there to check security; they were there to look like they were checking security. Soon enough it was time to return to Havana and they got on the seven o'clock flight.

10

KATE TRAVELLED QUIETLY in the Sikorsky after leaving McCaul behind on the ground. She really worked great with Boyd but he wasn't much of a conversationalist, to say the least, and he slept and snored loudly just about every time he wasn't shooting film.

And it was highly unlikely that the little Cuban pilot would be in a position to tell too many secrets. She started making notes from what had happened in the past week to the point the previous day when she ran into McCaul at the bar.

But she just wasn't entirely into work after their night together. Her mind kept going back to him and their evening and night together.

'The last thing I need right now is to get tied up with McCaul,' she thought. 'He's too damn stubborn and he's never in Atlanta. Plus I got a career to think about, dammit.' Then she noticed his name doodled around her note pad. 'Okay, well, maybe I'll think about him a little bit.'

She looked over her map of the Guantanamo region. There were a lot of lines close together, which meant, she thought, that there were mountains. She drummed her pen on the map. She was bored and looked out the aircraft's window. As far as her eyes could see was scrub ground, much verdant and lush, some areas burned out by the sun. On the horizon she could see a slim blue line that was sure to be the sea. In Cuba, she thought, you're never all that far from the sea.

She leaned back in her seat and remembered how they had met. It had been at an art gallery. No it had been at a government reception of some sort. A little over two years ago, she remembered, because she had just turned thirty four and had decided that if she didn't get her big US break that year she never would. And she had pushed her agent and she had gotten her first stringer assignments from CNN.

They had been introduced by their host, Claude, a greasy French consulate employee of some sort who had previously been shepherding her around the party like she was his mistress, even with his dowdy wife trailing behind. She had used McCaul as a reason to ignore her host by acting a little drunk and spilling her drink on his sleeve. She had rushed to get a napkin and club soda and offer it to him, intending to then move on.

But when she had returned with the cleaning materials she had taken a different look at him. He was standing by himself, in the corner of the room; perfectly calm and relaxed but with both inner and outer strength; reviewing the room with a pleasant but unsmiling expression as if he were a big sheepdog looking over his flock. He stood straight with big shoulders and a little cowlick on his short light brown hair, his suit was a little shabby, his tie a little cheap. He had really looked quite adorable.

The consulate guy had invited her to dinner at the Intercontinental Hotel along with a group of others and she had dragged McCaul along. They hadn't sat directly across from each other but close enough to chat over the course of the evening, although he hadn't been a big talker. She could tell he was interested in her but seemed sad. He had to leave and did, but left her a promise to get together sometime. But they hadn't exchanged numbers. She was disappointed but figured if it were meant to be, it would be.

Then, on the way home the most romantic thing ever in her life happened to her. Unexpectedly. Like they were meant to be together always. And the few fleeting hours after remained in her dreams whenever she was falling asleep and lonely.

McCaul was trouble. She wanted, no, she needed, other things in her future. But why not with Mike? Things would unfold as they should, she thought. She hoped.

They were over the mountains and with the rise in elevation not that far from the peaks. Kate noticed a lot of smoke coming from a plateau. She carefully negotiated her way to the co-pilot seat.

"Ronaldo - what's that?"

The little Cuban pilot turned and looked. "I go closer." He flew within a thousand feet of the smoke. She could see that it was some kind of camp; there was a cluster of tents and there seemed to be a lot of activity going on.

"Ronaldo, where are we?

"We're about one hundred kilometers from Guantanamo, Señora."

"Where's the American base?"

"Oh Señora, the base, it not near the town. It on the sea. And we can't get close because of air force Americanos."

"Shoot". Kate had hoped to get some video of Cubans looking desperately through a barbed wire fence at the promised land. But that wasn't to be.

It looked like her trip was wasted. Then she had a brainwave. There was nothing to lose and maybe she'd get an interesting story or something.

"Ronaldo, can you get us somewhere close to that camp we flew over without them seeing us? Where the smoke was."

Ronaldo changed course and in a minute, they were near the camp but on the other side of the mountain at several thousand feet and out of sound and sight."

"Ronaldo, take us down!"

"Señora, where I take us down? We over a mountain!"

"Just find a place."

Ronaldo circled quickly out of sight of the camp and within two minutes dropped precipitously and landed in a small plateau within a kilometer of the camp.

Without waiting for the rotors to stop, Kate jumped out of the plane carrying a tiny digi-cam while her massive colleague had some larger technology. Boyd pulled on a camo Tilly hat.

"Ronaldo, which way?"

"The camp is in that direction," he pointed, "about one kilometer. It is over that ridge."

For once Boyd led Kate to their destination. He was awkward and out of place almost everywhere, but wanted a story as much as she did and moved surprisingly quickly. Even with the physique of a polar bear.

The climb was enough to be tiring; Ronaldo had found a little plateau without much foliage, but it was steaming hot. Kate unbuttoned and removed her shirt and tied the sleeves around her neck and draped them over her bra.

The duo reached the summit and were able to follow the smoke from the clearing from there. Kate wondered what they were about to find.

They smelled the encampment before they found it. They had both been in similar scenarios and had enough presence of mind to be silent and invisible. There didn't seem to be anything like a sentry so it was probably a harmless village.

Kate signalled Boyd to hunker down while she moved into the underbrush to check out the ground. She returned in about five minutes and whispered in his ear, "No sentries. But it looks like a military camp of some kind."

Together they moved silently toward the camp, Kate forcing her adrenaline levels down; maybe this was her Pulitzer. It wasn't the risk of getting killed that bothered her. It was her not getting her story on air.

As they drew closer the sounds of the camp got louder. They came up to a collection of underbrush, with enough light to reveal the encampment. They crept to the edge and looked through the foliage, being careful not to disrupt any.

Before them was a small camp, about a dozen structures, mostly four-man tents, some away from the sleeping area; likely an armoury near the edge of the jungle. In the clearing, there were about two dozen possible combatants, all dressed in rough clothing, a few casually carrying weapons, several wearing pashtun style headwear. The men were all swarthy and dark haired, which only meant they weren't Swedes.

Boyd carefully started shooting long-range footage. Kate took out the digi-cam and silently moved around the perimeter. As she left Boyd three of the men in the camp began firing into the jungle on the opposite side, obviously checking their weapons. Kate saw a hooch nearby and crawled past the edge of the jungle and into it. It was filled with crates and she shot about thirty seconds of footage and carefully withdrew back into the foliage.

Boyd kept shooting and after about fifteen minutes he felt Kate move back beside him. "Let's go."

The two moved carefully. They appreciated the story wouldn't count unless it was aired, and there was no one shooting footage of them shooting footage for the story. They carefully took three times as long to get back to the helicopter as it had taken to get to the camp.

Ronaldo was sitting patiently when they arrived.

"Señora, you okay?"

"Ronaldo, get us back!"

- # -

The skinny kid weaved his way around the crowds of people plugging up Reina; the broad avenue that the Castros had dedicated in the name of one of their symbolic heroes, Simon Bolivar.

The avenue, one of the more significant thoroughfares in Havana and one tourists seldom visit, was busy with ordinary Cubans living their ordinary lives. Mothers were buying loaves of bread with their meager pesos, the lucky ones with a few CUCs were also renting DVDs that they would bring to their circles of friends and family to pass an evening. Those without a family were buying ham sandwiches for dinner for a pittance.

On every block there were women looking for a lover and men looking for women younger than those who were making themselves available. On almost every block one of the women would find a current or former lover in the company of one of those younger women and loud arguments and slapping and yelling would result. Small crowds gathered round each battle royal shouting advice, many laughing, while others tried to pull combatants apart.

The kid avoided these noisy bouts of emotion; he was unusual among the men of his age with whom he had grown up; he didn't participate in romantic adventures. His mother had brought him up in the church and he had even married his beloved novia in the Sacred Heart of Jesus Church that he was just now passing.

Early in the morning he had, as he always did, prayed for sustenance for his family from his saviour. But this devotion didn't always seem to be heard every day and this had been one of those days.

He was a student and got a tiny allotment from the government for he and his family, but even combined with his mother's stipend, was still not enough on which to survive. Like all Cubans they relied on the black market to feed themselves.

He had never resented the rough scrabble that he was forced to endure to support his wife and child and mother. Life was difficult in Cuba for everyone, he knew; he deserved no better than anyone else. On most days he was able to return home with milk and some protein; some days a quarter chicken that his mother would turn into a casserole that would feed the entire building which the four resident families shared.

But on this day it appeared he was destined to come home with nothing, unless his fortunes improved.

His spirits picked up when he saw a stout, mulatto man in a white linen suit walking toward him, one arm enwrapped with that of a stunning coal black woman, the other ending in a hand holding a cell phone pressed against an ear.

The kid slowed down in hopes that the older man's phone call would end and he'd be noticed. Lucky for the kid, it did, and the man noticed the younger guy and nodded to him.

The older man said, "Amigo, mi nombre es Manuel."

The kid said, "Señor. I am Joel."

"You work hard, Joel, and someday you will be able to help other people.

They chatted for a few seconds and the older man gave the kid a ten peso convertible note. The young guy thanked him effusively, rushed over to a bodega and then rushed home; dinner for his family and milk for his baby in the ubiquitous Cuban 'jaba', a simple plastic bag, that was about the most important of items that every Cuban always had in their pocket to carry found treasures home.

11

MCCAUL AND LARUE WERE FLYING BACK on Globalair's Airbus that routed from Halifax to Cayo Coco to Havana and then back to Toronto. One downside of flying charters to Cuba is that most of the flights returning home to Canada were either ridiculously late or stupidly early.

There were plenty of seats so LaRue and Mike took separate entire rows to stretch out.

McCaul's night before with Kate had brought back all the warm memories that he could recall from their time together. He thought of her; eclectic, gorgeous, smart, eternally positive and genuinely really sexy. All remembrances of his heartbreak were disappearing. So was his occasional morose view on life. In just over twenty four hours, he thought, 'I love me again.'

Relaxing and watching the lights of civilization disappear he remembered when they had first met.

It was a French embassy Beaujolais Nouveau party. Mike had noticed her, but she looked totally preoccupied with a pudgy French diplomat so he was surprised when she came over. As it worked out the pudgy diplomat invited them out to dinner and they'd gone to a fancy restaurant with a big group speaking French and neither of them had noticed anyone else.

Mike had had to leave before dessert, though; he had had an early flight south. So about one in the morning he gave Kate a peck on the cheek and left, feeling lonely and incomplete, his heart pounding. As soon as he turned the ignition key he realized he hadn't even gotten her phone number. Que sera, sera.

Mike had made it a couple of blocks north on Yonge St. and with only a thread of hope he pulled into a parking lot, out of sight, behind a library. He'd seemed drawn to the place for some reason. Sitting in the drivers seat with the top down he had sighed frequently, played La Boheme at maximum volume, left the door open and let the fates have their way with him.

It wasn't long; maybe ten minutes.

Pav and Mirella Freni were searching for a lost key on the floor and he had just touched her tiny, frozen hand. Headlights had appeared around the corner from off Yonge Street. Mike saw the Co-Op taxi logo and a door swing open. It was her. He hurried out of his car, caught his foot on the brake pedal and almost fell on his face.

She reached back inside to drop bills for the driver, and then came running into his arms. They spun around kissing; Rodolfo and Mimi. He asked her how she knew he'd be there. She had said, "I don't know, Mike. I just knew."

Serious romantic activity followed for the next year. But she had gotten a job with CNN, moved to Atlanta and Mike hadn't heard from her until yesterday.

Mike stirred from his trance as the landing announcement came from the pilot.

Their flight back from Cayo Coco was just about on time, just after 9 o'clock, and they got to again enjoy the lovely air of the Marti Airport. It was less muggy than when he'd arrived from Cancun, and it was evening, so the air-suspended taxi coal dust was solid not liquid but it still created a nasty film on the streets, sidewalks and people. They got in a cab, and arrived back at the Telegrafo about 20 minutes later.

He wondered how Kate was making out down south. He suspected that Ronaldo knew his way around from being Emmanuel Gant's flying taxi so he didn't worry about him. But Kate was the opposite of risk averse. He hoped Kate would be back by midnight.

"Lucien, how about I treat you to a Cuban sandwich."

"Sure."

They stopped into the Telegrafo bar and a bulky Hispanic server brought them menus. LaRue ordered a Havana Special, rum and pineapple juice, and Mike got a Bucanero, a stronger and more full-bodied Cuban beer than Cristal.

The menus had four different ham sandwiches, one with cheese, one without, one with salami and ham, one with salami, ham and cheese. They both took the salami, ham and cheese. The sandwich came with sliced tomatoes and shaved radish.

McCaul asked LaRue, "So what's your schedule tomorrow?" He bit into his sandwich. It was pleasing but plain.

"I'm meeting a driver early tomorrow on the Prado. What do you think about our new friend Felix?"

"He's standard Government Issue. Will likely want to position himself to take credit if there's any credit to take and blame us if anything goes wrong. I won't trust him. I am wondering about that bunch of rebels in the northwest he talked about."

LaRue said, "I don't know anything about them." He chugged the rest of his cocktail and stood, leaving his half eaten sandwich. "I need to go up and pack a few things and get some sleep. I should be back in a day or two."

"Fair enough. Let me know if you need help or anything."

He said, "I will, Amigo".

Mike stood, they shook hands and LaRue ran up the stairs to his room.

Mike got back to his sandwich. It was really, really bad, but somehow really, really addictive. After finishing, he immediately wanted another and eyed LaRue's uneaten half.

While they'd been chatting a grizzled old gringo had wandered into the bar. He was mid-height, thin as a rail and had the hard chewed up look of a gambler or musician. He nodded, Mike nodded back and the guy joined him.

"Don Hughes."

"Mike McCaul."

"How's the grub?" He spoke with a twangy upper New York State accent.

"Unbelievably deliciously bad. Try one."

He looked at the menu and ordered one and a mojito.

"What brings you here, Don?"

"Music. I teach drums at Buffalo U and play in a few bands."

"What do you think of the place?"

"Not crazy about the government, but I don't like ours much either. Music is way, way good and the drummers are the best in the world. I learn and then I teach."

"How do you get down here?"

"Cross the border and fly from Hamilton on charters. Sucks since the greenback hit the skids. Used to be cheaper to live here than in Buffalo." His sandwich arrived; he exchanged it for a 5 CUC bill and signalled for another beer.

McCaul asked, "Yeah, but what do you really think about the place? Are the Castros evil or just insane?"

"I don't think the Castros are evil. I firmly believe that Fidel and Raul believe that they are doing the right thing. Whether he is doing it or not is the issue. Castro said sixty years ago that history will absolve him, but we're still waiting." His sandwich arrived and he took a bite.

"I know Cubans who love Fidel and I know Cubans who hate him. I've never met the man but when I come here I see cops and troops everywhere. Is that evidence of a police state or is it evidence that Cubans are violent people? I think the former.

"Cuba's a very enigmatic place. In many ways it is an afterthought of days gone by. I just love the music, cigars and love watching their women dance. I don't go to beach resorts, I go to Havana for the jazz clubs."

McCaul chuckled. "Yeah. Too bad foreign policy makers didn't hold your view and do a little more of that."

As he bit into his sandwich Mike pondered having another. But he resisted and finished his beer.

"Good meeting you, Don. See ya around."

"Ya, see ya around."

They shook hands and McCaul worked his way back through the lobby and out into the Prado.

He turned left from the hotel and started on Neptuno walking away from Parque Centrale and Calle Obispo, west toward Centro and his place. It was dark, very dark, and the alleys were all blocked off from vehicular traffic by cannon balls partly sunk into the concrete.

McCaul sauntered through the dark alleys and passed singles and couples leaning out of doorways, some laughing with each other, some noticing him with just a hint of malevolence. The only light filtered out from half opened doorways and uncurtained windows. Each corner was home to a PNR policeman, blue bereted, dressed in grey and armed with a baton. Everyone was unsmiling. This was a Cuba not showing its friendly face to a visitor.

91

He passed the pseudo Buena Vista Social Club and heard a ruckus. Rather than the cheerful place of before, it was quiet and McCaul noticed a scuffle with two of the PNRs subduing a black man none too passively. The man had one of the resin patio chairs above his head and both of the paramilitaries had their batons in hand. It was Kate's friend, Eduardo. The chair went flying, the batons descended and all was quiet. Havana, as hopeless economically as it was, was showing its talent at policing. McCaul walked on. There was nothing he could do.

He passed a couple of paladares and discos, some obviously high end, others catering to the peso trade. Every couple of blocks he noticed signage for the local CDR likely busy ratting out locals who might not be entirely true to Fidel. He noticed a wall sized graffiti sign, 'Viva Fidel'.

After about a kilometre of walking along broken pavement and through foreboding alleys Mike decided to walk back and check to see if Kate had gotten back to her hotel.

As he got closer to the hotel and passed a little bodega, he was surrounded by hustlers; guys looking to squeeze one more dollar into their pockets before returning home to their wives and children. One thin, light-skinned guy with curly hair was particularly persistent in ignoring McCaul's "No Gracias," and spoke enough English to get his attention.

"Please Señor, my babies need meelk. Mi nombre es Shoel, like Noel, but with a shay. Whaaas you name, please Señor. Can you buy my babies milk?"

Mike stopped to listen.

"Señor, Señor, Fidel, he only gib meelk for babies til they four, then only one liter a week until fourteen. Babies need milk to grown, you know, Señor?"

Mike gave in and offered the little guy a CUC single, but he shook his head and said, "No Señor, you hab to buy. You cand gib me money, the policia they take it from me, so you hab to buy the meelk."

McCaul walked back with the young guy toward the bodega. "I'll help you out, Joel." It only took a minute for Mike to get the milk, give it to Joel, and feel better about himself, and worse about the Castros.

Mike went into the Telegrafo and checked for Kate in the lounge and at the front desk. No sign of her.

McCaul took a Panataxi back to his apartment. He checked and had an email from Jud telling him to call the Canadian Embassy whenever he got back and provided the number. Mike did and his call was answered immediately by an obviously tired but alert assistant under-secretary on the Ambassador's personal staff. She had a slight French accent.

"Hello, Mr. McCaul, I'm Jeannine Tremblay. I have a note here from our Minister informing us of your important trade mission to Cuba and instructions to provide all the assistance we can."

"Thank you, Madame Tremblay, I understand that I have had a meeting arranged for me? Is this so?"

"I have a note here from the Ambassador, dated this afternoon, that this is arranged and confirmed. We have already requested an audience with President Castro for a convenient time the day after tomorrow. His staff has suggested eleven or fifteen hundred hours. Are either of these times suitable?"

"I think the morning would be better." Based on his reputation, Mike figured the Jefe would likely make them wait for a couple of hours anyway.

"Please arrive at the Chancery at 10 am for a briefing with Ambassador DeGrassi, and for travel to President Castro's office."

Mike thanked Ms. Tremblay for her help, hung up, and went to bed. Before he fell asleep, he wondered if he would ever see Kate or LaRue again.

12

LARUE AWOKE JUST AFTER DAWN, showered, dressed in his cream suit and packed a travel bag with rougher clothing and basic toiletries. He donned a prized and ancient Montreal Expos baseball cap, packed a water bottle and a handful of granola bars, left his room quietly and walked downstairs to the lobby. The main floor was empty without any sign of human presence and another glorious Habana morning was emerging brightly through the hotel shutters.

LaRue was to meet his ride just before 0800 when the PNR officers were going off their night shift and were tired and not likely anxious to waste any time with possible unfriendlies. He had about an hour to kill so he took advantage of the gift of time to settle into a patio chair at the Francesca pastry shop between the ancient Inglaterra Hotel and the Telegrafo. He strolled up to the counter, exchanged pleasantries with the cashier and selected a sinful chocolate croissant and ordered a Café Americano and a packet of Cohiba cigarettes.

LaRue usually only smoked when in a theatre of operations, and then only while waiting. It helped him to settle down and focus his thoughts. For a soldier, life is a lot as Papa Wallenda described his: "All of life is on the wire. The rest is just waiting." Being a soldier requires months of patience and an ability to pass time, while always staying sharp, to be able to survive a few minutes of adrenaline, terror and violence.

He returned to his patio table, sat and lit a cigarette. The smoke was strong, remarkably flavourful and extremely smooth. And in his current situation, it was not likely that lung cancer was his greatest health risk.

While he was smoking, an old fellow, likely a war veteran, offered him an English version of Castro's propaganda rag, "Granma", named after the boat that Fidel had commandeered to travel from Mexico to Cuba. But like all "facts" from the government, nothing in the paper came close to reality.

His coffee and pastry arrived and were both delicious. He thought Cuba was world class at desserts but mostly a soup kitchen at main courses. While he sipped on his coffee he looked at the people around him, the locals almost all rail thin, the turistas almost all over fed. The sun's heat was starting to create waves on the asphalt and the benches in the Parque were filling up with Habañeros anticipating the Latin American League baseball game in the afternoon.

A thin, mulatta women approached him from the street after exchanging nods with the waiter. She pointed at his cap and spoke desperately to him in Spanish, "Señor, I beg you for your hat. My casa had a fire and I have no money to feed my children or to buy them clothes."

She seemed sincere, and although the cap was one of LaRue's personal treasures, she needed it more than he did. He passed it to her and she bowed in deep appreciation, "My children will honour you in their prayers".

He reached in his pocket and passed her a five CUC note and she began to sob. He comforted her with his hand on her shoulder and she left. The waiter came over with an unrequested fresh coffee and nodded to him with a smile.

One of Havana's huge camel buses, a diesel tractor hauling a trailer filled with people, roared by the patio spewing toxic fumes for yards. Dozens of little cyclo-taxis scurried out of its way like a school of minnows escaping a shark. LaRue stubbed out his cigarette, finished his coffee and went for a walk.

Turning right out of Francesa's and right again by the Teatro, he ambled down San Rafael. Even this early in the morning there was a steady line of stands along both sides selling Cuban sandwiches and curios and a steady stream of black men and young women whispering "chica?".

One girl was totally alluring, café latte skin with emerald green eyes. LaRue said, "No, gracias," and wondered whether an elderly Russian bureaucrat, now living somewhere east of the Urals, ever thought about any children he may have left behind in his previous posting.

Interspersed with the collections of merchants were groups of men circled around card tables playing dominos. The competition was verbally fierce and LaRue stopped in to watch a game, enjoying the repartee as a spectator.

He felt like a Cuban and revelled in the laughter and snide comments of the participants. He offered around his Cohibas and was enthusiastically accepted by the group; perhaps one with a few more pesos, but as a friend all the same. A shaky member of the audience offered him a bottle of Habana Club and LaRue took a short drink to be polite.

LaRue felt not the least bit conflicted, although he had not come close to revealing to McCaul what his real mission was, here in Cuba. He hoped McCaul wasn't to be harmed by his duplicity, but ultimately that was not his priority. His fate was not McCaul's fate.

LaRue left the domino game with handshakes and smiles all around and walked back to and crossed the Prado. Once he reached the other side he started strolling north, toward the Malecon.

He kept his eyes on the Prado looking for a blue Ford panel van. He also kept his eyes peeled for snooping PNRs as surely his driver was. Even though it was time for a shift change, there were still three PNRs on either side of the road in front of and across from the park. They were alertly noticing people acting abnormally and still harassing slippery looking hustlers desperate to scrounge money for breakfast from tourists.

LaRue saw the van approach on the opposite side of the Prado, driving slowly in the other direction. The driver gave LaRue a nod of recognition and LaRue continued his pace walking away from the park, past his hotel.

LaRue stopped to light a cigarette and was able to confirm that the driver was making a u-turn behind the line of taxis parked in the middle of the boulevard near the Capitolo. LaRue resumed his pace and noticed the police had thinned out after he left the busy tourist area.

In a few moments, the van pulled over, the passenger door opened and LaRue jumped in. They spoke in Spanish. "Mi nombre es Soto, Señor."

Soto's van was clean, in rough shape, but the radio worked great and was playing Gloria Estefan and LaRue had to almost shout to be heard.

"Call me Cien. Thank you for giving me a ride," LaRue shouted back.

Soto was small, late twenties, light skinned, slim with curly close-cropped black hair. Interestingly enough, he had on a Toronto Argonauts blue T-shirt along with his well-worn blue jeans.

"Look Cubano, Señor Cien, we drive through the city and Miramar. There are many policia."

Assuming he looked non-Cuban, LaRue removed his cream jacket and placed it in the back seat. He said, "You can keep this, Soto. Where I'm going I won't need it." He messed up his hair and rolled up his sleeves. He hid his duffle under blankets in the back.

"Señor Cien, it is a great honour to meet you. Señor Machado, he say you a very important and strong hombre." Soto spoke without his eyes leaving the Malecon; he drove efficiently, expertly shifting gears in his old truck with only occasional grinding and successfully avoiding potholes. He zipped along the Prado to the Malecon.

"Soto, tell me where we're going."

"I head to the sierras, Señor. I cannot tell you where for now. You will meet Comandante Machado, I can tell you this."

Soto drove along the Malecon, passed Meyer Lansky's Riviera Hotel, through a tunnel and emerged in Miramar, Habana's seaside embassy and international business area.

The buildings and houses resembled Miami, LaRue thought, and he was pleased that not all of Cuba had been devastated by fifty years of Castro rule. But Fidel had the demand for creature comforts by foreign diplomats to thank for this relatively modern part of the city, rather than solid economic policy.

They drove along 5th Avenue past the huge medieval castle that is the Russian Embassy and Soto sped in and around the newer taxis and nicer diplomatic luxury cars.

Soon enough Soto entered the highway and the duo passed dozens of Cubans looking for rides or trying to sell sad strands of garlic and other sketchy agricultural goods.

The highway looked to be of 1960's vintage, without potholes but with wear and weeds peaking out of cracks in the pavement.

They passed through thousands of acres of pineapple and sugar cane fields and Soto turned off toward the north coast and Pinar del Rio.

A million years before, Cuba had been under the great ocean and over time much, but not all, of the former limestone seabed had eroded. When the seas withdrew the eventual result had been a stunning mountain range consisting of huge flowerpots called mogotes surrounded by incredibly lush and fertile plains. Perfect for growing the best tobacco in the world.

Soto passed through a small village and in a few minutes was driving through winding roads bounded on both sides by steep portions of the mountain range festooned with foliage and leaves the size of Smart Cars. After another half hour he slowed, pulled deeply into the underbrush and beckoned LaRue to exit. Soto brushed away any sign of tire marks, rearranged the underbrush and rejoined LaRue.

He led LaRue through heavy jungle.

"The whole mountain range is a honey comb of caves, Señor Cien. Very few are able to travel them without getting lost, some people have died trying. My cousin is a guide at Memorial "Los Malagones" we are going to. Our families are from here, and our fathers were famous among peasants to save the Revolucion from enemies inside of Cuba who opposed Fidel. Now, we are not so sure our padres, Señor Cien, that they did the right thing."

The duo came out of the forest into a clearing at the base of a massive mogote. As they crossed the clearing and approached a small village LaRue had first contact with life: a family of tiny baby blue pigs, rolling in the dust, snorting and all in all enjoying a perfect day.

"Hola!" The greeting was followed by the entrance into the clearing of a small and thin Cubano with an obvious resemblance to Soto. They hugged and Soto introduced his cousin Luis to LaRue. LaRue noticed a massive statuary and surrounding monuments.

He asked, "What are those? Can I see them?"

"Sure, Señor. Is the memorial." The three strolled over to the site.

There was a huge bust of an incredibly ugly man.

"The man you see is Leandro Malagón, he was the leader of our peasant warriors, Señor, who captured the counter-revolutionaries supported by the USA after Cuba was set free. He and his men were led by Comandante Camilo Cienfuegos. You know this man, Señor?"

LaRue replied, "Yes I know something of this man, Luis. Tell me of him, por favor."

Luis put his hand on his heart. "Señor, mi padre, he say Camilo the best of men. Very brave, Señor and very kind. All of his men loved him. Some of our fathers fought with him from Camaguay all the way to Habana and he never left one man behind, and he never allowed any man to die foolishly. He was a great man and great general, Señor."

LaRue nodded his head slowly several times and shuffled his feet in the dust.

Soto interrupted, "Señor Cien, I must go now and return to Habana with a compañero." Soto and his cousin hugged and offered mutual hasta luegos.

Luis and LaRue walked away from the memorial toward a stream running out of a cave in the mogote cliff. LaRue thought it would be their destination but it wasn't. They walked past the cave and around a corner.

LaRue had thought that he had been dropped near his destination. But the duo continued on for at least a half hour though tobacco fields, past lonely farmhouses and cane fields. The sun was oppressive and soon he was sweating profusely.

A woman came up to them from one of the farmhouses holding a bag.

"Señor, a present for you."

He accepted the bag and looked inside. There were a few dozen Robustos undoubtedly made by the same family that had probably farmed tobacco on this patch of earth since long before Fidel had taken it from them.

He gave her a twenty-dollar CUC and she gave him a hug.

They continued on and finally came to another huge mushroom mountain, but this one much more massive than those they had passed before.

Luis put his arm around LaRue's shoulders and guided him further around the mogote. "This is a secret passage to our camp, Señor. It would be of no value to invaders, it is too difficult a climb for soldiers, but is good for two men without weapons."

They came upon a passage in the cliff so narrow that both men had to enter sideways and up they went. Luis had a flashlight and kept it lighted to facilitate the climb. Never was the passage wider than four feet, in several places it was barely two. While in places it was steep, there were natural hand and footholds and it was a fairly easy, if tight, climb. After about twenty minutes, with Luis leading the way, there was a hint of light and soon they emerged into bright sunshine.

The minute the men came clear of the cave, there was a query, a password given and a sentry came forward.

"Señor, I must leave now. This is Montana, he will take you to Comandante Machado."

Luis turned and went back down the way he had come and the sentry took LaRue away from the cave opening onto the mogote's mostly flat apex.

Within a minute they started to encounter men and came to a stone works of dark limestone rising a dozen feet beyond the plain on top of the mogote. The fortified area was fifty meters in diameter with a single entrance. The walls were built in and around the jungle that existed on the platform of the mountain.

Visible to LaRue above the earthworks was a naturally rocky "keep" probably a dozen yards across. This would be the place where the few survivors would make their last stand in the event of a disastrous scenario. A huge bushy broad leaved tree topped it. When viewed from above, if the crew was under cover and fires were extinguished, the camp would be invisible.

Scattered around the exterior of the defendable area were hundreds of men, some cooking on smokeless hibachis, some cleaning weapons, others playing soccer on small cleared areas. All appeared to LaRue to be happy, shirtless, and clearly fit. A few, but not many, paid attention to LaRue.

LaRue smiled as he walked across the encampment with Canto in search of his cousin Carlos Machado. He had last seen Machado in New York City almost a half year before when the final plans for the adventure were being hatched.

He was impressed with the activity going on around him; men seemed alert and busy. He followed Montana past a few dozen tough looking guys playing soccer and doing high intensity calisthenics. One looked as wide as he was tall but was working hard to keep up and doing a pretty good job. His guide waved at the big guy who waved back. He said, "Señor, that is Ernesto, he is one of our leaders."

They walked up to Machado who was relaxing with a cigar and a couple of comrades under a huge shade tree. They smiled and stood up when LaRue and Montana approached and walked forward to greet them.

"Finally, Cien. What took you so long?"

"Primo, this is a long way from civilization!"

"It has to be, Amigo, there are eyes that want to find us." This is Sanchez and Garza. The two men shook hands with LaRue.

"Cien, let's go and share some comida and talk."

LaRue followed Machado to a Hibachi where a cook was frying rice with large chunks of fish, garlic, chilies, onions and soya sauce. The cook put a generous serving on each of two metal plates and crushed a half lime on each then passed them with forks to LaRue and Machado.

The duo strolled to a rock formation and each sat on a boulder and started eating.

"How are Brother Franco's children, Cien?"

"I have not seen them on this trip, but I have brought along gifts for all of them. Baseball equipment mostly."

"You are a good man, Cien."

"No, Primo, I am an ordinary man. It is the children that are good. I hope someday I can see them doing better."

"They will remember you forever."

"My forever may not be that long, Primo."

"God is on our side, Cien."

"God always ends up on the side of the winners."

Cien said, "I suppose you are right. God has not done much for all the people on this island who live as they do."

LaRue said, "How are we progressing?"

"We have the men, and we have the plan that you will need to fine tune. What we don't have are means of transportation and enough weapons, I am afraid."

"What do we have?"

"We have three two ton trucks that are not in very good condition, but our mechanics are working very hard on them. We have only a handful of sidearms and enough rifles for perhaps a dozen men, although we are short of ammunition. No automatic weapons and we will need to reply on Molotovs for explosives."

LaRue paused while he enjoyed some of the fried rice. "You're telling me we have no chance."

Machado said, "We have no chance unless we are able to recruit a large number of men from the Castros', but even they would likely not come with weapons. The police, of course, have their sidearms, but fewer then fifty soldiers are armed with automatic rifles in Havana at any given time."

Machado rose and filled a canteen from a large barrel and passed it to LaRue who drank.

LaRue said, "That is good news, Carlos; if Raul does not arm his men, then we don't have to shoot them and they will surrender easier and perhaps come to our side sooner. We need to find more weapons. What about friends from outside?"

"The Americans promised me support before I came here, but they have not contacted me, so I have no idea if they will help or not."

LaRue said, "What about from the Cubanos in Florida?"

"Again, big promises. They can provide us large numbers of automatic rifles and ammunition, but we have to arrange delivery. We can make arrangements through our friend in Havana for a high speed boat to do this, but we would need twenty thousand dollars in cash, which, Primo, we don't have."

LaRue said, "So if we can find money, we can get weapons."

"Yes, but time is also an issue. We cannot be in a state of readiness for much more than a week; we are sure to be found out and to be attacked if not by then. And we cannot defend ourselves."

LaRue said, "I think I may have a solution for all our problems, but I will need to make some promises and I will need agreement from a man that I believe is very difficult."

"Will you do this?"

"Yes."

The two men finished their meals, scrubbed the plates with sand and returned them to the cook and thanked him for such an excellent meal.

13

MCCAUL SLEPT IN UNTIL ABOUT TEN. He had no place to go and nothing official to do, so he took a long shower and put on a pair of navy Nike shorts and a plain white tee shirt with his runners. He buckled up a fanny pack filled with cash and descended to the lobby to begin his run to La Habana Vieja.

It was already stifling hot and humid and after about three blocks he was dripping with sweat.

As days get hotter in Havana, so does the stink in the barrios of Centro get worse. The garbage trucks, when they were operational, seldom lasted through a tour of duty and given the structure of the Cuban bureaucracy that has them hauled back for repairs, they never get to some barrios. So approaching noon, the air approaches unbreathable.

It was only a mile, and he sprinted the last quarter. He checked in at the front desk of the Telegrafo and asked for Ms. McKee's room. The phone rang a dozen times before he hung up. He rang LaRue's room, ditto.

He felt lonely. When asked, the desk clerks advised they had not seen either of them and they had been working since the previous evening. McCaul sighed and wondered what he'd do now. No brother in arms, no prospective love interest and no helicopter.

He assumed LaRue was somewhere in the Pinar del Rio area, so expected no help from that end. Where to find Kate?

Obviously, if he was going to find her, unhappily, it wouldn't be here and now, so he left the hotel and went for a walk. He thought, 'let her find me for a change'.

McCaul decided to stroll down Obispo again and feel at least for a little while like a real tourist. As he walked by the Floridita again, there were even more Hemingway resemblers.

He wondered what the deal was. Had these fellas lived the last dozen years or so continually being told they looked like Papa, and were they devoting the remainder of their lives to making pilgrimages to his old haunts like Moslems to Mecca? Were there, at this moment, dozens of Hemingways at Key West or in the bowels of the Toronto Star building, where Papa had once worked?

Or was the reason that, as an average guy, to afford a high-end trip to Havana that included $5 mojitos at the Floridita you pretty much HAD to be mid-fifties, with the resulting paunch, grey hair, and the post-middle-age-crazy feeling that a beard made you look more distinguished which provoked comments like, "You look just like Ernest Hemingway." McCaul figured probably some combination of all of the above.

Obispo was swinging, again, even in the morning. Mike wasn't too far down the street when his new friend Joel arrived. "Señor, Señor, thank you for the meelk yesterday. My baby smiled very much when she drank it."

Joel was, like most Cubans, of mixed race: he with a little more of a Spanish complexion than Afro-Caribbean with mid-length midnight black hair with loose curls.

"That's great, Joel. Why don't you show me around Habana Vieja, and I'll help you out again."

"Oh, Señor, I am the primero guide you can have. I know all the secret best places to visit."

"You like some ice cream, Señor?"

Mike hadn't had his fix yet so he said, "Absolutely."

Joel grabbed Mike by his arm and pushed him through a line up into a little window hacked out of a wall. Mike gave him two convertible single peso bills, Joel ordered, passed one through the window, and came out with two cones, one pink and one white. Joel held both out and Mike took the white one.

McCaul took a lick and immediately got his daily sugar high. It was delicate, it was cold, it was sweet, and it tasted like vanilla. Not like vanilla flavoring, but like real, honest to goodness vanilla. It was a taste experience one was sure to never find in Dairy Queen. And another good reason to come to Cuba.

Joel urged him down the street with his free hand while they continued enjoying their cones. Not having had breakfast, Mike devoured it like a ten year old would and finished it quickly and afterwards worked to regain his dignity.

Joel took Mike down a side alley toward the ocean, McCaul leisurely following, while Joel seemed anxious to get somewhere. The guide slid easily between a dumpster and a wall while Mike had a much tighter squeeze. As he got to the end of the dumpster, a guy hiding behind it stood up and pushed McCaul through an open door into a small room.

One guy got Mike in a headlock and another tried to hammerlock his left arm. Bad choice. That left McCaul's right arm free. He stomped heavily on the instep of the head locker and he eased pressure on Mike's head. Mike spun quickly in the direction of the arm lock, pushed a nose into a face with the heel of his right hand and cracked the other guy's nose with his right elbow. Both of McCaul's new friends sat down quickly.

"Don't move an inch," Mike ordered, and they complied, mostly. Well, they were moving a little, but mostly moaning with blood streaming from both noses. McCaul put his foot on the larger stubby one and pushed him back against the wall. He dropped his left hand to the floor and Mike stood on it, trying not to break anything. The smaller guy seemed to be down for the count. He had on a familiar looking cream coloured jacket.

"Okay, bub, you talk English?" McCaul addressed the stubby guy; his partner needed a few minutes to come back to life.

"Si, I speak English." He had a large, naturally tonsured head, with a fringe of salt and pepper hair neatly cut.

"Okay, Muchacho, who are you and what were you trying to do?" The guy tried to sit up, but it was hard for him to do with Mike's boot on his hand. "Will you be still?" The guy nodded. Mike lifted his foot and moved back a few feet to remove his opponent's chance to grapple.

"I am a priest who lives in the mountains. I am a member of a group of the Machado Cubanos who resist the Fidelistas who have destroyed the spirit and health of our people.

"We pray and work for the day when Fidel is deposed and jailed for his crimes." He sounded educated and spoke with the least accent McCaul had heard since arriving.

"Those words are death sentences, here, Muchacho. It takes a lot of bravery to speak that way."

"I am not afraid, Señor. I am not afraid of death. We will stop you and your company from continuing to support Fidel's atrocities and the evil he does to our humble and hard working people."

McCaul said, "I'm not a big fan of his either to tell you the truth. So tell me about your friend's jacket." The little guy was starting to stir, and by now He'd recognized it as LaRue's.

The smaller one spoke, "I was given it by our compañero, Cien."

"This Cien, he is French?"

"Señor, he is Cuban, but I believe he does speak French. He is a very sophisticated man. Very intelligent and brave. Compañero Machado is a cousin of his."

Aha. So. Maybe LaRue hadn't told McCaul his whole story. "Who is this Machado? Can you take me to see Cien?"

"Señor, I am not so sure this can be done. I will have to ask Comandante Machado and Cien if you can be trusted. Machado is our leader."

"What is your name, Father?"

"I am a Brother, Señor. Francisco Lopez Cerrano."

"Well, Brother Francisco, you might wish to have a discussion with your compañero, Cien, and offer him my greetings. He's my friend as well. I assure you and your compañero that our company has no intent of assisting the Cuban government in harming the Cuban people." The padre stood and his smaller companion rose to his haunches.

"How is it that you know Señor Cien?"

"We travelled here together. From Canada. That is his home and he works with me. And that is his jacket." McCaul pointed to his companion.

"This will be checked, Señor, and we can always find you if you are not sincere." He flexed his injured right hand and offered his left and McCaul grasped it. The priest reached over to help his friend to his feet, nodded, turned and left.

When Mike got outside, Joel was in the wind, long gone, and unlikely to be asking for a litre of milk from McCaul any time soon.

But McCaul wasn't too much the worse for wear, and he continued on down the alley in the direction Joel had led him. He wasn't too upset with the boy. How could he be? Joel was on the clean side of a dirty campaign.

After a few minutes Mike was through the narrow alley and back to Havana's version of civilization. There was a small park with a statue surrounded by a few park benches and a small-grassed area.

Surprisingly to McCaul, this wasn't a statue of Marti; on closer examination it revealed itself by way of a plaque as Miguel de

Cervantes. The metaphor was too obvious, Don Quixote's biographer watching over an entire country that was tilting at windmills.

Like most of the little parks and plazas McCaul had visited, this one had a few mutts nosing around. All were odd: some with big heads and tiny bodies, some the reverse. Some with fluffy ears, some with hardly any ears at all. Sort of makeshift animals.

To think about it, and McCaul did, the whole city was kind of makeshift: the dogs, the buildings, the cars, the streets, the economy. Catch as catch can. Make do with. He thought it could either be seen as sad for such a wonderful place to be so deprived of basic order or as a triumphant tribute to peoples' unsinkability.

A block down was the Bodeguita de Melia, another one of Hemingway's alleged haunts, but now more famous for five-dollar daiquiris. A block further down Mike came upon the Catedral, one of the oldest signs of the Spanish occupation. As he was about to walk by a doorway he saw his new friend Joel facing away. McCaul blocked his exit and had him cornered.

"Mi amigo," Mike said.

Joel turned and looked quickly for a gap to slip through.

"Hey, it's okay, Joel. I had a good meeting with your friends. Why don't we finish our guided tour?"

"You sure, Señor?" Mike nodded. "You want to see the Catedral?" McCaul nodded again, and the boy grabbed Mike's arm to take him up the front stairs of the ancient limestone masterpiece. The Cathedral shows its age: it's two hundred and fifty years old, but shows it well. They went through the massive front door and up one of the aisles to the front alter.

"Il Papa Juan Pablo Dos was here a few years ago to give Mass. Come see." He pulled Mike to the left side of the altar in front of a small statue of a black figure dressed in pure white with golden accents. "The Pope, he bless our Santeria god, Aggayu Sola."

This was obviously a big deal to Joel and probably to many Cubans with African heritage.

McCaul had read about the African Cubans' religion before he had moved to Havana. Santeria was the religion brought from a different continent and had survived the generations of their existence on the island, competing directly with Catholicism. On the mornings after special days Mike had occasionally seen headless birds lying in alleys, sacrificed to save souls if the Roman Catholic Church wasn't trusted to do so.

Over the centuries, Mike had read, African slaves had learned to avoid burning at the stake by consolidating their Gods with Catholic saints. He suspected that to the Catholics the statue represented San Cristobel, the Catholic patron of the Cathedral.

"It was very nice for the Pope to do this, you think?"

"Yes it was, Joel." The previous Pope had obviously seen something special in the Cuban people to make such recognition of a faith that would be seen as satanic or pagan by the College of Cardinals.

Mike wondered why he had taken this extraordinary step; it wasn't as if the Catholic Church didn't know the history of Cuban religious practices, and it's not as if they were a pluralist organization that's open to different philosophies. This was interesting. What was the Holy See up to?

Joel told McCaul more about Cuba, about what religion meant to the people. How most Cubans keep an altar of some form, Santerian or Roman Catholic, in their homes.

And over the course of an hour sitting in a pew he told Mike about the music, and the "clave": the beats and basic rhythm that directs all Cuban music. And how Cubans were able to survive their poverty because of their faith and their music. Even those who like Fidel.

They left the Catedral and turned right and joined a stream of people surely heading somewhere interesting. In a half minute they passed a couple of doorway vendors selling dominoes, and the strangest looking woman McCaul had ever seen: probably eighty, withered, but with a huge smile showing off chicklet sized false teeth. Her hair was high in a topknot, she wore turquoise capri pants and an orange sleeveless shirt. She had a huge stogie firmly in hand. Mike thought, she must have been really something back in the Meyer Lansky days.

Heck, she was now.

They continued across the ancient cobblestones and soon were within sight of the market, a few long lines of booths: fabric blowing in the breeze, lots of colour, a slight buzz of people laughing and haggling. Mike hadn't eaten all day except an ice cream cone and thought he'd grab a bite.

"Joel, can we get something to eat here."

"Si, there is food of China over there." He pointed to a white enclosed courtyard a short walk away and they went in.

In Mike's voluminous reading, he had read that thousands of Chinese had immigrated to Cuba in the 19th century and still made up about ten percent of the population of Habana.

As soon as they sat at the ubiquitous white resin tables, a movie idol handsome waiter with emerald green eyes and salt and pepper hair came over to take their orders. Mike let Joel order and a minute later the waiter returned with two beers and a package of "Popular" cigarettes.

"You don't mind, Señor?"

Mike shook his head no and Joel went up to the bar to get a light. He returned savouring each puff like a man facing a firing squad. Mike guessed that smokes were a real luxury when you can't afford milk.

McCaul noticed the place was called "Café la Torre del Oro". He wanted a smoke, but for at least the millionth time he was barely able to resist. A quartet was assembling next to the washrooms: a craggy-faced black bongo player with a Che beret sitting on a stool, a grinning, thin harmonium player, and a solid, graying guitarist.

They quickly started playing a high-spirited song with the words, "Quizas, Quizas, Quizas". In English: "Perhaps, Perhaps, Perhaps."

Perhaps it was about a person who wondered about something. But Mike knew it was about unrequited love. Very Cuban. McCaul remembered Nat Cole had sung it a lifetime ago.

He continued eating and chatting lightly with Joel. Joel told Mike about his little girl and his wife. They lived in Centro near the university; he was a student of science and received twelve dollars a month as a government stipend. Milk was three dollars a liter when he could get it. Mike thought, 'no wonder he needs to count on milk charity'.

A Fu-Manchued Chinese man dressed in a red dragon robe came toward their table, in his hand a tube of long bamboo sticks. McCaul had a toy set when he was a kid. They had been called Foo Chu sticks he remembered.

When the Chinese guy raised his arm his sleeve fell down his arm, McCaul noticed a mole with hair six inches long between his wrist and his elbow. He had obviously been touched by an angel or devil of some ilk and just as obviously had been awarded special powers.

He spoke to McCaul in English without accent, "Señor, I tell you your fortune. I will tell you the wisdom of a millennium from the prayers of Guanyin."

Mike figured the wisdom of a millennium would be worth a lot so he nodded and the seer sat and shook the tube until a stick fell on the table.

"Honourable Guanyin says you have a troubled way with women and that many think you are a devil. You will soon meet a woman who does not have this opinion. But I sense she is very difficult."

Mike was impressed and asked, "Yeah, but what about the wisdom of the millennium?"

He shook the tube and another stick dropped out and he studied it.

"Señor, Honourable Guanyin says that fortune never comes to fools. A wise man knows when to pursue his destiny and when to allow it to pursue him. You will soon need to make this decision. And Guanyin says that you are not a fool."

113

Mike shrugged and thought, 'I guess'.

The fortuneteller reached out his hand and Mike gave him a single. It was always good to know you're not a fool, but to those who aren't fools, it's not worth much more than a buck.

The food came and it was really good. Not up to Rigby's House of Chan on Eglinton, but very tasty.

A little seventyish paperboy with a bundle of Granma newspapers came into the bar, chewing away on a stick of gum and doing the Samba. He was joined on the dance floor by, of all people, Kate. Mike shook his head; 'now where in the world had she come from?'

14

SHE RUSHED UP TO MCCAUL, "Mike, God I'm MAD!"

"Mad? You're mad!! I'm the one who's been worried spitless for the last day."

"I mean, I'm crazy! You wouldn't believe what we saw down south." She snuggled against him. "God, the world is so perfect."

Mike was distracted for a second but brought to life by seeing Boyd plod into the bar's courtyard, a too-small straw sharecroppers hat on his gigantic head, topping a pair of loud sun specs.

Mike leaned in toward Kate to get closer. "Kate, I was really worried about you."

"Well, it wasn't as if I could call you on my cell."

"I know, but when you didn't get back last night and weren't around this morning, I figured I'd have to order up a brigade to find and rescue you."

"I'm sorry, Mike. Jeez."

The waiter came over and Mike ordered another round of beers, as well as a mojito for Kate and a beer for Boyd.

"Joel, this is my friend, Kate. Kate, this is our new guide, Joel." They shook hands and Kate sat down.

"So, dear one, exactly where were you for the last twenty-four hours?"

"Oh, Mike, after we dropped you guys in Cayo Coco we flew right over Sierra Cristal Park north of Guantanamo. It's unbelievably remote and beautiful. A real jungle."

Mike noticed Joel was pretending to watch the band, but was listening closely to them. "Joel, why don't you go get us some Robustos." McCaul gave him a twenty and Joel got up and left. Mike didn't expect to see him back.

"What did you see, Kate?" The drinks arrived.

"Well, we were going to Guantanamo to get some security fence footage. You know, Cubans trying to break through for sanctuary. Girls standing outside looking sad and dreaming of getting a gringo soldier to marry them."

"Please go on."

"Well, Ronaldo told me that the base was miles from the fence and I figured that it wasn't worth it. But we had flown over a camp in the mountains and flew back to take a look at it."

"So then you..."

"So then we landed and Boyd and I went in to see what was going on."

"Um hum?"

"Well, Mike, there's something going on over there. It looks to me like they've got a few dozen mean looking guys holed up. I bet they're a training camp or something."

McCaul moved closer. This was interesting. Something like this couldn't operate without the knowledge of the Cuban leadership.

"What kind of training camp?"

"Well, they've got a little tent city, and they've got shooting ranges, and things like that. We got great vid. I crawled around some of the tents and they've got lots of weapons. I got some stills and some digital video."

"And, what do you plan to do with this film?"

"Well, we already did it. We flew to Jamaica and stayed over to deliver it to our Kingston bureau first thing this morning to have it sent digitally to Atlanta for editing and production. I'm going to get it on the National News tonight. That's why I was late, so now it's someone else's problem to deal with."

'No', Mike thought. This was very definitely his problem to deal with. The minute this film was shown, she was almost sure to disappear, and he'd probably become lost while trying to save her. And the Navy Seals would hit the beaches soon after.

"You've got to hold it, Kate."

"Why would I do that?"

"Oh, just something to do with whether you want any of us to leave Cuba alive or not."

"Come on, Mike, Castro wouldn't dare touch a CNN reporter."

"No, come on, Kate. Once that video is shown all hell is gonna break loose.

"Kate, I'm not supposed to tell you this, and I can't tell you the whole story, but it's not good politically right now to shake the tree too hard."

"What do you mean?"

"Let me just say the US government is looking real hard for a reason to be a little more ambitious in their Cuban policy."

"Mike, don't bullshit me, what are you talking about?"

'Oh, boy', McCaul thought. Official Secrets Act enters play.

"Well, I'm not so sure proof like this would do anyone any good. Not the Americans, not the Cubans, not any visitors here, and for damn sure, not me and not you. If this gets aired, the first thing that's going to happen is that we're going to be sealed inside, and they will find us, Gant's helicopter or not. The second thing is the Yanks will do something serious. Maybe take over, and I don't know if that's good right now."

"But, Mike, don't you want to see the Castros get the boot?"

"I don't know, Kate. I definitely do know that I don't know. I'm meeting with Fidel and Raul tomorrow morning and maybe I'll have a better idea after."

"Mike, you're kidding. Can I come?"

"I don't know if that's a good idea, either."

"Mike, I don't know if I can do anything about the video. I mean the footage is being editted now and is due to be aired tonight."

Mike said, "Did you keep copies of the video?"

"Yeah, I dubbed it to a memory key."

"Let me take a look and you see if you can hold them back. Let's get back to the hotel."

McCaul left enough money on the table to cover the food, drinks and a generous tip, and the three of them left for the walk to the hotel.

Within a half block, Boyd had fallen a half block behind, taking pictures and videos of the surroundings, but Kate and McCaul didn't wait. They got back within ten minutes, but then realized they had to wait for Boyd anyway, because he had the equipment. So they went up to her room.

McCaul sat on the bed next to the telephone, while Kate opened the window and looked down into the Plaza. "Kate, will you do a deal with me to kill the airing if I give you something bigger?"

Kate turned around to face him. "Sure, if there's a good enough reason to. What?"

"Let's say there's something going on in Cuba at this very moment that no other media person on the globe has the slightest idea about."

She moved toward him and sat on the bed. "Start talking, Mike." She put both elbows on her knees and rested her chin on her hands.

"Okay, but if I tell you this, and you do anything to let the word out before everything happens, then I go to jail and thousands of innocent people die and you don't have a story."

"That might work. But I gotta get my story out of it."

"You pull back the story you got and I give you a bigger one when it happens. Yes or no??"

"Within a week."

"When it happens, but it should be within a week."

"Deal."

"Kate, call Atlanta."

She picked up the phone, made the call, argued a little bit with someone on the other end and it was done.

A second after she hung up there was a thud on the door.

A grunt came from outside that sounded like "Kate? You in there?" It wasn't the cops. It was Cameron the Cameraman.

She popped up and opened the door and the room became much smaller as Boyd entered.

"I brought the portable."

He proceeded to make happen whatever technical things that had to happen and soon they were looking at rough footage, preceded by Kate's standard intro she was reading off a sheet or paper, "CNN Atlanta. Assignment SGQ030902. Near Guantanamo, Cuba. Kate McKee Unit Producer. Boyd Cameron Cameraman."

She said, "There's probably an hour of footage, but only about twenty minutes at the camp." Kate fast-forwarded through a lot of tape, finally pressing play and previewing in fast forward mode. She hit the play button to show a fairly remote shot of a cluster of men. It was perfectly in focus, credit to immovable Boyd.

There were about a dozen men in the shot, all bearded, most in well-worn fatigues. Some were armed with AK-47s slung over their shoulder. There didn't seem to be much good cheer; they seemed to be serious, and there seemed to be a command structure. One very tall member of the gang seemed to be giving orders, and while salutes were not in evidence, there seemed to be a lot of respect being passed his way. There was about three minutes of footage in the shot.

"We shot this from a grove of trees about fifty meters away. It's high def, so we can zoom in on faces once we get the right technology. Let me go to the next scene."

The next shot was of a hooch. It had a thatched roof and open sides. The shot was taken from a low angle pointing up. Obviously, the shot was from a prone position. It was a little unsteady and slightly out of focus.

Kate said, "I shot this footage on a micro-cam. I thought it made better sense if only one of us got this close."

The shot revealed some crates, and although they were out of focus, the contents were obvious. They were Stinger and SMAW - Shoulder Mounted Assault Weapons - missile crates. Where there were missile crates, usually there were missiles not too far away. There were other familiar crates that carried ammo and some others that surely contained AK47s. All in all, the brief footage was explosive and not only in its content.

"Kate, for now can I keep the video chip?"

She shook her lovely head. "No, Mike. Thus is the stuff of which Pulitzers are made. I'm not going to give it up."

"You don't have to give it up, you've already sent a copy to CNN. I just don't want you to get caught with it, Kate. I mean this are dangerous. I've got a room here in the hotel, why can't I just lock it in my safe?"

"Why would it be any safer in your safe than in my safe? Huh? Tell me that."

She had a point there. Mike knew he wasn't going to win this one so he said, "Okay, that's fine. But give me a key to your room and your safe password. I might need it if they decide to shake you down or something."

"That's fair. But don't you dare take it unless it's a matter of life or death. I'll give you seven days and then I just have to give a go ahead to Atlanta." Boyd was unhooking the video player.

"Agreed."

"Okay." She took a pen out of her pocket book and a slip of paper and wrote down a four number code. "Here's my safe password and an extra key card."

"What are you going to do, Mike?"

"Don't know yet. I have to find LaRue and find some time to spend with my sweetie."

She gave Mike her million dollars a year smile and he felt helpless and totally in her grasp.

She said, "Can we have drinks a little later?"

"Let's see. I'm going to start to track down Lucien. How about tomorrow night for sure? I can fill you in on my sit down with Fidel."

"That would be great. About seven in the lobby?"

"Yup, perfect." McCaul started to leave and she followed him to the door.

She smiled, "Well, toot-a-loo." Mike looked back, smiled again and tootled off.

Well, McCaul's Kate situation was solved, at least for a few days. Now he had to figure out what to do with what he had.

It seemed as if his mission for Inglewood and the CIA was finished. He could file a report that would give them exactly what they wanted to hear.

He could leave tomorrow, proof in hand.

If he didn't mind gaining the eternal enmity of the girl of his dreams, and leaving LaRue to get out of whatever soup he was in on his own.

Which meant that nothing was finished at all.

So, McCaul had to do what he had to do. Get Kate safely off the island, her Pulitzer in hand. Somehow get a copy of the video for Felix. Find LaRue, see if what he was doing was good for world peace, and escape without Fidel, Raul, Zorro and who knows whom else finding out that McCaul had anything to do with anything. Easy.

McCaul took a taxi back to his place.

15

IT WAS EARLY EVENING and McCaul figured he could either start to track down LaRue tonight or wait until the morning. He hadn't talked to Webster in a while, so he thought he better check in. He called Jud at home on Skype.

"Webster here."

"Hi, Jud."

"So how does it go, Mike?"

"Where should I start? Well, I'm seeing Fidel and Raul in the morning and Colombian druggies or ISIS or some other nuts have an invasion force in the mountains."

"Say that again."

"I'm seeing Fidel and Raul in the morning."

"No, after that."

"You mean the part about the druggies or ISIS having an invasion force?"

"Well, yes, Mike."

"Hmmmm. Well. Our friend Kate has footage of a couple of dozen scary people at a hidden camp in the mountains. They've got a pretty big stash of weapons and look to be up to no good."

"Why Mike, what does that mean? How can we get our hands on her video for the Minister?" The moment of truth.

"Well, we already have our hands on the video, more or less."

"More, Mike, or less?"

"More or less," McCaul said, "It's locked up in her hotel room safe, which means it's anything but safe. A crowbar could set it free. But I've got her room key and password, so if we decide, we can get the video about any time we want."

"Well, Mike, do we want?"

"I'm not so sure." Mike scratched just above his right temple, ran his fingers through his hair, and his hand downward over his mouth and chin. "Can I have a couple of days to find out?"

"Mike, don't you forget why you're down there and your commitment to Minister Inglewood."

"Now how could I forget that, Jud?"

"One more thing. I've lost LaRue. He's somewhere in the hills of Pinar del Rio hooked up with who knows who."

"What was that?" McCaul could almost hear Webster's eyebrows rise over the phone.

"Can I hold off telling you for a couple of days?"

"If you need to, Mike, but for Christ's sake, be careful."

"You know me, Boss. Careful's my middle name."

"Mike, you have never met a careful you've ever liked."

Mike hung up; he opened a bottle of Cristal Lager, and watched bad TV for a few minutes; Cuban female gymnasts doing bizarre things with their sculpted bodies on industrially designed apparatus.

For the first time Mike noticed three Cohibas next to the television. Janisleyda must have left them. Mike opened the box, smelled the cigars and pocketed them. Outside of the normal poorly made contraband smokes, some cigar makers in Havana often try to smuggle a little of this and a little of that from their workplace every day to support their own cigar trading company. These were likely of this ilk.

It was just after six, too late for McCaul to chase down LaRue and too early to go to bed. Seeing as how his list of drinking buddies was rather short, he decided to clean up and try to find some new ones.

He showered and put on a plain white t-shirt, cargo shorts and thick wool socks under hiking boots. He filled one of the pockets of his shorts with Janisleydis' stubby Robustos. He locked up his apartment and caught a taxi on La Rampa and went to the Prado.

McCaul figured he'd end up at the Bar Monserrate where Damian, the sonero, had told him he was singing at nights.

Only a block from the Parque Centrale McCaul noticed a scimitar sign above one in a series of bedraggled buildings. His Spanish was bad, but not so bad that he couldn't translate "Arab Cuban Friendship Society" from Spanish to English.

He hung around on the street for a bit. He lit and smoked a cigar while standing on the broad boulevard. He walked down the Prado. If there is a more beautiful boulevard, he thought, as tired as it is, then he hadn't seen it. The mosaic in the promenade in the middle of Paseo de Marti was tiring out from its many, many decades of couples strolling its length and fifty years without any repairs or maintenance.

But its gigantic shade trees that had outlived almost all of the old Marxist dictators, but two, more than made up for any little flaws one could find in the ancient mosaic artistic genius that Fidel's workers had besmirched with cement patches.

As always, the Prado was moderately busy with kids playing hackysack or soccer with a ball facsimile, couples arm in arm and artists trying to sell their work.

There was one of Old Havana's inevitable priestesses in her white colonial garb at a card table on a stool smoking, as they inevitably did, a massive cigar.

She looked up at McCaul with a knowledge of himself he felt he was without. She didn't as much as blink or make a facial expression. She didn't have a come-on to try and magically make a peso move from his pocket to hers. McCaul found that unusual. Perhaps she knew a little more than the Chinese guy with the hairy moley arm did. For a place that didn't seem to have any good fortune at all, they sure had a lot of fortunetellers.

McCaul dropped his rapidly declining cigar in an empty sink that someone had wisely provided a century ago and sat down.

He passed a 10 CUC bill across the table to her but she didn't appear to notice.

She took a long drag from her cigar and moved her face toward McCaul's and blew a steady stream of the smoke from her lungs through her nostrils at his face.

"Señor."

He moved toward her. She spoke in broken English.

"We will have a hurricane in three days. No one else knows. Keep your clothes dry and stay warm with your woman. You will be betrayed by someone who is close to you."

McCaul got up and started walking toward Bar Monserrate.

She said in a louder voice, "Trust no one!"

McCaul thought, 'Better than the Fu Chu guy. At least something useful and that would prove itself right or wrong in the near future.' He had no doubt that he would be betrayed; these adventures always had some form

126

of betrayal attached. As far as the weather report, McCaul figured, if Accuweather can't be right in the morning for that afternoon, what chance would a rum swilling, cigar smoking priestess have to get it right? But, McCaul thought, his fortune could be much, much worse. He reached in his pocket, pulled out another Robusto and lit it. He came to the corner of Neptuno, across from the Telegrafo and leaned against a light post.

A few lovers walked by while he smoked and watched. None were of anything close to the same general age, nor for that matter, of similar skin tone.

While sucking his cigar he sneered in the males' general directions. Not with typical Canadian holier-than-thou smugness - because undoubtedly some of these older fellas were Canadian - but to at least confirm in his mind how wrong is sex imperialism. None of these guys were handsome or charming, and likely not even rich. But they feel this way because their paltry tens of dollars can buy them this self-opinion in Cuba from desperately poor girls and boys.

There wasn't a lot of action at the Friendship Society; barely a scent of Turkish coffee wafted across the wide street. But before he finished his stogie, a couple of interesting characters arrived at the place. Both were well dressed, one sinister-looking, mustachioed fellow that resembled Zorro's alter ego in typical bowling alley Cuban formal garb down to the white shoes, the other in what seemed to be pajamas and sandals. Both were smoking big Montecristos and both were laughing. They went inside and didn't come out before Mike stubbed out his cigar on a palm tree, so he started walking back toward Obispo and the Monserrate Bar.

As he was passed the Prado y Neptuno restaurant he heard the sounds of blaring salsa.

"Senor!"

Standing across the broken concrete on the other side of Avenida Virtudes was Manuel.

127

"Come to party! Have a cigar?" The bulky Cubano was grinning, standing next to a flamboyantly dressed woman with flowing black hair, large hoop earrings and long red finger nails.

McCaul crossed the rubble and Manuel reached out to grab his shoulder. "Come, we're having my birthday party." Manuel let his date lead him upstairs and allowed Mike to precede him.

The smoke in the staircase was thick as pea soup and Mike entered a room filled with partying people. There was eardrum shattering salsa coming from a huge ghetto blaster while the partiers were dancing, every man holding a bottle of Havana Club rum in one hand, his dance partner in the other and a cigar between his lips. The girls were dressed like movie stars, all with ebony hair in long ringlets and stilletto heels. A few wore sunglasses and had Prada handbags.

They were in a party room above a restaurant and when there was a lull in the music a waiter in dirty whites entered with a huge tray containing a chopped up suckling pig. He placed it on a table and it was immediately descended on by a cluster of revellers.

Manuel stood back and beckoned to McCaul who came over. He took two Robustos from his jacket pocket, and snipped the end off one with a deadly looking cigar cutter and then took the other, did the same, and gave one to McCaul. He lit them both with a small propane torch of a lighter.

"Mi Amigo, how is your project doing?"

"I don't have a project, Manuel."

"I think I know different, McCaul. You hang out with people I know. And I know what they are hoping to do."

McCaul didn't show his concern. He had to resist acting as if he cared.

"What you need to know, Michael, is that you are not the only ones who want to fix things for Cuba."

"Now what do you mean, Manuel. I don't want to fix things here."

"Ahhh. But your friends do. And if they do, you probably do. And I know your friends. And they have competition."

"Huh?"

"Raul pays his spies less moneda than I pay mine."

"What do you mean?"

"There are some people in Raul's own government that would like to see the Castros disappear."

McCaul took a sip from his rum. "Who?"

"You will see. But you have to know this. They have plans to remove the Castros that they look to start in three days. If I can help you. I will. You know how to find me."

McCaul looked at the ceiling and rubbed his face. What did Manuel mean, what did he know and what should he, McCaul, do about it.

"Okay."

McCaul took a long draw from his cigar. "Okay, Amigo."

"McCaul, I am your friend and you have very few here."

Mike nodded and walked down the narrow staircase.

- # -

Ramon Duarte Borges hated most people that he had to deal with. This Arab was just such an example. Since Cuba had been placed in dire financial circumstances by the loss of the Soviet Union by the Bolsheviks and the Venezuelan economy had failed, Cuba's security chief often had to work with races of people he found inferior.

The Chinese were, to Duarte, a race of worker ants who were unable to think on their own and were physically weak. Occasionally he had to deal with Mexican or Colombian drug merchants, who, even for him, were frightening. He was disdainful of all such American aboriginal races; Duarte's ancestors had exterminated Los Indios in Cuba.

But worst of all, to him, were the Arabs. He thought them only a generation past living in tents in the dessert and were obnoxious in their ostentatious spending of their oil riches.

This one was among the most obnoxious. He was a special delegate from Iran, here to discuss that country providing Cuba oil extraction services and weapons for its military. The Chinese had made an offer to trade weapons for the right to exploit Cuban offshore oil, but the Castros were hesitant to sacrifice what might be their only opportunity to gain economic self-sufficiency.

Both Castros hoped that the National Iranian Oil Company might be convinced to construct and operate the extraction program for only a commission per barrel.

Duarte had his doubts and trusted the Arabs not at all.

Having been dropped off by his driver at the roundabout at Neptuno and Prado, he had walked a few dozen yards before he noticed his meeting subject walking toward him from the other direction. They met exactly in front of the Cuban Arab Friendship Center, offered each other perfunctory greetings, shook hands and entered.

Duarte followed his subject, Abu Bahoz Al-Bhadi, into the dark main room of the centre. Bahoz ordered coffees and lit up a pipe; Duarte countered with a massive Esplendido cigar and settled in to serve what was sure to be an unpleasant and very trying evening.

16

TO GET TO BAR MONSERRATE McCaul had to pass the Floridita and again wiggle past a gaggle of Hemingways. He wandered down the alley behind the Fine Arts building, and was greeted with a huge smile and a catcher's mitt handshake from Alexi, Monserrate's gigantic ex-Olympic boxer doorman.

A few years before on vacation in Cuba Mike had happened to meet another member of the famous Cuban Boxing Team and had finished up the evening at a disco with several of these pugilists and Alexi had been among them and their coterie of pleasant looking females. McCaul had looked but didn't touch, especially out of fear for his life if he had happened to pick the wrong one.

Damian was doing a set and nodded his head toward Mike between notes by way of a welcome.

An older fellow in a golf cap walked by Mike and offered him a Cohiba Robusto and Mike gave him a CUC in return. Probably 95% of all the Cohibas in the world were fake and half of them sold in Cuba. Mike sniffed it and checked the band. It wasn't real, but then again it was a buck and felt pretty solid. The guy introduced himself as Felipe and lit it for Mike and he sat at the bar to watch the show.

One unhappy thing about Havana, for McCaul, was that its saloons don't have many Cubans in them. Only people with dollar equivalents can enter and not many locals have extra cash to throw around on five-CUC mojitos. But of course, in the interest of enhancing tourism spending, Fidel's people were pretty welcoming of hustlers who bring along a turista or two to spend a dollar or twenty. So crowds were often matched up, local and guest.

McCaul noticed that the scrawny American guy he had met at the Telegrafo was sitting at the side bar, chatting to the bartender and an equally scrawny red haired woman.

The guy waved him over and McCaul approached him. The guy's eyes were slightly blood-shot and he welcomed Mike with a slight slur, even this early in the evening.

"Don, right?" They shook hands.

"That's me, this is Roz." Roz was a fairly attractive but overly tanned woman who, once she said "How do you do?" was easily identifiable as English. Mike shook hands with her.

Damian was leading an up-tempo song and scraping a guiro, Oswaldo was on keyboards. Don Hughes was drumming on a stool as if he was in the band and producing a remarkable result.

Don passed Mike a new Mojito that had been sitting next to his nearly empty one and ordered himself a fresh one. Mike offered his thanks and took a sip. It was a double.

"So, Don, what's your real story?"

He stopped drumming.

"Mike, buddy, I don't know. I don't live in Buffalo. I'm stuck in paradise."

"Not a bad place to get stuck."

"Not so great if ya ain't got no home to ever go to."

Mike took a drink of his Mojito.

"You live here, Don."

"Yeah. I split up with my wife last year, she took everything up there including half my pension, which leaves me just enough to get by on down here. I'm working on a book in my spare time. Which is almost all the time."

Mike finished his Mojito and ordered two more, paid and gave one to Don. "Havana ain't Buffalo, Don."

"Nope, it's a lot nicer."

Damian finished his song to a standing ovation by the few dozen people present.

He and Oswaldo came over to Mike after his song and sat down next to him, the opposite side of Don. Mike started to order them mojitos but the singer made a vicious face and did the universal finger rubbing symbol for "too expensive" and said "cervesa, por favor," so Mike got them beers.

The Cubans and Mike used their best efforts to chat for a while over a couple of drinks. Mike had often observed that women have a difficult time communicating with each other when they don't speak the same language. Maybe because they were far too effusive and have much more to say.

Men, though, opined McCaul, whenever these language issues arose, got along very well with sign language, pointing, grunting and using a pidgin form of each other's languages. After all, there were very few topics that hold male interest long enough to warrant using words at all, and they all know what they were: the booze, the game, the boss and the girls. Oh, and among the bourgeoisie, the golf. With Cubans, the music. So he, Oswaldo and Damian managed to get along, get what each was saying, laughed lots, and Damian dragged McCaul out the door, with Don

Hughes and Oswaldo trailing behind, to go to another place after a slightly less adept sonero took Damian's place.

The singer pointed and grunted and wiggled his fingers and Mike figured out that the destination was in Centro, and they could walk, but they would miss a lot of the show if they did. Not wanting to miss a minute of a show that Damian the bolero master would take him to, Mike hailed a cab and off they went.

They travelled about ten minutes to and along the sea wall and Damian had the driver stop at a corner. There wasn't a light in sight, but the sky was clear and Mike was able to tell a five from a ten and paid the driver. Damian pointed across the bay toward Miramar and the lights of Meyer Lansky's old Riviera Hotel. The waves were smashing up against the sea wall, and billowing twenty feet into the air and crashing into the street and all around them and it was about the most spectacular thing that, Mike thought, by which he had ever been enveloped.

The Malecon thoroughfare and promenade is a stunning, almost surreal, place at night. All along its length of a few miles are old mansions that at one time would have made Boca Raton's inland waterway castles look meek in comparison. And they were all devastated by time, lack of care, occasional hurricanes and over a century of consistent salt-water contact.

The sea wall sidewalk was busy with people: Mike watched a happy northern couple, arm and arm with a bottle of Veuve Cliquot in her hand and a cigar in his, a Havana couple laughing and joking. A couple sharing a bicycle and several of those extra-generational north-south pairings he disliked so much.

Damian pointed across the Malecon and the duo managed to avoid the traffic and walked up the hill. They were on Avenida 23, "La Rampa". Although it was late, the street was filled with couples and their local "guide". There were a couple of dimly lit bodegas, and a busy café or two. In a couple of minutes McCaul and Hughes followed Damian as he entered past a sign "La Zorra y el Cuervo" and down a set of stairs. The doorman hugged Damian and Oswaldo and when Mike offered two 10 CUC bills the old man hugged him too.

"Mike, here es you heard the primo major musica Cubano. Es grupo de mi amigo, Gilberto. Venido."

McCaul followed.

The music was at full beat as they entered the modest music hall. Damian was moving fast so McCaul had to pick up his own pace to keep up.

Damian was bear-hugged by a huge bear of a guy who he introduced to McCaul, who then bear-hugged Mike. Then a tall thin fellow vigorously shook Osvaldo's hand and then Mike's. Then a beautiful Latina gave Damian a wet kiss and Mike one on the cheek. Then another sturdy, hairy fellow kissed Damian and thankfully, for Mike, only gave him a pound on the shoulder. All these greeting activities were remarkably performed in perfect time to the music.

Everyone seemed to know Damian and he in turn everyone else. Even the conga player managed to unnoticeably interrupt his commitment to the music to give Damian a wave.

Damian pulled Mike to a table and introduced him to a blonde, definitely unCuban, woman.

In a Jersey accent she said, "Hi, I'm Sue."

If she could speak English, and her accent indicated this, McCaul thought she'd be a powerful ally for the night. McCaul noticed Don Hughes circling close to the band. Oswaldo had already moved to the keyboards.

Almost everyone moved to the music. It was hard not to, it was all around the crowd, within each and every person, beckoning and stimulating them all. Half the audience was dancing with others, the other half were dancing by themselves. A few lonely souls were parked in a corner talking. McCaul thought they were probably Canadians. McCaul suspected this because he'd gone to an Afro Cuban All Star concert at Massey Hall and Juan de Marco had to plead with the audience to get up and dance. Even Germans would be unable to resist dancing to these tunes, even if they did it badly. As a Canadian, McCaul therefore felt justified to resist sharing undue body movement so he stifled his own worldly urges. Sue, as a Jersey girl, did similarly.

McCaul focussed on the band and the music. The group was young: teens and early twenties. The music was Afro Latin Jazz, with the Cuban beat: the clave; the root, the rhythm of all aspects of Cuban music; the instrumentation, the vocals, the dance steps. The players were spectacularly and enthusiastically immersed in this world.

McCaul was blown away by the power, imagination and creativity of these horn bleaters, conga beaters, bongo bangers, guitar strummers, harmonium pluckers, Güiro scrapers and Maracas shakers. He thought one needed to be there to appreciate it. Hands were slapping skins at speeds beyond the ability of eyes to follow, perfectly in combination with every other player. An assembled mélange of rhythm, high tones and low rumbles, thumps and squeals and shakes and scrapes were all in imperfect harmony but with an identical beat. Mike closed his eyes and he could hear them all, when he focussed on one instrument, the Güiro, a dried and hollowed gourd, he was able to pick it out of the fantastic mélange perfectly. The music was intercellular. There was even a violin sounding otherworldly in this performance.

In the Cuban way, the music wound up and down and up and down into a climax that didn't seem would ever end. But then the bandleader, an older Spaniard, worked his magic and with the clash of everything at once, it finished. Everyone in the room at once sighed.

And then the small audience of a few dozen began whistling and applauding and howling and cheering. And the band bowed, then bowed again. Then they set their instruments down and calmly joined their adoring fans who brought them cold drinks. Several dropped by to offer greetings to Damian and in turn to Mike after he was introduced.

After a moment or two the bandleader joined them. He kissed Susan before he hugged Damian. He offered McCaul his hand, "Buenos Noches, Señor. I am Gilberto Valdez Rodriguez."

McCaul offered his greetings, "Your English is impressive, Señor."

136

"Señor, during Fidel times," he said, "one cannot make a living doing music. I have been a travel agent for almost thirty years, so I work very often with Americanos, English and Canadian visitors. I was in Canada, Toronto, last week, at the university, to teach them how to play drums.

"Toronto is a beautiful city, but very cold, and the music is not very good. But I try to make it better."

McCaul asked him about his musical group.

"Oh, my muchachos. They are street musicians. Habana street kids who live for their music not just for the bread on the table. They will eat tonight because of playing tonight. But tomorrow, if they wish to eat again, then they must play again."

Damian tapped Mike on the shoulder. A basket of Cristals had appeared. McCaul gave the waiter twenty CUCs and signalled to Damian to have beers taken to the players and gave him another twenty.

Gilberto took one. "Music to Cubans, Señor, is like air to breathe. Like food to eat. We don't have much, here, but we have our family and friends, and we have our rum and our novias and our music. And we have our, how should I say, our intimacies. And to save our poor souls we have our religion.

"Señor, I can walk down the street in New York and tell if the coloured man walking ahead of me is Cuban. I can tell by the way he moves his hips. Señor, Cubans even walk with the clave." He laughed and Mike joined him. A very likable man.

"Have you met Sue?"

Mike nodded.

"Sue is very dear to us. Each year she is able to arrange with USA Immigration to accept a small number of our muchachos to study in America. And she arranges full scholarships for them at some of America's best universities for music. Even Julliard."

McCaul was impressed.

"How did you end up down here doing this?", McCaul asked her.

"Just like everybody else. I'm a music teacher in Manhattan and I came down here one time with some girlfriends to study the music but mostly to get some sun. We started hanging out at the Casa de la Culturas and one night I hooked up with one of the musicians. One thing led to another and now he's home in Westchester with the kids."

"Susan, that is very, very cool."

"Aaah, it's nuthin. The kids they let me bring home are solid citizens and world class and they teach other kids up there more about music and drums than they'll ever learn from their professors. We run a couple of fundraising concerts a year to cover travel for the kids and get some money to their families. It's fun and some day one of them's gonna win a Grammy and maybe let me keep it for him for a week or two."

"No Grammies yet?"

"I only been doin' it for six or seven years, but we got kids in the top Latin bands in the country and before long they'll have their own."

The grupo stirred, and a few stood and started back toward the stage. Damian saluted McCaul with his cervesa and indicated he was going up with them.

A flautist, a bongo player and a guitar player joined Damian with his maracas at the front of the little stage.

The flute, then, "Dos Gardenias Para Ti."

McCaul's breath was taken.

Susan said, "This is so typically Cuban. It's about a man who gives a woman two flowers and he tells her that if one dies he knows that she's been fooling around. Stupid Latino machismo, but romantic as hell."

Mike chuckled and said, "That's funny. But true." He signalled to the guy who was delivering beers and he provided another round and McCaul gave him another twenty.

Gilberto leaned toward McCaul. "Damian, you know, anywhere else he would be a star and rich."

"Why does he stay?"

"He's got a family and a mother in Las Tunas, Amigo. If he were to leave Cuba, his kids would be stuck in purgatory or worse. Fidel doesn't like people who are tourist attractions leaving unless he gets to keep the money they make. When I go to teach in Canada or the USA I don't get paid, Fidel does. I just go to do what I love doing."

McCaul thought, 'these Cubans are a different breed of human. As communal as anyone and as capitalist as most.'

Gilberto stood and said, "Thank you for enjoying our music, Señor. Tell people about us when you can."

McCaul stood and shook hands. Gilberto went back up on stage with the rest of the band and the entire group got behind Damian who started a song about Cienfuegos, which rang a bell for McCaul. It was the name of that guy whose picture was on the wall at the restaurant Mike had visited with Manuel.

Gilberto announced loudly in English, "This is a song about a small town named like one of our great heroes finally getting its guanguancho music. Cubans find anything a good enough reason to write a song."

It was a great night for McCaul. Hanging out with his new musical maestros, learning about Cuban music, and having music pulse through his body. But he had a date with Fidel in the morning and he had to leave.

He looked around for Don Hughes and finally saw him standing near a corner of the grupo, studying the timbales player like a craps player studying the dice.

McCaul decided to leave Hughes where he was. He had about a hundred dollars in his pocket and gave all but cab fare of it to Susan to entertain the band. If some of the cash ended up buying the kids eggs in the morning, he wouldn't mind.

139

Susan stood up and gave McCaul a hug and he waved at Damian and left.

Don Hughes never noticed McCaul leaving; he was too wrapped up in watching the performance. His hands were red and swollen from clapping out on whatever hard surface he was near, but he couldn't stop, he had to be a part of it. He stared intently at the Timbales player, then the Conguero, then the young woman on the drum set and back again.

He was drinking and inhaling the music (or it was drinking and inhaling him); trying to watch all three of the percussionists at once. The piano player added to the rhythmic collage with a stunning "montuno", a percussive and rhythmic use of an instrument that non-Cubans only use as a principal instrument.

Don had travelled Cuba in search of a moment exactly like this one. He had watched and played with some of the most respected Cuban musicians, but this performance, this new generation of child musicians, were doing things he had never seen done before.

He never went near the dance floor at these concerts because any time he did he felt like a country hick trying to dance hip-hop. But his feet were moving constantly. The musicians, the dancers, the listeners, the watchers were all one. Sweat poured off the faces of the musicians and the dancers because the energy never stopped. Don was soaked but he didn't care. He was experiencing this event with every fibre of his being and didn't leave the place until the last rhythm was played.

17

MCCAUL GOT UP FEELING A LITTLE ROUGH. He showered, dressed in his nicest, suit and walked down and into the street. He caught a Panataxi to the Canadian Chancery, the Ambassador's residence in Miramar. The trip took about fifteen minutes and Mike got out in front of a locked gate guarded by two Cuban soldiers in dress greens. One checked his passport against his clipboard, and the other opened the gates for him to enter.

He was greeted at the door by a bulgy, burr-haired and red-faced guy who greeted Mike by name in a loud voice and accompanied him into what he thought is called a drawing room.

The butler had a slight Spanish accent. "The Ambassador will come to meet you shortly, Mr. McCaul. Might I get you a coffee?"

McCaul nodded please and relaxed on an enormous leather armchair. There was a laser-printed copy of the on-line version of today's Globe and Mail on the coffee table and he paged through, looking for something of interest. Reports of mistreatment of an RCMP whistle-blowing undercover agent interested him for a moment and so did a story of a funding scandal in the Federal Department of Public Works. Either of these articles could have been published in the 70's, 80's, or 90's.

Many of the government's ills are systemic, and wouldn't be cured until the system was.

The bulky butler entered, "Mr. McCaul, Ambassador DeGrassi will see you now."

McCaul rose and followed Jeeves down a hall into the Ambassador's home office. He rose to meet Mike, and walked around his desk to shake hands. He was late fifties and a little cherubic, with fluffy white hair parted on the right and he was dressed in a light blue linen suit with a red tie and white shirt.

"Mr. McCaul, welcome to Havana." He sat back on his desk and indicated for Mike to sit.

"Thank you for seeing me, your Excellency. And thank you for setting up the meeting with such short notice."

He laughed, "No excellencies around here, Mr. McCaul. Ted is fine."

McCaul liked him. He seemed to have a little bit of the Cuban spirit in him.

"Well what do we have up our sleeves for the Beard and his brother, Mr. McCaul? You know that he is officially retired."

"Mike, please." McCaul said "Well, Amb..."

He lifted his hand to stop McCaul.

"I hear that he still has both hands on the steering wheel, Ted. But Raul has his foot on the brake."

He chuckled and nodded.

"Ted. I don't have to tell you about the importance of travel to Cuba to our firm, nor how important our travel is to the economy of Cuba."

He nodded.

"Our volume of business has gone down considerably after the terrorist attacks, hurricanes, oil spills, economy meltdown and other stuff. We've seen travel rebound to Florida, but without a better feeling of confidence in the security of Cuba's leadership, we figure that travelers will start to avoid coming here."

"And you wish to have the President and Former First Secretary Castro confirm a reason for confidence."

"Yup, but we also hope Mr. Castro will let us conduct our own evaluation of security provisions at his major airports, so that we can run a P.R. campaign aimed at our travelers."

"Is that all, Mr. McCaul?" DeGrassi leaned forward.

"I'd like to request a privileged pass of some kind from the Cuban government, to allow me freer access to certain secured facilities."

DeGrassi took a sip of coffee and moved his upper body closer across his desk.

"Don't bullshit the official representative of the Canadian government in Cuba, Mr. McCaul. I know what you're up to. Special treatment from Fidel might be more of a problem today than it would have been yesterday. I have a report here that you're on Cuban Intell's watch list."

"I heard that. But I don't have the slightest idea what that's about, unless it's because I've been hanging out with a CNN journalist."

"We know a lot more about you than you might like, Mr. McCaul. But your secret's safe with us. You know the Cuban authorities are real leery of nosy foreigners. A few months ago they shot and killed a Danish kid for just walking next to military headquarters. With Fidel's health they're more paranoid than ever. And you're here on a guest worker visa. They can pull that back any time they want, if they get really suspicious."

"How's Fidel's health? That stumble from the stage a while ago and his stomach problems?"

"Hard to say. After he fell down in Santa Clara, some said he had a stroke. Our people studied the tape, talked to our intelligence friends. He tripped and had a heavy fall. The crowd surged forward and the guards had a hard time getting him up and out. We guess a sprained ankle, a bruised hip, shoulder and face. Maybe a fractured arm. We'll get a first look today.

"He's amazingly durable. He had a serious small colon problem and probably a touch of prostate cancer, but it looks like he's through it for the time being. But he's almost 90."

"What about the so-called succession?" Mike asked.

"It's so-called bullshit," he said. "Fidel feels he owes Raul, I don't think he really likes him very much, and has let him run his security and military gigs, but always with a hand firmly on his privates. Raul wouldn't last a day without Fidel's sponsorship and won't be around very long if Fidel ever dies. Fidel is loved, Raul is hated."

He continued, "Fidel certainly showed who's the boss with Lage and Perez Roque. They were his designated post-Raul successors and he kicked their cans when they started acting like they enjoyed it."

"What's really going on here? Tell me about Cuba, Mr. Ambassador. Ted."

"I've only been here a year, so I only know what I've been told, and that's that it's an island of lies. Nothing here is as it seems and everyone lies to survive."

"Do tell."

"Young Cubans have to lie to stay in school. Old Cubans lie because lies are the only opinion they've ever been allowed to have. Castro's politburo lies about everything it does, and just about everything everyone else does; especially the USA. The Castros spew lies constantly but are so extracted from reality that they seem to believe them."

Mike nodded and smiled.

"Fidel lied his first day on the job. He lied when he "temporarily" suspended free elections when he took power. He lies about his health care and his education and the equality of Cubans, Mr. McCaul, but, as in Animal Farm, the pigs are more equal than others."

McCaul chuckled.

"Loyal Fidelistas, virtually all of Spanish extraction, get all the good jobs and are rewarded with pleasant homes in nicer areas like Vedado and Miramar. Those who unfortunately are not in favour, who are almost all black, live in tenements on narrow streets filled with rubble that serve as both sewers and playgrounds.

"There's only way to survive here, Mr. McCaul. Theft. Or at least what Fidel considers theft. It's participation in the black market. All family members scrounge for anything of value that they can turn into cash.

"Fidel lies when he pretends that the black market isn't the only way that people prevent starving."

McCaul asked, "What kind of things do they scrounge?"

"Oh, might be trinkets and trash to sell to turistas. Workers in tobacco factories try to sneak out enough tobacco and labels to make a cigar a day at home. The factory workers get a box a month that they sell. Grannies dress up as Santerian priestesses to have their picture taken by tourists for a buck. Children look for kind foreigners who will give them a peso because they're cute. Girls dream of having a child with a rich Canadian and, if the Dad has at least some ethical standard, getting child support."

"What about the prostitution?"

"Yes, there's lots of it. I'm hardly a moralist, but these guys feel rich and handsome in Cuba by throwing ten dollar bills around like man-hole covers and I don't like it much, but it helps people survive."

He rose from his comfy ambassador chair.

"Let's go and meet El Jefe Maximo and his hermano."

McCaul stood and they walked back to the main entrance.

"Mike, you've met Jorge?" He pronounced it George, not Horgay. Mike again nodded hello to the burly butler.

"So, Jorge, we are off to see the Señors Castro today. It should be an easy trip."

Parked in front was the Ambassador's black Mercedes, a Canadian flag on the left front corner panel. They headed east and took the thoroughfare up the hill past a series of estates and lovely houses, and around the famous Colon Cemetery.

Jorge was no less than a maniacal equal to all the drivers Mike had ridden with all week, just a lot faster and in a lot more solid vehicle. So the trip was a little less scary, plus, McCaul didn't get a travelogue, so all in all, for him, the trip was quite pleasant.

They approached Fidel's headquarters from the west, through the Plaza de Revolucion and the National Theatre and by the Interior Ministry, with its massive steel wall mural tribute to Che. Then they turned right in front of the Marti Statue and the thirty-story Memorial Tower; near the place that Fidel stands for hours to preach to his millions of recruited admirers.

Across the plaza was the communications centre festooned with antennae and dishes of every size.

They turned right on the other side of the adjoining park, and stopped at a security booth manned by a single armed soldier in crisp green fatigues and a peaked cap. He came to the window and Jorge produced a sheet of paper that must have been an authorization of some kind. Whatever it was, the soldier raised the barrier and they drove up the driveway to a long office building.

The building was the headquarters of the Communist Party of Cuba, built for some reason in the fifties, with a lot of glass. They stopped at the front door guarded by two more soldiers. One came to again check out the authorization and then allowed them to exit the car.

Jorge stayed chatting with one of the soldiers, while the other took the ambassador and McCaul in the front door. Another guard waited at a staircase on the left side of the lobby.

It's a very simple building, like bureaucratic office buildings around the world. Being inside, McCaul could think of at least a dozen almost identical buildings in Ottawa alone. The interiors reminded him of high schools he had attended; steel staircase railings, lots of linoleum, mustiness and sickly green paint.

Their guide passed them and their authorization document on to the staircase guard and he indicated that they should ascend ahead of him.

At the top, they were guided to the left and into the left back corner of a medium-sized rectangular boardroom that looked out on the Marti Memorial. There were about a dozen or so simply designed ancient wooden chairs around a plain rectangular table. On the wall across from the windows was a picture of a middle aged Fidel, chest and chin pushed out. On one side of Fidel was a picture of Che, and on the other a print, probably of Jose Marti in action. Facing McCaul and DeGrassi, next to another door, was a banner "La Revolución es Justa y Apenas!" "The Revolution is Fair and Just!"

McCaul wondered if Cuba has an official sign painter, like other countries have poet laureates.

They waited for over two hours.

The soldier was still standing beside them, all with their back to the window facing the door they had entered. Their guard was definitely discouraging any small talk or snappy comments. The atmosphere did not encourage any gay repartee between DeGrassi and McCaul, either. So time went by for them at the speed of a calendar.

They chatted quietly about their hometowns, his in British Columbia. Both of them offered deep regrets about the ongoing scandals back home. They tried to talk about hockey, but neither of them had been fans since the Canadiens had last won a Cup. Mike updated him about the Blue Jays, he hated baseball. The ambassador tried beginning a conversation on families, but both of them were single. Mike made sure his fingernails were clean enough to meet with a dictator. Mike hummed Besame Mucho and tried to remember the taste of the pollo and the dinner with Manuel.

McCaul thought, 'Nelson Mandela did this for twenty seven years, alone'.

Just as McCaul was examining his hand to see if it would help to maintain his sanity if he chewed a finger off, he heard a bustle outside the room and an obviously much more senior soldier entered.

Their new host was dressed in a khaki dress uniform, adorned with much fruit salad and brass. Their long time little green friend snapped to attention and offered a very crisp salute. His colleague gave a much simpler motion to his right eyebrow and stepped quickly toward the two men. They stood.

Mike recognized the General. He had seen him the previous night on the Prado. He wasn't wearing his white shoes today.

"Ambassador DeGrassi, it is good to see you again. Introduce me to your colleague, please."

"General Duarte, this is Mr. Mike McCaul who is Vice President of Globalair, an airline that carries over three hundred thousand chartered tourists from Canada to your tourist destinations every year."

"Mr. McCaul, it is a pleasure to meet you. Of course I know of Globalair and have met the Chairman Señor Webster several times. I am a Second in Command to President Raul Castro, of whom I am sure you know. I am in charge of security of all Ports of Call in Cuba, including airports, harbours, marinas and non-regulated egresses."

McCaul suspected this was most likely the guy who had sent six Cubans to a watery grave in a '57 Buick a while before, as well as sunk the makeshift rafts of hundreds of other desperate but hopeful émigrés. The General sat and the others followed suit.

"I understand you wish to discuss security concerns about your airline travelling to the island. President Castro and the Former First Secretary have no roles in these areas on a day-to-day basis, but will allow us to join them shortly as a courtesy.

"So, Mr. McCaul, exactly what security concerns do you have? You know, of course, this Republic values security very highly. We have no terrorists on our island, and we have very strong procedures to prevent them from coming to Cuba. Unless, of course, American security is so incompetent they allow their prisoners of conscience to escape from their concentration camp in Guantanamo. Mr. McCaul, the greatest risk to security in Cuba is from Americano capitalist fanatics, not people from other continents."

McCaul responded, "I respect the high level security procedures in Cuba, General Duarte. But, I hope you understand our company has made an extremely large contribution to the economy of Cuba. And our investment currently contributes almost a tenth of all foreign currency generated by tourism in your economy. We have commitments to financiers for our airplanes, and if we have empty seats because of consumer apprehension, then we have to find alternative destinations to fill them.

Degrassi said, "Global tourism is very likely to come to Cuba along with American tourists, General. So is Islamic terrorism.

"In order to properly inform our Transport Ministry, as well as our consuming public, we need to be assured aircraft and passengers arriving to and leaving from Cuba are absolutely at no risk."

"Mr. Ambassador, it is impossible for anyone to enter Cuba who is not invited to enter Cuba. You cannot buy your way into our country, nor is it possible to land an airplane without permission. Even small boats are boarded if they do not have proper authority."

McCaul thought, 'This guy is a tough nut, but so am I', so he challenged him, "General, I know and you know that twenty dollars allows anyone to walk through the VIP gate at the Marti Airport and it's pretty much the same in all the other ports of entry."

"Sir, if anyone is caught accepting a bribe in Cuba, they face very serious charges. What is it exactly that you wish President Castro to approve and authorize for my action?"

"General, I require a Letter of Permission to examine security procedures at all airports we use. I also require a Passage Permit that will explain the importance of my mission and allow a visitation by myself and my colleague to any non-military installation."

"That is a great deal to ask, Mr. McCaul. Ambassador, what is the position of the Government of Canada in this matter?"

DeGrassi sat up very straight and stiff. He was no longer the gregarious host; he was now the dedicated diplomat.

"General. The Government of Canada places its highest priority on the safety and security of its people and assets. As you know, our hoteliers have divested many of their properties here because of economic concerns. As well, several planes full of Canadian travellers have been treated abysmally at your airports.

"I have been directed to advise the Government of Cuba that an unacceptable evaluation of security measures in any country could influence our trade policy as it relates to access of transport carriers to and from that country.

"In effect, General, a refusal to allow an acceptable examination of security procedures by any country could result initially in a travel advisory to our citizens to that country. This might be followed by more serious measures."

Duarte stuck his nose in the air, "But of course, Ambassador, by discouraging Canadians from travelling to Cuba, you will be hurting the investments made by your own citizens."

DeGrassi blustered, "Our hotels lost money for many years because of Cuba's employment policies; we hope we will not see the same problems occur with our airlines."

McCaul spoke up, "General, our policy has been developed with other key stakeholders in our industries. They agree that it's a bigger risk to their business if our people are not confident in travelling to your country. Globalair's investments are in marketing not in hard assets; we can shift our ad dollars and our flights in a day to Costa Rica or Jamaica, or even Costa Rica if we cannot prove our confidence in the Cuban experience to our passengers."

"Well, this is a very serious matter, Ambassador DeGrassi. I'm sure that President Castro will be very disappointed with such a position."

"That's why we are here today, General. We wish to assure President Castro our request is reasonable, given the global circumstances, and we hope this concession will be seen as a means of further development of mutual economic interests."

"Well, Ambassador, we will see if the President is able to make such concessions, given the global circumstances. Sergeant Fuentes!"

The previous companion entered and snapped to attention.

"Please ask the President's secretary if he is ready to see us." Fuentes saluted trimly, did an about face, and left the room.

McCaul and DeGrassi sat there for a few moments, unspeaking. Not even winking or gawking at each other while anticipating their invitation to meet the great bearded one. DeGrassi had been here before, but not McCaul, and he was wondering what he was going to see.

Fuentes returned in about two minutes, clicked to a halt and spoke to Duarte directly. "The Former First Secretary and President are ready to meet you and your guests, General Duarte."

The General stood and turned slightly to proceed down the hall ahead of Degrassi and McCaul. They followed him out and back past the staircase and into an anteroom at the start of the other corridor. It was interesting that the building was virtually empty. It seemed only the Castros' personal staff were in the building at this time of day. Either that or there was a mass evacuation because of their visit. Maybe there was something more going on.

At a desk in the anteroom was a late middle-aged, slightly dreary looking Cuban woman. She stood and knocked on a door to her left, and passed through it into another room.

A moment later she returned, "Former First Secretary Castro and the President will see you," and held the door open to allow them to enter ahead of her.

McCaul allowed the Ambassador to precede him into the Castros' office, thinking a familiar face, especially an official one, would be advantageous. General Duarte followed them.

Entering, the office smelled musty: sort of like old potatoes, maybe a hint of cinnamon. Sitting at a large reddish coloured desk in a wheel chair was el Jefe. He was wearing a short-sleeved white shirt with blue checks. His large rectangular spectacles were steel rimmed and facially dominating enough that at first Mike didn't notice his need for a razor and a comb. His skin was waxy and he was slightly shaking, like he was either hung over or palsied. Raul stood to greet them and waited for them to be welcomed by his brother.

Castro's secretary translated.

"Mr. Former First Secretary, thank you for agreeing to see us today."

Fidel stayed seated, although he did raise his body slightly to extend his arm across his desk, "Excellency."

DeGrassi moved forward to shake Raul's hand. "Mr. President..."

Raul backed off and sat down, he said awkwardly in English, "Gentlemen, please sit and be comfortable, you are with friends."

DeGrassi spoke in English, though he had told McCaul on the way over he was fluent in Spanish, and Fidel's assistant translated. "Mr. President, this is Michael McCaul, a Senior Vice President with Globalair. This is Canada's large airline that delivers over three hundred thousand tourists to Cuba every year."

The Canadians both looked at Raul for a response but it was Fidel who responded. He slowly shifted his glance to Mike and spoke in strongly accented English, "Señors, sit down and be comfortable." He settled back in his chair. He seemed like a grumpy grandfather. He continued in rough but comprehensible English.

"I was pleased, a few years ago, to visit Canada for the funeral of my dear friend, Pierre Trudeau. You know we have been friends for almost fifty years. We shared many enjoyable times at baseball games and at fine dinners.

"Do you know we share many ideas; I especially like his views on providing education and medical care. I believe he enjoys my ideas on pluralism, about the criticality of offering equal opportunity to all people in a society. Did you ever meet my friend, Pierre, Senor McCaul?"

"Yes, Mr. President, I met Prime Minister Trudeau when I was a young boy in University. He was a very impressive man, very intelligent, and charming." After his aide translated, Fidel smiled broadly. Obviously, Fidel was not only weak physically; Trudeau had been dead for years.

He chuckled. "Yes, my friend Pierre is charming. He is a very good athlete, you know. I call him Pedro and he calls me Fedo."

The Ambassador and McCaul nodded their heads in an attempt at stimulating finality to the tribute to P.E.T. Now that they had listened for a few minutes, Mike thought that the man had lost his bag of marbles.

"But, of course, you are not here to talk about my friend. You are here to talk about some economic issue about tourism trade between Canada and our Revolutionary government, I expect."

"That's correct, Mr. Former First Secretary. Mr. McCaul is here to discuss with you the importance of confirming your airport security arrangements so we can continue to invest in and develop our tourism trade with the Republic of Cuba."

Fidel pursed his lips slightly and sat more upright in his chair.

"I can remember when the Americans invaded our Republica some years ago. They allowed Cuban people to starve when they appointed dictators for decades, and then they refused to assist them when we built a democratic republic. The Americans hate us because we are surviving without their help. We are not like your Canada; we do not depend on America for security and to feed our economy.

"But, Mr. Ambassador, as you know I am retired and only a counsellor to my brother, the President. It is best if he responds to your request."

153

Raul leaned forward, "We are of course very interested in having good relations with all of our neighbours in the Americas. I have had some very good and positive meetings with the President of the United States. Unfortunately his underlings in his Congress are not helpful.

"But General Duarte is responsible for these security issues and I can assure you there are no risks of any kind in Cuba for your travellers. We have no terrorists in Cuba, except for those financed by the locos in Miami."

McCaul could see DeGrassi fidgeting in his chair. They could not make their request until they had a means to enter the conversation without offence. Raul nodded toward Duarte and the General rose to pour Fidel a glass of water. The older man favoured his left side and his cheekbone had a noticeable bruise.

Once Castro had finished his drink, DeGrassi took advantage of the lull to open his side of the discussion.

"Mr. President and Mr. Former First Secretary, it is important to Mr. McCaul's company that we find a way to offer confidence in your security to our Canadian travellers for insurance purposes as well as safety. We have a requirement to see first hand the anti-terrorist procedures you have in place."

Fidel was looking DeGrassi in the eyes but seemed to not be paying attention. Raul's pursed his lips. When DeGrassi finished his sentence, Fidel again spoke.

"Mr. Ambassador. You and all your travelling public are guests of Cuba and are given the benefit of the personal security apparatus we have built in our democratic republic. As guests, we expect you to act in a manner complementary to our modest style of cooperative existence. But we welcome your presence here and wish it to continue."

Raul said, "As friends of the Republica, we might be prepared to offer you this access. Of course, it is only normal for our republic to expect compensation for this concession. We would like the Canadian government to more ambitiously try and persuade the fascist American

154

Congress to give their population true liberty by allowing them to visit Cuba without worry of penalties.

"But, until we come to this agreement, now that you have been informed of our need, we shall offer you authority to visit any relevant area of security you wish.

"General Duarte, you shall make yourself available at any time to the Ambassador of Canada to accompany he and Mr. McCaul for examination of Cuban security measures. Now, Gentlemen, I must ask you to leave. We have urgent affairs of state we must look after immediately, and we have already spent almost one hour with you. General Duarte, please accompany our guests back to their transportation."

Duarte stood, as did DeGrassi, so McCaul felt dragged along. Raul stood and shook their hands and Fidel rose slightly to offer his hand to the Ambassador then beckoned to McCaul. He moved forward and Castro extended his hand. Mike took it. It was thin, waxy and cold; like his hand at Madame Tussaud's in Niagara Falls.

"Please arrange to say hello to my friend, Pedro, for me. Tell him Fedo says hello. He is such a fine man."

"I will, Former First Secretary. I will." McCaul backed away and nodded before he turned to join DeGrassi. By then Fidel was already seated and McCaul's last memory of him was of the great leader examining the fingernails of the hand he had just shaken. He wondered if the old man was counting his fingers.

In a couple of moments, McCaul and DeGrassi were back down stairs, ready for departure. They had to wait with General Duarte and a soldier while the limo was called. Mike noticed it parked about two hundred yards away, at the very end of the driveway, by the guard booth at the entrance, where the driveway met the public road. He suspected Fidel's people took no chances that they might have had anything deadly in the trunk. Or maybe to make sure no one had snuck into it to seek asylum while it was parked.

As Jorge got closer, the General said his goodbyes.

"Ambassador, Mr. McCaul. Thank you for your visit today. I will make myself available to accompany you on any visits you wish over the next few days. Please call my office with a day's notice when you have this need." He extended his hand to the Ambassador, and then to McCaul, and he left.

Jorge pulled up to where they were standing, jumped out and hurriedly opened the back door for them to enter. He nodded to the soldier, now standing at ease, the duo jumped in the back seat, and the roared away.

Everyone present knew Duarte would never be available.

McCaul was kind of shocked with Fidel's condition. It was hard for him to believe that the Cuban people had depended on a dictator that detached from reality.

"Who's really running things, Ted?"

"Honestly?"

McCaul nodded.

"Honestly, no one. There is a bureaucracy to control the basic things, but all they accomplish is to make the transportation system not work, the electricity and water supply be shaky, the food not get distributed, and the people get their tiny monthly stipends.

"Fidel and Raul are figureheads, emperors of ice cream. They only play at running things, and Fidel always says that Raul is in command, but always takes full authority back whenever he feels like it."

He finished, "Well, that was that. Not what we hoped for, but it is certainly not a perfect world."

Mike agreed, "No, it certainly isn't a perfect world."

"Well. Sorry, Mike. We tried."

"That's okay, Ambassador, nothing you could have done."

McCaul had certainly accomplished Felix's mission for the CIA, but he had made his one heck of a lot tougher. Duarte would know any time he was poking around anywhere, that he was doing it without any authority. Otherwise, he would have called for his attendance. This made much of what McCaul wanted to do difficult and very, very dangerous. And as they drove past the Colon Cemetery tombstones, Mike wondered what would happen on this island when, make that if, Fidel died.

Cuba barely survived with demented leadership. Without any at all, who in heaven knew what might happen.

"Jorge, could you drop me on La Rampa?"

"For sure, Señor."

DeGrassi said, "Mike, I'll offer our assistance but at this point I don't think we can really help you out with the old fart."

"Ted, I think he needs more help than I do."

DeGrassi laughed. Jorge pulled the limo up kitty corner from the ice cream park and soon they were surrounded by a mass of twelve-year-old boys hoping to get a bauble from the car's contents.

Jorge exitted the car and shooed the pack away and spoke to them in Spanish. They obligingly lined up. They were likely well experienced at being ordered to line up.

Ted gave Mike a bag of a dozen lollipops with Canadian wrappers. These might come in handy, Mike."

"Thanks, Ted. Too bad this won't work with Fidel."

He laughed, "His candy is much pricier, Mike. Take care. Let me know if I can help."

Jorge opened his door and McCaul walked by the line of kids giving each a small gift from the Canadian government. It probably would mean more to them than Canada providing a favourable trading policy for Cuban rum.

18

DUARTE HAD WATCHED THE Canadians leave and then motioned for his own car. His luxury class black Audi pulled up and the guard marched over sharply and opened the rear door and Duarte got in. He told his driver to go to his headquarters at Villa Marista.

As they started the ten-minute trip to his home base, Duarte flipped open his cell phone and called ahead. "Eugenio, I will arrive in a few minutes and expect you to be there to meet me. I think we have solved the riddle that is Señor Mike McCaul."

Ramon Esteban Duarte Borges settled back in his seat. He removed his peaked cap and ran his right hand through his graying blond hair; a legacy of a dalliance by a forgotten ancestor with a visitor from America. He lit a cigarillo and watched the palm trees on the boulevard pass by as his chauffeur weaved in and out of traffic.

Villa Marista had been a Roman Catholic boys school before Fidel had taken it over and refashioned it as a detention and re-education centre for people of all ages, genders and religious beliefs.

For more than fifty years its renovated dormitories and grounds had served Fidel well in keeping those failing to see the wonder of la Revolucion from fomenting dissent.

It had been a convenient place for Castro to keep dozens of Bay of Pigs survivors who hadn't the cash to be ransomed, anyone who had decided to be "anti-revolutionary", and, most recently, a jail to simple protestors whose wives, women in white, now protested on their husbands' behalves across La Habana.

Duarte had been appointed in the 80's to find corruption within the highest levels of the Cuban military. While he had found none, he had understood his orders and had arrested three of the army's highest-ranking officials. One was Arnaldo Ochoa, a war hero, a life long friend of Fidel's, and one of the most popular public figures in the entire island. In Castro's Cuba, this has always been a capital crime.

He had delivered Ochoa's coup de grâce at his execution; depositing a nine mm round in the back of the war hero's head.

Duarte loved seeing the look of fear in the eyes of his new inmates and the defeated despair in the eyes of long-timers. Once he had actively participated in interrogations, but in the last few years he had mellowed and left the wet work to others.

He was committed to his cause and convinced of its righteousness. He believed that those who refused to accept the greatnesses of the current Cuba and its leaders did not deserve the benefits of acquiescence. He also thought the Castros were weak ... and getting weaker.

His driver pulled off the busy thoroughfare, turned around a few side streets and into the prison courtyard. He parked adjacent to the baroque marble and stone chateau that was the former residence of the Marist school's principal immediately north of the main prison facility.

His executive officer, Eugenio Famosa, stepped forward, opened the limousine's door and Duarte exitted.

"Come for a walk, Eugenio, we have some items to discuss."

Duarte led his aide to the baseball diamond located adjacent to the prison. There was an informal game going on between off duty guards and their friends and family members, but it was being played with all the ferocity, and some of the skill, of a World Series seventh game.

Duarte lit a fresh cigarillo. "We have a request from the ambassador from Canada to allow a representative of a Canadian travel agency, our suspicious amigo Mike McCaul, to examine our security arrangements. This is, of course, a ridiculous request as there are no security risks here. So this means that they have something up their sleeves and it likely means that this McCaul hombre is as we thought; a secret agent planted probably by Los Americanos."

"What do you wish us to do?"

"I want to know every person he meets with and every person he talks to. If they are Cuban you are allowed to arrest and interrogate them. Understood?"

"Yes, General."

"How are arrangements to eliminate the noise coming from that damned internet woman."

"It is very difficult, General. She still manages to get her stories published by others. We have interrogated her, warned her of prison and threatened arrest but she is always surrounded by others with film cameras. Since she had her book published she is quite impossible. We do have our agents responding to the lies on her website, but they are overwhelmed by the locos in Miami."

"Ay Caramba. Well, keep her under observation and if she breaks a criminal law arrest her."

"Eugenio. One more thing. Pick up that American musician. I want to know if he's involved in any of this."

Duarte dropped and stepped on his cigarillo. "You may go to your duties, Eugenio, and report to me tomorrow morning. I believe I will watch beisbol for a while."

Duarte didn't like baseball or any sports, for that matter. He thought athletes were wasting energy that could otherwise be used for the good of all Cubans.

So he spent his time half watching the baseball players thinking of ways to eliminate his adversaries. The athletics went unnoticed as he devised ways of eliminating the risk from criminales such as McCaul and the damned internet woman and reaching his destiny.

Duarte despised the youths who acted as pimps for fallen women or as common capitalista salesmen for illegal restaurants and other lawbreakers. He looked most actively for those who took advantage of the rights earned by others; those who drove illegal taxis in cars awarded to war veterans and those others who rented out the residences granted to their parents for service to the revolution. He would demote, and had demoted, National Revolutionary Policemen who had not aggressively prosecuted such enemies.

To Ramon Duarte Borges, the black market needed to be eliminated. In his opinion, the ones who depended on it, instead of working hard for the benefit of all, were anathema and should be jailed.

He had few things in his life that he did not fully control. He lived spartanly, had never married and had never accepted parentage for any children he may have left behind. He demanded compliance and obeisance from every subordinate and respect from every superior.

He was an opponent to the new freedoms being discussed by his superiors. To the Miami newspapers he was a hardliner and he was proud of being known as such. But the chanchos in Miami had no idea how hard he wanted his line to be.

He was a man to be feared by anyone whom he might perceive as being an anti-revolutionary. As head of the Intelligence Directorate he had more power than anyone save the Castros and he believed that if necessary, he could exercise more authority than they had.

He was the true protector of the revolution. But first in his desires was to replace the senile leadership at its head.

The wondrous revolution could only succeed through strength and Duarte saw himself as Cuba's backbone. He would derail any plans to upset his plans for Cuba's sovereignty by McCaul, the Castros, the internet woman and anyone else who dared threaten it.

He entered the main building, went to his private quarters, changed into military fatigues and packed his toiletries, undergarments and personal weapons into a duffle and left for a short trip to the airport by auto and a longer one by helicopter.

19

THE ONLY POINT OF REFERENCE McCaul had to find LaRue was his friend, Brother Francisco Lopez Cerrano, the padre with the weak hammerlock and a bent nose. All Mike knew was that he was in Pinar del Rio, but not where. Knowing of the glue that binds all Catholic fathers together, Mike suspected that if he could find a Catholic church somewhere in the northern mountains, then he could get a message to him, and, hopefully to LaRue.

McCaul changed into some more rugged clothing, ran downstairs and outside toward a taxi and pointed him to Parque Centrale.

Joel was waiting there, looking for some milk-buying bleeding hearts. Mike thought that it couldn't hurt to have him along, he could vouch for McCaul with Lopez's friends. For that matter, he could likely take Mike to Lopez. He wondered what the chances were that Ronaldo the pilot would be near the helicopter. Not having his cell phone number, as if the young Cuban would have such a device, he'd hope for the best and go out to the airport. McCaul looked around and didn't see any grey uniforms and walked up to the little guy.

"Hola, Señor."

"Hi, Joel. Want to go for a ride?"

"Where to, Señor?"

"The mountains in Pinar del Rio. I want to talk to your friends again."

"You want them hurt, Señor?"

"No, Joel. I want them to help me find my friend. I need to meet with your friend, Brother Francisco. Do you know where he is?"

"Si. He is in Vinales. I can find him. Okay. I go with you. Ees a long trip. How we go?"

"Have you ever flown before?"

"Flown, Señor? Like aeroplano? No, I have never flown before."

"Good, you'll be in for some fun." They walked across the lot and Joel led him to a taxi surely driven by a friend and contributor to his milk fund. They got in, McCaul told the driver "aeropuerto doméstico." They left and pulled in front of the terminal in about twenty minutes.

Ronaldo was sitting on his haunches, chatting with some friends, laughing and smoking a cigarette. He saw McCaul and Joel and stood up, brushing his hands on his pants, and walked quickly over to grab Mike's hand and shake it enthusiastically.

"Señor McCaul. Señor Gant's heli-chopper is all ready for you."

McCaul decided he needed to at least apply a little common sense for what they were doing. No sense in letting Gant in on what he was up to.

"Ronaldo, we're going to Vinales, I want to get some real fresh Cohibas, and Joel here knows the best place. Can you fly us up for the day?"

"Oh, si certainly, Señor. We are ready to go right away."

Joel and Mike settled themselves in the luxurious leather seats, Joel's eyes as big as plates. The rotors began turning and in a minute they were airborne.

"Want a drink, Joel?"

"Señor, yes, what you have?"

"A coke." Mike reached over to the mini-fridge, took one out and gave it to Joel.

The young guy was in all the way, and Mike needed him at least as much as his baby needed milk. "Joel, will you die for a free Cuba?"

"I not like it, Señor, but if it make a better life for my baybee, then yes, I die, but not be happy about it."

"Everything you see around me is a secret. Entiende?"

"Si, Entiendo, Señor."

"You know what my friend and your friends are trying to do, yes?"

Joel nodded.

"Do you want to be a soldier, Joel?"

He nodded again.

"Will you do what I tell you to do? I'll make sure your baby gets all the milk he needs."

"He is a niña, Señor."

McCaul laughed, Joel looked confused.

The flight took just over a half hour and they started to land in a valley, surrounded by several mogotes and not far from a rustic looking little town. The skies were more overcast than in Havana and the palms trees more aflutter. Ronaldo was a master, though, and landed the rotorcraft without any damage to McCaul's dignity. Mike was a little anxious about aircraft ever since he had an Air Canada jet almost land sideways on a flight to Las Vegas with him aboard.

They exited the Sikorsky and McCaul gave Ronaldo a handful of small bills to entertain himself while he waited for the afternoon. "Amigo, thanks for the safe landing. I'll be back by six o'clock." Mike had a drink date with Kate he didn't want to miss.

"No problem, Señor," Ronaldo replied and he started walking around the chopper and checking it for damage.

Joel dragged McCaul toward a seemingly pleasant hotel high on the ravine. "We will meet mi amigo Erno at Los Jasmines."

In about fifteen minutes they came to a steeply uphill hundred-meter path and ascended to the hotel. In the courtyard, Joel, still breathing normally, went up to an older, grey haired black man. He and Joel exchanged hugs and kissed each other's cheek. They laughed and smiled and talked happily in Spanish and Joel introduced McCaul as his friend. Erno shook his hand warmly, although he regarded Mike a little suspiciously.

Joel kept talking. In a minute or so, Erno reached into his pocket and pulled out a pair of keys joined by a long woven leather thong and gave them to Joel. They traded some more pleasantries and Joel was soon hauling McCaul by the arm again, out of the hotel courtyard and into a small parking area. They got into a beat-up motorcycle and sidecar, with Joel astride the bike, Mike in the sidecar. They pulled away, heading to parts unknown. McCaul felt like an idiot hunkering down in the sidecar.

They took a road from the hotel toward the village back down the hill and motored through its outskirts until Joel found a road that looped back around the other side of the valley where the chopper was parked. Mike noted that Ronaldo was busy cleaning it. They roared down a paved road for about twenty bumpy minutes before they turned into a narrow gravel path.

After climbing further along bumpy roads for about a half hour they started up a narrow road, really little more than a path. By this time McCaul's teeth were rattled and all his change had bounced from his pocket into the bottom of the sidecar. McCaul put his sunglasses in his guayabera pocket and buttoned it. His teeth kept rattling.

It wasn't long before they pulled into a little village, distinguished from their point of view only by a central plaza fountain in front of a small but well built limestone church. Joel stopped and un-straddled the motorcycle and McCaul took this as a cue to dismount himself. He left his change in the bottom of the sidecar, re-installed his sunglasses and followed Joel toward the church.

They walked up the few steps and entered. There were a half dozen parishioners, some seated and hunched over, others on their knees praying for good things to happen or repenting for bad acts or naughty thoughts.

Joel genuflected and crossed himself before he led McCaul up the aisle to a door immediately to the right of the altar. They both had to duck as they entered the sanctuary. The two walked up a narrow hall where Joel knocked on another door. They heard a summons to enter, and did.

Brother Francisco looked up and removed obviously old reading glasses.

"Mis Amigos." He stood and walked toward Joel and McCaul smiling. He hugged Joel. "Señor McCaul, I am very sorry about our small conflict. It was a terrible mistake. I spoke with our mutual friend last evening, and he told me you are to be treated well." He shook McCaul's hand while grasping his shoulder with his other hand.

"Why you come all this way to see me, Compañeros?"

McCaul said, "I want to see my friend, Cien, and I need you to take me to him."

The priest gave McCaul a shocked look and raised his index finger to his lips, "Dios. Quietly, please. Fidel has spies in every building, including this one, most of the time. My friend, this would be very dangerous, and maybe not so good for you and not so good for me."

"And why is that, Brother?"

"Señor, people will die who know where are Cien and his compañeros. Fidel, and Raul and Duarte will imprison anyone who knows where they are and remains silent. It is safer if few people know."

McCaul said, "I understand, Brother. Will you take me to see him? Joel can stay here, if it's not safe."

167

"Is okay if you call me Franco, Señor McCaul. If Joel does not know, then he cannot tell. I will take you, but it is a very difficult trip, and we should leave soon. We will walk most of the way."

"Can we fly?"

"No, Señor. We cannot fly. This is a secret place we are visiting."

"Okay, let's go. Joel, can you keep yourself busy here?"

"I will find something, Señor."

Brother Franco stood and put his spectacles into a case and then into a pocket. McCaul and Joel stood as well and followed him out a side door. There was an ancient, but immaculate red Lada there.

McCaul reached in his pocket and pulled out some bills. "Joel, here's some money to keep yourself out of trouble. Don't spend it all on milk."

"Oh, gracias, Señor Mike. I will buy some cigars I can sell to gringos."

On a Cuban scale Joel was getting rich from McCaul's generosity, but it troubled him not a bit.

The priest and Mike said their goodbyes to Joel and got in his little Lada. It was clean, started quickly and they were off.

They drove for several minutes alongside flat fields, a couple of which had small herds of huge scrawny hump-backed cows foraging around largely bare fields looking for any form of sustenance.

"We call the cows Cuban Unicorns, Señor. We know they both have horns but most of us have never seen one." He chuckled. "You know that if you kill a cow in Cuba, you go to jail for viente anos, but only siete if you murder an hombre. That shows the value of people to the Castros."

After a half hour they came to a cluster of shacks and Brother Franco pulled off the road and parked his car next to one. A guy came out of one of the shacks using his straw hat as a fan to provide some relief from the heat. They got out and Brother Franco walked slowly over to greet his friend with a brief hug and a few quiet words.

He introduced him to McCaul, but he didn't use Mike's name and he shook the guy's hand and nodded.

Franco said to Mike, "Silvio Canto is our security guard for this route. He is another son of the Malagones who has realized that Fidel has destroyed the pure beliefs that were expected from the Revolucion."

McCaul asked, "Who were the Malagones?"

"They were farmers who fought for Fidel as a militia against those enemies who still supported Batista after the revolution.

"If Canto sees an aircraft or anyone suspicious come this way he puts wet leaves on the fire for his still and we stop all movement at the camp. We have heroes like Canto surrounding our main camp."

They followed Canto into and through his tiny shack. There were a couple of large barrels laying on their side alongside a rack of empty bottles. A homemade distilling unit, looking like a Rube Goldberg contraption, was a few metres away.

The shack and Canto's booze factory were on the edge of a cane field. Canto picked up a machete and beckoned McCaul to follow which caused him some trepidation. But the Cuban just walked into the field, smashed down a few cane stalks and pressed them with a cranking device into a fluid that dribbled into a small bucket.

McCaul wondered what he was doing until they wandered back to the shack. Canto picked up an unlabeled bottle of liquor and poured healthy portions of this brew into three water glasses, then topped each off with the sugar syrup from the cane press. The distiller held his glass up to toast McCaul and Brother Franco, they all clinked and snorted. It was a remarkable boost to McCaul's spirits; strong as battery acid and sweet as a sugar cookie. Mike thought about asking for the North American distribution rights but decided that could wait until he was done his work here.

Canto the sugar presser and Franco chatted briefly, the priest pointed toward a mountain on the horizon and the two visitors offered their salutations and continued their trek.

They hiked quietly through the cane fields for a half hour and McCaul's hopes of getting back on time for some fun were growing dim. They entered a tropical jungle.

The only sign of human existence in their surroundings was the path they were walking along. Overgrowth had been macheted enough to allow them passage; in places the path was a leafy tunnel and they were surrounded by foliage. All around them were cackling and whistling birds, and occasionally an insect of monstrous proportion dropped on one of their shoulders. One time this happened, McCaul jumped and frantically brushed the bizarre being off. McCaul could stare down a drug dealer with a Mac 10, but almost fainted whenever he came across big ugly bugs.

After grunting through the leafy tunnel for about twenty minutes two men in fatigues stepped in behind McCaul and commanded him and Franco to stop. Even though McCaul feared the insects more than the AK's pointed at his back, he raised his hands. Brother Francisco did the same.

"Hola, Brother." The taller one, who looked as old as a Cuban mahogany tree, smiled and shouldered his weapon, walked the couple of steps to the padre and embraced him. They talked in Spanish, chuckled and smiled and the padre directed his friend toward McCaul.

"Leon, this is Cien's comrade from Canada, Señor McCaul."

McCaul's new friend smiled widely and gave him a vigorous handshake.

"How ya doin', pal?" Leon said with, surprisingly, an obvious and strong Brooklyn accent.

McCaul laughed, "Leon, how the hell did you ever get here?"

"It's a long story, buddy, I only got back here a few years ago - I was in Noo Yawk for forty years!"

The padre took McCaul's elbow. "Come, Señor. They will take us to la Campo Machado."

They started to follow the two friendly fearsomes about another mile over varying, and more lush terrain.

McCaul took another look at Leon. He was about seventy, thin as a rail with a grizzled beard and a broad smile, "So Leon, back to your story, how the hell did you get here."

"I was a dealer at the Capri. Meyer's guys got me on a boat in 59 and got me a job at a bar in Miami for a while.

"Then they got me in Brigade 2506 at Baio de Cohinos. I jumped out of an airplane on my twenty-fifth birthday, April 17, 1961. I got caught and spent a while in prison but Joe Bananas bought my way out and I moved to New Yawk and ran a card game for forty years. I met Machado up there. I came back to visit family three years ago with fake ID, but really to hook up with General Machado and his gang, so here I am"

"Tell me about the Bay of Pigs, Leon."

"Ah, it was an effin disaster. There were about fifteen hundred of us. We'd been trained in Guatemala and flew out of Honduras. It was supposed to be a big win in the skies but our guys got shitty old Marauders when the Commies had T-Birds.

"Kennedy let us down big time. He didn't want us to win - he'd made a promise to someone he wasn't gonna get involved. The turd. He moved the invasion to where there weren't no guerrillas so we didn't get any local help. Then he dropped us in a swamp at night.

"We killed our share, but if we had been given one fuckin' Sabre jet the world would be a different place today."

"What happened to you?"

"Ah, I got caught. Got tangled up in some concertina wire and shot in the ass. I spent a year in prison on the Isle of Youth because of my ties to the mob. It wasn't very much fun."

He held his right hand up. "They cut off my trigger finger the first night so I couldn't shoot, but I've learned to shoot with my pussy finger. They broke the soles of my feet so I couldn't run, and they still hurt, but I get around okay."

Leon introduced McCaul to his shorter and bulkier partner. He was shyer and so was his handshake. But his smile seemed genuine and his eyes were clear and honest. So Mike shook and smiled.

They came to a cliff side and were guided around a corner, stepping over a meandering stream via a series of stones and into a low cave opening.

Brother Franco provided a travelogue, "All mountains in Pinar el Rio cover caves, Señor. Some are a hundred kilometers long."

This one seemed easily that long and mostly uphill and they were all sweating badly after a half hour. They passed several sentries, most of whom were playing dominoes and all of whom were smoking cigars. After a while new scents carried by a cooling breeze reached McCaul's nose; indication of many humans not too far distant: a little cordite, a hint of cooking food, a faint aroma of unwashed armpits.

Finally, they reached a wide opening and exited the cave, looking straight into a manned machine-gun nest.

The camp as they approached it was highly defensible. The plateau area of the mountain they were on was fairly flat and was on the highest point of ground for many miles. Most of the mountaintop was covered by towering, bushy trees. Under one was a tiny and antique backhoe. Mike suspected there were various explosive goods planted around the perimeter to discourage unaccompanied visitors and unwanted relatives.

He could see a fortified area in the middle with stoneworks.

Among the men scattered around the clearing McCaul noticed Francisco's friend from the alley in Havana, still with a plaster over his nose and still wearing LaRue's jacket.

Francisco's little nose-busted friend shuffled over to join the visitors, showing off an embarrassed smile, "Señor, I am sorry we assaulted you in Habana."

"I can see that. I'm sorry you were hurt." Mike said, and shook his offered hand. "Can I see my friend, Cien?"

"Yes, Señor. Follow me." Mike did and they entered the fortifications one-at-a-time through a narrow passage; McCaul immediately behind busted-nose and before Friar Tuck.

20

DON HUGHES OFTEN WALKED with a pair of bongos that he carried on his shoulder with a belt. He never knew when he might get a chance to play and he never wanted to miss an opportunity that might arise. Today he had his bongos and a fairly expensive digital camera to play the role of a journalist. He had in his camera case some business cards that positioned him as a freelance journalist and had samples of "his work".

His work for the Americans, he assumed it was the CIA but they had never introduced themselves that way, gave him just enough cash to survive normally, better than ordinary Cubans. His mother was French-Algerian in background so his skin colour, and excellent Spanish, usually allowed him to pass as a Cubano.

He had a girlfriend and most nights he stayed with her, although she was becoming less friendly and accommodating because he staggered to her place more often than not a lot more drunk than sober. Sometimes he was so depressed that he wondered if he shouldn't end it all. He was a failure as a husband, as a musician, as a professor and wasn't even a very good spy. He had no confidence that things would ever change. He had been writing a novel for a year, thinking that maybe he could do a tell all book under a pseudonym and make enough to keep a residence back in the USA.

Don took a semi-obligatory digital snap shot of the Che metal statue installation on the Interior Ministry. Almost every tourist who ever visited the place felt a need to do so every time. It was just something that everybody did.

He kept an eye on the exit off of the Avenida Independencia into the Communist Party headquarters where the Castros kept their offices.

When a car made such an approach, and stopped at the guard booth, he pretended to take a picture of something else, while actually capturing the visiting car. Most of them were late model European sedans.

Over the next hour he took about a dozen pictures, both of cars and of general scenery. He smoked about a half pack of H. Uppman cigarettes, drank most of a bottle of Habana Club rum and thought about finding a place to grab another bottle. The National Theatre was next to the Plaza, and they had a nightclub there, but he doubted that they would be serving booze to tourists in the early afternoon.

So he wandered over to the 100 metre tall Jose Marti tower and decided to try and climb to the top. Don wasn't very far from the entrance to the tower when he heard a noise behind him and turned to see an army guard, dressed in greens, running up the slope toward him.

Don was smart enough to know the gig was up, and began running past the tower, toward a street that he knew led to the bus terminal where he might be able to get a ride.

He couldn't listen in on a telephone conversation that was taking place up in the tower.

"General Duarte, the foreign agent that was infiltrating the Jefe's headquarters is back, and has just made another attempt to surveil the area. He is fleeing. We wish your instructions, General."

"Capture and if you must, kill him. We have too many of these, and need to discourage them," came the simple response.

Hughes didn't know he was running toward the Cuban Defense Ministry building, just across a street and up a hill, but directly en route to his bus stop destination. By now, the guard in the Marti Tower had phoned through to guards at the Cuban Pentagon, and they exited the Ministry running directly toward Don with the shouted instructions of General Duarte ringing in their ears.

The American musician was sunk.

He turned left down Avenida Territorial straight toward another couple of army guards and stopped. Even in the most high security places in Europe, at this point guards would do no more than apprehend a trespasser, and politely check out identification before driving the innocent subject away from the danger zone.

Don raised his arms in surrender, and waited. The first guard on the scene fiercely stuck him in the face with the front sight of his AK-47. The second guard pulled out his side arm and shot him twice, one grazing his forehead, the other in his stomach. Hughes bled out on the ground in a few minutes.

21

RAMON DUARTE WAS DRIVEN IN A NEW Audi from the airport to visit his mistress to calm himself. He could not appear nervous or excited when he visited Fidel in his office so he had expelled his anxiety with violent sex.

He passed quickly through the security stop at the Plaza de Revolucion entrance to Castro's headquarters. His driver stopped at the entrance and a uniform officiously opened his limousine door and properly saluted.

Duarte exited informally and entered the Communist Party Headquarters without any fanfare. He went to the security desk and the guard stood and saluted.

"I was called by el Presidente's secretary to meet with him immediately upon my return. Is he in his private quarters?"

"I believe so, Generale. Should I call?"

"No."

Duarte rushed by the guard and strode confidently down the corridor and up a flight of stairs to El Jefe's private quarters. Fidel had three residences in La Habana, but often preferred to sleep in his headquarters surrounded by security staff where he felt more secure.

He passed quickly and without being stopped at two security checkpoints with only one guard even looking up. But that guard dropped his eyes the instant that he recognized Fidel's visitor.

He entered the ante-room to Fidel's private quarters. Normally Castro's secretary would be present, but with his declining responsibilities this time she wasn't present.

He knocked and entered Fidel's bed chamber.

Castro was in his pajamas, snoring in a cushy armchair, his television tuned to a Pan American baseball league game. Duarte removed a syringe filled with insulin from his pocket. He removed one of Fidel's slippers, tested the syringe and inserted the needle between two of the old man's toes which caused him to stir. Then he pushed the plunger, pocketed the syringe and left.

The guard looked up as Duarte left the private quarters. "The First Secretary is sleeping. He should not be awakened until the morning."

Duarte calmly left the headquarters and had his driver speed to the military airport. His next step to taking command of Cuba needed to get underway.

Duarte met his subordinate Juan Carlos Garcia on the helipad, buckled his seatbelt and slept during the three hour flight. Garcia woke him as his command Mil-8 helicopter started it's descent into the jungle. In the back were twelve of Duarte's meanest and most personally loyal scrappers.

He looked over the side and saw the LZ being cleared of people and suffered the bumpy and as always rough landing of the obsolete Russian aircraft. The chopper bounced when it hit ground and he waited until the rotors started slowing before he and Garcia unbuckled and stood. Occasionally one of the rotors on these relics would break off and decapitate someone.

He and the rest of his company were wearing simple camo fatigues and simple camo baseball caps without any insignia. The rotors stopped, Garcia slid open the door and they all deplaned.

They were in the middle of a military camp and were approached by two swarthy men in dirty cotton clothing and one more modernly dressed in jeans and a golf shirt. All wore sandals.

"Garcia! Have your men prepare lodgings."

"Yes, General."

"Generalisimo! Welcome. I pray that you had a comfortable trip."

"I pray very seldom, Abu, very seldom."

"Please, let us eat. We have goat."

Duarte followed the Arab to a mat in front of a large tent. A spit was being turned by a young Arab over a fire. On the mat was a platter of flat bread, a bowl of yoghurt and a bowl of fruit and vegetables.

Abu Bahoz Al-Bhadi said, "Please General, share in Allah's gifts." He indicated that Duarte should sit and Duarte did.

The young arab sliced off hunks of meat and placed it on a platter and put it on the mat between the two older men. Duarte reached into a pocket and withdraw a package of handi-wipes.

Al-Bhadi lifted a vial of arak and poured some in each of two small bowls. The men toasted.

"So what would you have us do, General, what is your plan?"

"On Saturday, next at dark, you and your soldiers will dress in army fatiques and travel by truck through the night to Matanzas. You will be met at the miitary base there and given quarters for the night. Then you will be given arms and travel to the government headquarters at Plaza de Revolucion and arrange yourself in ranks of ten."

Duarte lit a cigar, inhaled and exhaled.

"You will act ONLY on my direct orders. I expect you will never have to fire your weapons. Understood?"

"Yes."

22

ONCE THEY ENTERED THE STONE palisades it was easy for Mike to notice LaRue. While smaller than most of his men, he stood out; leaning over a makeshift table with a collection of maps, surrounded by taller men seeming to look up to him.

LaRue was bare-chested, and rapidly bronzing and when he turned and saw McCaul, he broke into a wide grin. He hadn't shaved in the last couple of days and his stubble had become a solid shag. While McCaul didn't know Larue that well, his first impression had been that Lucien was a neat freak and seeing his comrade so untidy seemed strange.

LaRue spoke to his men in Spanish and they all shook hands or slapped him on the shoulder and wandered away.

Mike walked up to him.

"McCaul, you found me." He grinned as he talked.

"LaRue, your aunts need razors."

"We don't have razors in the camp, Mike."

"Nice place you got here. How come Fidel hasn't found you?"

"Cost too much gas. Fidel hasn't got the resources any more to do random fly-overs to look for suspicious characters. Plus we've got our own spies and we're careful. Come join me."

He led McCaul over to an alcove between a couple of small boulders topped by leafy trees.

LaRue said, "So. My secret life."

"You know, McCaul, I didn't lie to you, I still have aunts that live not far from here. And I've got a cousin I'll introduce you to." There was a pot of coffee on an adjacent hibachi and he poured some in two tin cups and passed one to Mike. "Please sit."

They sat on some rough-hewn benches, facing each other at a 45-degree angle and LaRue lit a thin non-banded cigarillo and then offered McCaul one. He accepted and lit up as well. It was probably hand-made somewhere on a nearby farm and likely the finest small cigar made by man.

"I've always wanted to come here and try and help out. I've even supported an orphanage that Brother Franco looks after for many years. It was just a coincidence that my mother told me about a cousin living in New York. I tracked him down and learned the whole story."

McCaul asked, "And the whole story is?"

"The whole story is, Amigo, is that my father was not an anonymous Cuban man who escaped to Canada to become a lumberjack."

Mike said, "Do tell."

"He was one of Fidel's closest friends and his brother-in-arms. His first name was Camilo. That's my middle name. His last name was Cienfuegos. And from this comes my first name, Lucien and my nickname, Cien.

"Fidel sent him on a plane trip, but my father found out that Che had arranged for the plane to be shot down. He and Fidel didn't like people who were more popular than them. So my father made the pilot fly to Miami. He had some fake docs from the CIA and went as far as he could

181

by train and as far from civilization as possible. Ended up in New Brunswick and worked as a lumberjack until he died of cancer."

Cienfuegos name kept coming up. This time from a source that changed everything. So this was the bloodline of he who was to be McCaul's personal warrior.

Mike told him he had read and heard of Camilo.

LaRue had a last drag of his cigarillo and stubbed it out on rock.

"Maybe you know better than I do. I knew him not as a legend, but as a son to a father who had led a secret life before I was born. He never talked about his past. And he died when I was young.

"But from my cousin, I heard many stories of his life. When his plane supposedly disappeared my mother was allowed to leave for Canada and her travel costs and a small pension were provided by Fidel.

LaRue signalled to a passing soldier wearing a white golf cap with a maple leaf flag on the side. A minute later the guy returned with a bottle of rum moonshine. The two toasted and McCaul coughed. Without the sugar syrup it had the kick of a moose.

"Lucien, tell me about Che."

"Ernesto Rafael Guevara de la Serna. Where should I start? My mother said he was a passionate man. He believed very much in liberation and communalism. But his comrades called him Chancho, which is a word for a pig, because he never washed and he smelled very badly. This became Che as his nickname."

LaRue paused.

"I don't know if he was brave as much as he was foolhardy. My father told my mother Che would go into battles to be noticed, not to win. He was not a very good general. He was brutal with those who he controlled as prisoners.

"There is a funny story, Mike. After the Revolution was won, Fidel called all of his closest friends and advisors together, in the old Capitolo,

182

to form a cabinet to run the new government. He asked if anyone wanted to be Head of the Bank and no one raised his hand. So he asked if anyone was an Economist.

"And Che put up his hand and Fidel said, Che, you are now Head of the National Bank.

"After the meeting, Che asked Fidel what a banker did, and Fidel said, Che, you held up your hand when I asked if anyone was an Economist.

"And Che said, Oh, I thought you said a Communist."

LaRue began laughing as he told the story and McCaul broke out laughing when he finished. LaRue said, "One thing is, Señor, that Che was not all that great a liberator at all. He did not include those with brown skin in his liberation. Nor the artists, professors and students.

"Che is not one to laugh about, he was a terrible tragedy. When there was peace in Cuba, he wanted to wage war against the people. He personally executed hundreds of innocents in la Cabana and when he ran the prisons. He killed them because they were not Communist enough and he imprisoned artists because they did not do hard labour to serve the revolution. He imprisoned and murdered hundreds of university students and professors if they did not fully embrace his Marxist philosophies."

"How did he and Fidel get along at the end?"

"He is only known as a hero because Fidel could not have afforded to have the people have bad opinions of his Compañeros. Che did not go to Bolivia to free people from capitalist enslavement on his own. Fidel sent him there because he was causing so much trouble here.

"He even wrote Che's farewell letter to say he was carrying the revolution to the rest of Latin America to make it look that they were still friends. Che and Fidel never spoke after he left, and in Bolivia, Che was an even bigger failure. He took hundreds of local people to the grave with him, by starting an imaginary war for no reason."

"When he died it is said that he begged to be ransomed, and cried to not be killed and urinated on himself he was so afraid, even though he had a fully loaded weapon after ordering others to fight to the death.

"Nothing that is said and written by Hollywood describes Guevara as who he really was."

LaRue continued, "You know that Fidel is very difficult with those who might challenge him? You know of Arnaldo Ochoa?"

McCaul said, "No. Tell me."

"Arnaldo Ochoa was a neighbour of Fidel's growing up and served under Camilo in the Revolucion. He came late to communism at Fidel's standard, but led Fidel's adventures in both Ethiopia and Angola to promote communism.

"He was much loved by his soldiers and their stories of his leadership made him much loved by the people.

"Mike, it is a very dangerous thing in this country to be loved by many if you are not Fidel and this killed Ochoa.

"So Fidel invented corruption and drug selling charges and had him shot by a firing squad. After he was murdered Cubans painted red 8As everywhere. Fidel does not like those who might threaten his power.

"And Huber Matos he threw in jail for 20 years for what he called sedition, but really because he did not wish to be as friendly to Russia as Che and Fidel. He had Huber arrested in Camagüey and brought back to Habana for trial. He is still alive in Miami and still hates Fidel."

"Then there was William Morgan. The Yankee Comandante. He actually did plan to overthrow Fidel when he realized that the promise of the revolution was a lie. So Fidel put him in front of a firing line."

McCaul asked him if he wanted to replace Fidel.

"Not me," he replied. "My cousin Carlos. He'll replace Fidel.

"Come, we'll meet him."

184

They both had another generous sip of the firewater; this time McCaul managed to be a man and not screw up his face or gasp for air and LaRue took him toward the inner circle.

A man McCaul assumed was Machado was chatting with another soldier as LaRue and he drew near. Machado noticed the two and guided his companion away with a gentle hand on his shoulder. The soon-to-be leader of a free Cuba was clean-shaven, taller than LaRue, but with a resemblance, especially in his broad smile.

LaRue introduced Mike to Cuba's messiah and Machado offered his hand and shook Mike's firmly. He spoke in English, only a little accented, perhaps slightly with a New York accent. He urged them to sit on the stone benches to his left.

"Señor McCaul, Cien tells me you are a man to trust and you are welcome to our camp. We have important work here and I hope from our discussions you will join us in our challenge."

McCaul didn't say no, but he withheld a yes.

"Señor, if you do not wish to hear what I will tell you, then you may leave now. You will be escorted back to your transportation, and we will trust that you will tell no one of what you have seen here. If you do not stand now, then I will tell you what we wish to do."

McCaul stayed sitting. He was in on it.

"Señor McCaul, in 1998 the Pope John Paul the Second visited Cuba and visited our barrios and churches. He gave mass in our ancient cathedral in Havana."

McCaul nodded. He had learned that from Joel.

"Il Papa also found time to secretly meet with me and a small number of my friends." Machado nodded at LaRue.

"We talked about our country and how deep our roots of faith have always been, despite more than a generation of enslavement under Fidel's Marxism. He offered his spiritual support for our people and prayed with me.

185

"We also discussed the other worries that Cuba must face. How much our people love music, and how our population has been degraded because of Fidel's poverty and how our young women are raped by foreign pigs to gain money to survive."

McCaul nodded again.

"The Pope, he pledged his political support."

'God almighty,' McCaul thought, as he restored his jaw from around his knees. "What does that mean?"

"The old Pope... John-Paul made a commitment to place Cuba under his protection in the event that we are able to achieve a new freedom. After he died his successor sent us word that he would keep this promise. The new Pope confirmed this. We believe that this will allow la Cuba Nueva to receive international recognition and reconstruction funds sooner. It has taken us this long to put our revolution in place."

McCaul's lips went numb and his fingers and toes tingled. 'Whoa,' he thought.

"We will establish an interim parliament that will be led by President Francisco Lopez Serrano, who you know as a priest, I think. He is a humble man who has the love of all who know him. I will act as Prime Minister until we have free elections. The first cabinet will be padres and other men of faith from across the island."

"Señor, la Cuba Nueva will be a religious democracy, based on the principals of community, rather than politics. Our country will be simple, and our people will be happy and healthy.

"We will build an economy based on ecology and our musical culture and control the tourism attractions built by investors from other countries, but allow them to function without political interference. There will be no Lucky Luciano in Cuba Nueva, but I expect we will allow some casinos in our more depressed regions."

"We will have a free market economy, but it will result from the communal local ownership of lands and factories by workers. We will not tax our people, but will tax businesses and tourists in a normal manner."

McCaul sat stunned, unable to even mouth enthusiastic approval. For a second he thought he might applaud, but managed to stifle his urge. He thought, 'What a wonderful solution to the ills that have assaulted and plagued this beautiful land for hundreds of years; since the first time that Catholic explorers visited and ravaged the place'.

This new connection to the Roman Catholic Church would make Cuba bulletproof. No one, not communists, not capitalists, not even secular humanist do-gooders would ever be able to think about controlling Cuba militarily or economically once it became a Vatican protectorate.

McCaul wanted to know more, and his eyes spoke for him, he thought, but Machado chose that moment to stand and walk them away from his post.

"We need your help, Señor McCaul. Can I ask you to work with Colonel LaRue to devise our plan? The Cuban people will honour your name in their prayers forever, I promise you."

"Señor, this is quite an interesting thing that you describe. I don't see how I could say no."

Machado came toward McCaul and they gave each other a comradely embrace. After they gave each other a firm handshake and parted; McCaul with LaRue and Machado back to his planning.

LaRue led Mike over to one of the hibachis and pulled two half chickens onto tin plates. He gave McCaul a canteen and he filled it from a cistern and LaRue passed him his share of the victuals.

"So what do you think, McCaul?"

McCaul finally found his tongue and told him, "LaRue, I can't imagine that there is any other way that Cuba could ever get out of its mess."

LaRue chuckled and bit into his pollo.

McCaul said, "And I gotta think that his solution makes a whole lot more sense than anything Fidel has done in the last fifty years." LaRue smiled.

They sat down again and ate. Mike noticed LaRue had a fancy portable phone and he pointed at it.

"A few weeks ago, I got a new Gold Visa and bought a half dozen satellite phones with open accounts. I've got one for you." He handed it to Mike. "I snuck them here in a suitcase. I even got little manual chargers." He tossed one to Mike.

LaRue said, "Let's get down to business. We have a plan that calls for us to take down Raul, eliminate Fidel and control the headquarters of the television and radio stations, the Interior Ministry, the Intelligence Directorate and the Havana Barracks. If we take the centre, we take the whole."

"Tell me more, Cien."

"McCaul, Fidel has many important friends in many important countries. We need to find a way of eliminating him, without eliminating him, if you know what I mean."

Mike knew what he meant. There are enough Marxist friends of Fidel around the world to restrict a free Cuba from enjoying the benefits of the United Nations and all its agencies for years. Dictators own half the member nations of the UN and a free, capitalist Cuban democracy might not be welcomed. Fidel would need to depart gently.

Reports that McCaul had read suggested that Fidel and Raul were likely short of Bill Gates when it came to wealth, but were at least as financially able as a typical Cuban pro athlete who had escaped their 100% tax rate by sneaking out of a hotel at a Pan Am Games and playing for the Yankees. The brothers probably are members of the Sukarno / Marcos / Duvalier club that go to seminars on how to salt away bags of cash in secret places.

"LaRue, I think we can get temporary safe haven for Fidel and Raul's early retirements, if we need to." McCaul handed the phone back to LaRue.

"Good, McCaul, Good. But we also need better weapons. We've only got small arms and our plans need at least a dozen Stinger missiles, some RPGs and fifty Shoulder Mounted Assault Weapons. We have money to buy them, bullion buried in caves near here by American mafias after they were removed.

"In all your travels, McCaul, you must know where we can buy these?"

"LaRue... You may not need to buy them."

"Mike, what do you mean?"

McCaul told him, "I know where there's a stockpile of Stingers and weapons that can be gotten here in Cuba. But not without a little work."

"McCaul, what the hell are you saying?" LaRue said.

"Kate found some sort of terrorist camp in the Sierra Cristal in the southeast. Is it yours?"

"News to me. Who are they? What are they doing? How do we get them?"

"She's got video you can look at. There's a few dozen guys, maybe terrorists or drug dealers. They're got enough stuff to invade Miami. We'd need to go in at night when they're asleep and finish them off before they wake up."

"Very, very interesting."

Mike said, "We can also count on some support from a third party government."

"Now, who might that be?"

"You can guess. It will be covert, but it'll be there when we need it," McCaul said.

LaRue asked, "What do you need to pull it off, McCaul."

"We need about twenty men to be sure; the chopper, of course. Likely a thirty cal mg, four grenades each and AK 47s. We also need to have most of the guys find their own way home to be able to load up with goodies to bring back."

"Let's do it," LaRue said.

Now all McCaul had to do was figure out how to make it happen and pay for it. He had to assume either Webster would supply the cash, or his bank would give him a second mortgage on his house to refit and repair the chopper. Assuming it didn't get Stingered, in which case, he thought, even his friendly neighbourhood bank manager might have conniptions and be forced to say no. Mike had equity in his place, but not a million bucks worth.

McCaul said, "Part of the deal I've made is to bring Kate in on this."

LaRue said, "I have discussed her with Comandante Machado, and we will need her to tell the story. So this is okay."

McCaul said, "I'll pick them up and bring them back and get you the chopper."

LaRue drew a rough map of a secure place near the main camp where Ronaldo could land the chopper.

McCaul thought it was also time to update Webster on his progress, if it could be called that.

"Can I use the phone, again, Lucien?"

"You can keep it, my friend. The number is on the back."

McCaul punched in Webster's number and amazingly, from a mushroom shaped mountain in the Cuban jungle and heard Clarence Wong's voice say hello.

"Clarence, is Webster there?"

"Yes he is, Mike. One moment, please."

"McCaul! Where've you been?"

"Hi, Boss. At the moment, I'm about twenty metres from the next President of the Cuban Republic."

"What!"

"I'm up in the northwestern mountains of Cuba with Lucien LaRue, about fifty or sixty guerrillas and the next President of Cuba."

"Mike, this is nothing to fool around about."

"Jud, this is no duff. I am telling you the absolute truth. I suspect you might like to know more."

"I will spew my scotch out my bloody nose if I don't."

"Okay, here's the Cole's Notes version. There's a rebel group that has formed in the northwest part of Cuba. It's led by a guy who, as fate would have it, is Lucien LaRue's cousin. Kate McKee is in Havana and discovered a terrorist camp of some kind in the southeast mountains."

"Holy crap. What will Earl and The State Department have to say about this."

"The best I can figure is that the US is at least supportive if not partly behind it. But the biggest thing is that the Vatican is behind it fully. They've already pledged their economic and political support."

"You're kidding me."

"I kid you not."

"Well. That's a pickle. This is hardly what you agreed to do with Earl, is it now? We do have a contract."

"Jud, LaRue wasn't supposed to be the saviour of Cuban democracy, and the Pope is supposed to stick to his flock, and Fidel was to bring freedom to the Cuban people."

"Ah, Mike, you're right. So what are you going to do?" He could hear the ice cubes in his Bowmore as he took a sip after speaking.

"Well, Webster. I think I'm in all the way. We're going to raid the Al Qaeda camp, steal their arms and take over Cuba."

Mike heard the sound of what was likely his Bowmore, ice and glass dropping and a muffled "damn".

"Boss, you still there?"

Webster reverted to his Scottish burr. "I'm still here, lad. Ya shouldn't a told me. I dropped my whiskey. Now, whatever am I going to tell Earl?"

"I don't think you're going to tell him anything, Boss, until it's over one way or another. And there's one more thing. We're gonna turn Gant's chopper into a gunship. Someone is going to have to buy him a new one."

McCaul heard him call Clarence and ask for another whiskey.

"Mike, do you have any idea what that aircraft cost?"

"I dunno, a million?"

He said, "Mike, Manny told me that thing cost him ten million dollars before the new interiors."

Webster heard him gulp.

"Well, then, I guess we better win this thing."

"Well, lad, considering the stakes, and the investment Manny already has in Cuba, and the economic possibilities that a free and friendly Cuba has for us, I suppose we can see our way around this. But please try and make sure none of Manny's hotels are hurt and do try to save yourself, okay?"

"I promise."

"Stay in touch daily, Mike, in case we have to pull together some sort of rescue. If you get in trouble I can get a team based in Bermuda there in six hours."

"I will, Jud, if you don't hear from me by dark every day expect the worst. This phone I'm calling from has a GPS and beacon, I assume you got some tech weenies who can figure out how to track it."

"You remember Sampson? He could track somebody down from the beam on their wrist watch."

"He was in Jamaica, yes?"

"Yes. And you take care."

"I won't."

"I know." He hung up and McCaul clicked off.

Mike had two problems. One is that he had to wrest the chopper from Ronaldo's control, while charming him into flying his crew around. That wouldn't be easy and would cost more than money.

The other problem was that he didn't have the faintest idea where the bloody Al Qaeda camp was. Which meant Kate. To do that would cost an unbelievable sum.

He dialled the Telegrafo and was able to get through to Kate.

"Kate McKee," she said.

"Mike McCaul," Mike said.

"Hi, Mike, what's up?"

"Everything's up, Kate. What cha doin' in the morning', babe?"

"Stop kidding around, Mike. What have you got in mind?"

"Pack some sturdy clothes, Kate. We need you, Boyd and the video up here."

"Up where?"

"Secret place, hour or so north of Havana. I'll meet you at the domestic terminal, Ronaldo will be waiting for us at 0900 hours."

"Judas Priest. This is what you told me about, isn't it? It's awesome, I won't sleep all night."

McCaul hoped she was excited by the possibility of spending time with him. He suspected instead she was excited that McCaul was paving the way for her Pulitzer. Ah, love.

"Get your sleep, Kate. You'll need it. See you in the morning. Nine at the Domestic terminal."

"Mike, I still won't sleep, but I'll try. Night." They each hung up.

McCaul told LaRue he was heading back to Havana to get Kate and Boyd. LaRue gave him his satellite cell number and a list of others and accompanied him to find Joel.

Joel was playing with an AK-47 and getting amused grins from a couple of LaRue's scrappers. It was obvious he was in his element and wanted a new Cuba as much as anyone else did.

"Señor, I think I stay with the hombres and become a fighter, hokay?" he said.

"Joel, I suspected you'd be a hero someday when I first met you. What about your family?"

"They be hokay. Mi Madre is with them."

McCaul offered his hand which Joel shook and twisted into a brothers' grip. He released and gave McCaul a hug who hugged him back.

Busted-nose led McCaul back down the mountain; they had a route that was much faster, but impossible to navigate uphill. There was a panel truck hidden away in bushes when they reached the valley and they headed off toward Vinales.

McCaul found Ronaldo alert and ready to defend his S-92 with his life. Little did he know what McCaul had in mind, which was probably a good thing. They were back at Marti airport in an hour and Mike was in bed a little after one with an arrangement to meet Ronaldo back at the airport at nine in the morning.

23

KATE HAD TOSSED AND TURNED ALL NIGHT and finally awoke, disappointed that she had slept alone. Her life now had two paths and she wasn't entirely comfortable with this latest event involving Mike. But she also thought she might even be less comfortable with her new life in Atlanta.

She had missed Mike desperately when she had first moved to CNN. Atlanta was a strange place; the men who had pursued her were rude, aggressive and never saw beyond her visage and shape. The reputation of southern gentility there, she thought, was likely a century out of date.

She disliked the city; it was a doughnut, no one lived downtown, people hesitated to even visit there at night. And her neighbourhood, she was renting a condo in Norcross, was as barren as Mississauga. Strip malls and car dealers.

She thought she would like to find a cake, have it and eat it too. She suspected she had much in common with Scarlet O'Hara, even though she had disliked her in the movie. Fiddle-dee-dee.

But Kate was still a Canadian small town girl from St. Catharines and she still had her mother's and grandmother's values. They had both been married to their husbands until with death they had parted.

She wanted Mike to die in her arms, in forty years, and she wanted to be a news star. Could she have both?

She showered, got dressed and knocked on Boyd's door. They were running late and he was even surlier than usual when he found out he wouldn't have time for breakfast. He grunted something about not having had any bacon for a whole day.

The night before he had burned the video of their exploits in the terrorist camp onto a flash drive. Boyd grabbed his battery pack, playback unit and mini-cam while Kate put the chip into her carryall.

Kate pushed the elevator button three times, but it seemed to be stuck on one.

"Boyd, let's take the stairs."

With Kate leading, they started down the open staircase. One step down and the elevator doors started to open, three steps down, and Kate glanced at the elevator. Four steps down and two Cuban soldiers stepped out of the elevator.

Kate remembered the video chip in her bag. "Boyd, hurry!"

Kate pushed Boyd forward as the soldiers arrived at Kate's room. By then Boyd's thuds on the stairs could be heard and Raul's men turned around and noticed the fugitives.

"Alto!"

The two didn't. The Cubans were after them.

Boyd, fully as wide as the staircase and loaded down with equipment, stumbled and tripped Kate. The Cubans, unburdened by anything more than sidearms, were running headlong down the stairs and connected with the bulk of Boyd. One knocked his head into the battery pack and the other went teakettle over testicles down the stairs.

Boyd rose awkwardly, amazingly, despite the big crash neither he nor any of the equipment seemed damaged. Kate, being quick and light on her feet, had managed to avoid any serious contact and was fine.

The Cubans, though, were down for the count. One was bleeding profusely from above one ear while the other had landed on his chin and was unconscious.

Kate and Boyd climbed over the wounded Cubans and quietly opened and went through the stairwell door into the lobby. Trying to avoid attention, they slowed their escape until they got outside where they jumped into the first available cab and escaped.

For the moment.

*****

McCaul woke up about eight, hair mussed and eyes cloudy. Could have slept in all day. His message light was on. Remarkable, really; he was in the third world and had a message light.

He checked his messages, it was Hadrian Felix telling McCaul to meet him at the Hotel Nacional at eight o'clock; that he had news that would change everything. McCaul scratched his day old whiskers and chuckled. 'Change everything! Well, this'll be fun.'

McCaul cleaned up in a hurry without a shower, ran down the stairs and then ran down the hill and got to the Nacional's magnificent boulevard driveway with its towering Royal Palms, twenty minutes after waking up.

He entered the hotel and found Felix laying low amongst the yellow pillars of the Hotel Nacional lobby looking at pictures of long dead visitors from Hollywood. He was dressed in a linen suit and was wearing a matching Panama hat and smoking a monstrous cigar.

"Sorry, Felix. I didn't get your message until this morning."

Felix looked at McCaul like Mike was about to ask him for money and said seriously with a mafia / Texas accent, "Fuhget about it. Let's walk."

He gave McCaul a cigar and lit it and they exitted the back door of the lobby onto the patio overlooking the Malecon. They strolled past the guests enjoying their morning coffee outside and past the outside bar, now closed. They reached a collection of a few chairs right on the edge of a cliff that directly overlooked the crashing waves of the Caribbean Sea and sat. Two innocent turistas smoking great cigars and enjoying magnificent views.

"You live here?"

"For a little over a year. Just up the hill off La Rampa."

"What's it like?"

"A thrill a minute." Inhale. Puff.

"Girls?"

"Not yet. Been too busy."

"You're in a growth business, McCaul."

"Yup."

"Never got noticed?"

"Not really, though rumour has it they know I'm here, just not who I am or what I do. I go into the Globalair offices a few times a week and try to look like a typically lazy regional security boss."

"I hear you hooked up with Machado."

"Yup".

"We know Machado," he said, "and he seems like the kind of guy we can do business with." Puff. Exhale.

"How are you coming with your assignment?"

McCaul knew this moment would come. Big puff. Slow exhale. "I met with the two boys and their head of security."

He said, "I know. I arranged it. Duarte? He's a real card."

Mike said, "Seemed like a wild and crazy guy."

"Trust me. He's not. He's a murdering goon. Is Fidel as gone as we hear?"

Mike said, "You kidding? He's one."

"I do not tell jokes, McCaul. I am a very serious motherfucker."

Mike said, "So what's it really mean. Bottom line?"

Felix said, "Means that the Castros are done. We figure there are already people lining up. And not all of them in Cuba... other than us. Truth is, that Fidel has a lot of love from a lot of Cuba people. He's a national treasure for all the older people, and most of the upper level functionaries are loyal to him, not Raul. "

Mike said, "Us?"

"Us. We're two hundred percent behind Machado. But he doesn't know it, and we won't tell him.

"So our question is, do we Manifest Destiny Castro's ass, maybe hit the beaches, or just wait and do something sneaky. A lot will depend on the call we make... You and me, Podner."

Felix stopped and blew a couple of smoke rings.

He said, "So the Castros gotta go. If we force change we like, it's over his dead body. We give him more time, then maybe El Chapo, Putin, the Chicoms or Saudi surrogates takes over. None of which we would like."

McCaul said, "Up to you guys."

"Here's the deal," Felix said. "You guys are gonna start his thing in the next few days. If everything goes good you've got enough guys and guns to take a lot down and maybe even take over. If it goes bad it won't even get on the evening news.

"That's just the way we want it. If it works, we want it to look like it didn't and if it sewers we don't want anyone to hear a peep about it. And regardless of what happens, we're invisible.

"Okay let's do it. How can we help?"

McCaul thought for a minute and stubbed out the stogie. "Well, we need aviation fuel. We need to be able to get some in Gitmo and have a supply up in Pinar Del Rio."

Felix nodded. "Can do. We know where their camp is, even if the Castros don't. I'll get a fuel truck up there for tomorrow morning and I'll set something up at Gitmo."

McCaul said, "One more thing, if they, I mean we, manage to take over, the new junta will need diplomatic relations to be announced immediately."

"Yup. No problem."

McCaul said, "And, they'll need reconstruction money. Say ten billion to start. A safe exit for a bunch of guys and their families. If it goes bad. And you gotta buy a helicopter."

Felix took a last drag on his Cohiba. "We'd figured on more. The State Department has a full-blown strategy for the transition with sixty B set aside. The other stuff is peanuts and we'll cover it, just give be a bill." He stood up and McCaul strolled with him back toward the hotel.

"Do what you have to do, McCaul, and we'll do our end. But no one's going to know we had anything at all to do with this. It's gonna look like a popular uprising. The people rearing up against the tyrants kinda bullshit."

"Okay, good, I reckon you guys know how to be invisible. I gotta get going, Felix. I'll keep in touch."

"No you won't, McCaul. Call me once in a few hours to confirm the fuelling stations. But I'll have a tanker near their camp and one at the southern end of the old McCalla Field runway in Gitmo ASAP. I'll get them to have a flashing light or something to bring your rotor-craft in. From then until Radio Free Cuba announces the new government, we've never met. If it don't work, we don't know each other at all. We'll pay our bills and that's it. Entiende?"

"I get it."

They moseyed back to the hotel lobby. McCaul looked at his watch; he had fifteen minutes to meet Kate and Ronaldo.

He said, "Good luck, Amigo."

McCaul said, "Gracias. Hasta la vista."

They shook hands and Felix turned away and walked toward the elevators looking cool and deadly. Mike exitted the front door, got into a taxi and told the driver to go to the Aeropuerto Doméstico.

24

WHILE KATE WAS EN ROUTE TO THE MARTI AIRPORT she missed the first of a steady stream of calls from Atlanta. While Hadrian Felix was chatting with McCaul, Felix, too, could not be reached.

Kate was being called by her Editor in Chief. Felix was being called by the CIA's Director of Intelligence. Both of them were missing desperate messages to contact them immediately, if not sooner.

Hadrian returned to his room and noticed his Blackberry beeping and flashing. He had a text that ordered him to immediately go to the United States Embassy along the Malecon.

Felix calmly took the elevator back downstairs and jumped into an almost new Toyota Camri taxi. When he arrived he was immediately ushered into a war room with a live video feed with CIA HQ in Langley. The Ambassador, Simeon Maris, was already in the room along with several staffers.

Maris nodded to Felix and said to Director Intelligence Perry Dalukis while staring into the camera, "Director, Hadrian Felix is here."

Dalukis said, "How are ya, Harry, looks like you're in a helluva mess down there."

"What ya mean?"

"A Miami Herald journalist was killed yesterday by Cuban police in Revolution Plaza."

Felix said, "Perry, you gotta be fucking kidding."

The local Chief replied, "I kid you not. This is a real problem, the Floridians are gonna go ape shit."

Felix asked, "Is he, was he, Cuban American?"

Simeon said, "We don't know. Our friends within Duarte's camp tell us that his name is 'Donald Gibson Hughes' and that his credentials put him with the Miami Herald, but the paper has no record of a Hughes working for them."

Felix said, "Fuck."

Simeon said, "Fuck what?"

"He's mine, at least he was mine. I've been using him as a stringer for the last year or so. I just got him checking to see if any unfriendlies from outside Cuba are visiting Fidel or Raul."

"Any way to track him back to you?"

"Not if he's dead. Never had anything in writing and paid him in cash. I don't know if he kept any records."

"You know where he lived?"

"He's got an apartment, I don't know where but he's got a girlfriend I can likely find."

Simeon said, "Perry, where is the POTUS and Cabinet on this?"

"Well, it's an election year. The Joint Chiefs want to park the Kennedy in Havana Harbour, State wants the Marines to hit the Miramar beaches and POTUS wants it to just go away and for us to keep it under wraps. I'm suggesting they put a hold on things until we get a better handle on things. And for now they're listening to me. But I better get them intell real fast."

Maris looked across the table at Felix. "Well, Buddy, what you gonna do?"

Felix said, "I'm kinda stuck. He's a stringer. I gotta track him back to see if he left anything nasty behind. Simmy, you got any resources for me?"

"I got our guy with Duarte. Can go back to him, but'll cost us a lot, probably a green card, and we'll lose us a key asset."

The Chief Spook spoke up from Langley. "Here's what we're gonna do. As of this moment none of us has ever heard of the guy. As far as we know the Cubans have murdered an innocent reporter and we're pissed off about it.

"We been effed up before by rabbits like this guy keeping notes and even writing effin books. So let's clean up any mess that might be out there before it happens.

"Simmy, you try and get the guy's address however you can. Now. Harry, you try and chase his place down, too, toss it and make sure it's clean.

"We gotta beat the Cubans to this. It costs what it costs. But do it now, people."

Dalukis flipped a switch and the screen went dead.

Simeon Maris said, "This is heavy shit, Harry. I can get my guy in Cuban Intell to meet you at the Coppelia if we absolutely need him. But if he knows where this guy lived it'll be too late, anyway. See what you can dig up on your own between now and end of day."

After his call Felix rose, shut off his phone and left the Embassy before he started to think very hard. He lit up a cigar and started walking east along the Malecon toward the only place where he might find some tracks of the dead guy: the cafeteria across the street from the high-rise hospital. Hughes had told him a few times about how he ate most of his meals there and was having some sort of a relationship with a woman that worked there. So that's where he went.

25

KATE AND BOYD WERE WAITING OUTSIDE the terminal when McCaul arrived just a few minutes after nine. He walked up to them and could see that Kate was agitated and even Boyd seemed to be quivering a little.

"McCaul, hurry up," Kate said. "We got to go!"

"Whoa, Kate. What's the hurry?"

"No time to talk, the Cuban police are after us."

"What do you mean us?"

"Well, me! They were at our hotel room, and Boyd knocked 'em both out. C'mon, let's go!"

"Boyd knocked them both out?"

"Yes, COME ON!"

"Okay, okay." McCaul led his CNN crew through the front door of the terminal and found Ronaldo sleeping awkwardly on a narrow wooden bench. Amazingly, he was snoring. Probably dreaming of someday being invited to live with Dad.

McCaul shook the little pilot gently and he started and fell off the bench, swearing in Spanish.

"Oh, Señor McCaul. I am sorry, I fall asleep on the hob."

McCaul assured him everything was okay and asked him if he was ready to fly. "The Seek is gassed and ready, Señor."

They boarded and Ronaldo booted up the rotors and off they went.

"So what's the panic?" Mike asked Kate.

"Well, we were in a hurry. You didn't give us very much time to get up here, and Boyd was bugging me about needing to eat. We'd copied the video last night and deleted the videos from the cameras and grabbed our stuff." She stood up and got a bottle of water from Boyd's camera bag.

"The elevator seemed to be stuck on one, so we decided to go down the stairs. But just as we started downstairs the elevator opened and two Cuban cops got out; you know, the guys with the berets and grey uniforms." She took a drink. "They walked toward my room and I told Boyd to hurry, and they noticed us and told us to stop."

"You didn't stop."

"Nope, we didn't stop and they came after us. Boyd kind of slipped and tripped me against the wall, and the cops were running fast and they fell downstairs and smashed their heads on the stairs. There was blood everywhere. Then we walked outside, got a cab and came up here to meet you."

Everything had changed. If Duarte and his gang knew something about Kate, then maybe they knew something about her visit to Guantanamo, which meant they might know something about the video, and possibly that she was flying around Cuba in Gant's chopper.

Hopefully, her two visitors were just pilot ants and would need to go through a half dozen channels to get word to someone who could put all the pieces together and cherchez la femme, her friends and her helicopter.

McCaul figured they needed to hope the Cuban Marxist bureaucracy didn't work any faster than the Canadian version. If so, then they likely had a day or two, maybe three or four. But they couldn't bet on it - McCaul knew they were in a police state, which probably encouraged efficiency in such matters.

They had, at most, two days to have everything happen.

McCaul went up front to join Ronaldo. When he got there the little guy was joyfully singing a little Cuban ditty.

"Señor McCaul. It is such a beautiful day, is it not?" He had no idea, whatsoever.

McCaul agreed. "Yup. Ronaldo. There's something I need to tell you."

"Oh si, Señor McCaul. What is that?"

"Well, Ronaldo, we are commandeering you and the helicopter."

He let go of the stick and for a second there McCaul thought he might crash them.

"Qué?"

"Well, we're hiring you for a thousand US dollars a day. We need your helicopter to set Cuba free from Fidel and your helicopter needs you to operate it."

"Santa Maria, Señor. That is very good. Una mil dólares por dia! Santa Maria." He was shaking with joy. McCaul didn't think he heard anything after the money part.

"We need to take your helicopter, Ronaldo."

"Oh, Señor, eez not my Seekorsky. Ees Señor Emmanuel's Seekorsky."

"Not any more, Ronaldo. We just bought it and you're working for us now. We need it to free Cuba from Fidel."

"Oh, Señor, you can't free Cuba from Fidel. Fidel love Cuba, Señor. He no want to free it."

"Well, Ronaldo, we're going to use the Sikorsky to help Fidel change his mind. We might need to do some repairs."

"Some repairs, Señor?"

"Yeah, we, ah, have to renovate the interior, maybe take out a few seats, attach a few weapons, that sort of thing."

"Oh Señor, you can't do that to my baybee."

"How about this, Ronaldo." He looked at McCaul with a form of terror stretched across his face. "How about we pay you a thousand dollars a day and then sell your baybee to you for a dollar?"

"You serial? Honest? Now with that, Señor McCaul, you have ideal."

"Here's where we have to land." McCaul gave LaRue's map to Ronaldo.

He said, "I know this field, it is not far from where Che had emergency headquarters during war won against USA."

McCaul nodded, "bueno, mi amigo" and went back; they were only about twenty minutes away.

Kate had finished her water. "So, McCaul, what the hell is going on? We just screwed ourselves back there with the secret police. I brought the video and equipment. This better be good."

"Okay. I gotta tell you, because it's risky and it's not up to me for you two to put yourself in harms way."

"I'm no coward."

"I know. Okay. Here's what's happening. I've signed on with a movement to bring down the Castros."

"No way. You are effin kidding me. You're fulla shite."

McCaul chuckled, 'so much for his sweet, little innocent girlfriend'.

"I may be fulla shite, Kate, but not about this."

"So tell me already."

"Turns out that our buddy LaRue's down here to help push Fidel and Raul out and he's up in the mountains with a couple of hundred guys to do it with."

"His cousin is a guy named Machado who's the top guy. I'm helping them out and we're gonna go raid that camp you found down south and steal all their guns."

"Mike. This is huge!"

"I told ya so."

"No, I mean this is huge. Revolutions don't much happen any more, at least not in the Americas. I mean Cuba is a basket case but it's still relatively civilized and everyone kind of thinks that Fidel and Raul are bad but mostly harmless."

Mike said, "Tell that to the journalists he's got in prison."

"I want to be right in the middle of this and don't you even think about trying to stop me."

"Kate, you don't have to be in the middle to report your story. Fidel still has about a dozen operational fighter aircraft, a few attack helicopters and some surface to air missiles. I don't know how many planes he can get in the air and how long it would take him, but we have to do this all in the next forty-eight hours. It's really dangerous."

"Mike, I don't care about the danger."

Boyd woke up. "What about me!!"

"Boyd, don't be a pansy!"

"Kate, if you don't survive, you won't win any Pulitzer, at least you won't be around to pick it up. They know you're up to something tricky, and they're almost sure to know you have the helicopter, so unless we're very lucky, you and the chopper are already targets.".

"Okay. I'll stay away from the shooting, but you better take Boyd and he better get some pictures."

"Huh?" from Boyd.

"Can it, Boyd. You just stick with McCaul and get pictures."

Ronaldo yelled back for them to, "Bucker up, Por Favor."

So they buckered up.

* Near Vinales, Pinar Del Rio *

Ronaldo conducted some fairly intricate maneuvers between the mountains and brought the chopper down into a flat cultivated area surrounded by sheer cliffs. McCaul looked down and saw the other-worldly terrain of northwestern Cuba; the flower-pot mushroom mountains and greenery in every direction towering over cultivated fields. He saw a welcoming party preparing to meet them. Mike hoped it was friendly.

They had flown into a tobacco field near Machado's mountain encampment that included an old cigar shed with worker barracks. It wasn't planting or picking season and was vacant. When they landed, the welcoming party was at the door before the rotors stopped.

They got out and LaRue met him on the ground.

"McCaul, welcome back. We have our helicopter renovation team ready." There were about two dozen fatigued men waiting to demolish all of Gant's comforts and they got to work.

Hopefully, Raul and Fidel wouldn't have any eyes in the skies for the next couple of hours.

LaRue led them over to a shaded area and they were joined by one of his men.

They were chatting when McCaul's satellite phone rang. It was Webster. "Michael. It's me."

"What's up, Boss?"

"Something's come up. I just heard that Fidel Castro's died. You need to get to Havana and meet with the Company guy down there, ASAP."

McCaul said, " Whoa, whoa, whoa, whoa... What did you just say?"

"I just got a call from the US State Sec. The beard is dead. No duff. He's ordered me to order you to get down there and hook up with his guy in Havana."

"Jesus. Okay. We're at crunch time. I'll be three, four hours. Where will I meet him?"

Webster said, "No idea. They can't reach him. His cell phone isn't picking up. Be creative."

McCaul said, "Okay. What will I tell him?"

"Tell him to just call home."

"Okay."

26

THE CAFETERIA WAS A MILE OR SO FROM THE US EMBASSY and Felix decided to walk and shut off his phone so it wouldn't buzz and draw attention to him. It was a rare event for him to screw up; not that this was that, at least not yet, anyway. But he was worried, both about his rep in the Company and in burying anything that needed burying from Don Hughes' time on earth.

In Hadrian's world you didn't want to know your illegals too well, nor the reverse. If real names were never exchanged that was great and if all contacts were through a third party even better.

He had never asked where Hughes lived and had no interest in knowing. So he had a very flimsy formal relationship with his lost rabbit which was both good and bad. It was bad because he couldn't find Hughes when he needed him. It was good because he couldn't tell anyone if he was being forced to.

Felix had leverage on Hughes and had counted on that to have him keep his nose pointed in the right direction. He'd threatened the wanna-be drummer with a life-time ban from ever returning to the USA, except as a Cuban spy with prison time to follow if he didn't cooperate. He played hardball.

He had also promised Hughes the hope of a safe return and a decent pension if he did a good job.

Poor sap would never see Buffalo again, though. Too bad. Felix always acted heartlessly; it was part of the job. But he never enjoyed acting that way. Can't keep track of each fallen robin.

The only lead he had to pursue was the girl at the cafeteria so he started walking in that direction, zig-zagging along the relatively clean side streets of Vedado.

After about 10 minutes he approached the hospital, maneuvered to the cafeteria and entered.

There was a middle aged woman dressed in a shabby and plain house-dress sitting at a bar which was manned by a mulatto guy, probably sixty.

They looked at Felix like he was bringing in a large basket of excrement, but didn't rise up or move to intercept him. So he walked to the back of the place to meet them and took a seat on a stool at the bar.

If he'd waited for a greeting, he might have waited a long time; if there were to be a conversation, he would have to be the one to start it. So he did and he tried to sound as friendly and sincere as he could.

"Buenos dias, Señor y Señora. Como esta?"

The guy nodded and shrugged while she ignored Felix and lit up an H. Uppmann cigarette. Don Hughes' brand, Felix noticed; a few cents more expensive than Popular, so likely not something that many ordinary Cubans would buy with their own money.

Felix relied on the most tried and truest form of intelligence gathering. He made a show of taking a ten CUC note from his wallet, folding it, and placing it under the ashtray on the counter which was next to the package of cigarettes.

"I'm looking for the man who gave you those cigarettes." He pointed to the package.

A shrug from the guy and no reaction from the woman.

He waited a few seconds, then he reached forward and took back the ten spot and started to leave.

"Entiende, Señor."

Felix sat back down.

The hombre said, "He did not come here today."

"What about his girl?" Felix took the Uppman package, removed a cigarette and lit it.

The guy said, "His girl is our niña, Marisol. She is in our apartment. He pointed to the ceiling."

"Will you take me to her?"

"I will ask if she wishes to see you." The man stood and walked toward a doorway off to the side and upstairs. In a minute or two he came back down and beckoned to Felix to join him. Felix crossed to the staircase and went up.

The apartment was clean and neat and decorated in Habana Moderne, which is circa 1978 almost everywhere else. There was a 14" TV with rabbit ears, a boom box that would be offered for sale for five dollars in a Goodwill store and well cared for furniture that had likely had served its purpose for close to the age of at least one of the apartment's residents. The apartment was festooned with electrical wires and cables.

Sitting on the couch was an attractive Cubana, probably in her mid-thirties, with nicely cut dyed blonde hair; a tight pair of jeans and tee shirt showcasing her attributes.

She stood and offered her hand, "Hola, Señor, you are amigo of Donald? I am Marisol."

215

Felix shook her hand and lied to her, "Do you know where I can find him?"

She spoke English quite well. "He often stays here with me, but last night he never came so perhaps he returned to his own place. He rents a bed in La Habana Vieja from an old soldier named Pedro. It is on a corner at Plaza de Armas just across from the books."

"Does he leave any of his personal items here?"

"Some, but he has very little, just his drum sets and some clothing. He keeps his book notes and letters and private things at his other place, I think, Señor, because they are not here."

Felix said, "Say again, Marisol?"

"He has very little."

"No, after that."

"He keeps notebooks, I think that he records notes from musicians he meets and music he hears. Perhaps more things about what he sees. I don't know. Why don't you ask him?"

That changed things. Hughes dead was one thing and could cause no harm. Hughes dead, leaving who knows what by way of notes behind, was another.

"Marisol. I have to tell you something. Donald was killed late yesterday."

The girl looked shocked but not surprised. Felix suspected that for her, Don, as relatively poor as he was and even being a few decades older, was a meal ticket. His pension was a fortune for a Cuban girl, but she probably wasn't surprised because an Americano lover windfall was a long shot. One that was a decent man was even more rare. And if he hadn't been killed, chances were that he would have left her anyway.

They sat silently for a minute or two.

Felix said, "Where would his notes be?"

"At Pedro's place? I don't know where else."

Felix rose to leave. He knew where it was. He'd even bought Pedro a cervesa one time. He thanked her the best way he could, he opened his wallet, gave her five ten CUC notes, and descended the staircase to begin making his way to the oldest part of Havana.

* White House *

The U.S. Director of Intelligence, Perry Dalukis, took a helicopter to the West Wing and walked down the wide corridor toward the Oval Office. The POTUS would not be happy. Dalukis waited in the ante room and was soon joined by the Secretary of State, Bill Hamilton, and Admiral Lucas McCain, Chairman of the Joint Chiefs of Staff.

McCain asked, "What you got, Perry."

"Nothing yet from Felix. He'll clean up whatever he can. Last word on his rabbit is not good. The guy kept notes, but we don't know what's in them."

Hamilton said, "Fuck. Fuck. Fuck... Scary. I hate going in that room without having all the answers."

Dalukis said, "It's what we got and is what it is."

The door to the office opened and the President's secretary, Mrs. Dickens, ushered them in. The Boss was seated at the Resolute desk. He looked tired.

"Have a seat."

Mrs. Dickens had arranged seats in front of the desk and they sat.

The President held up and waved the briefing notes and stood.

As they were making their way take their seats, Dalukis' phone buzzed again and he looked at it and answered and listened and said: "Jesus Christ, Fidel Castro just died."

The President said, "What!!! Holy shit! Call your guy back. You sure?"

Dalukis said, "I can't. That was our guy with Duarte. He had a quiet minute to call and he can only call me. And I don't know if I can trust him anyway... Cuban officials lie like bad wigs."

The President said, "Holyyy shit! Then what we gonna do, men. Tell me NOW!" He clicked his intercom and said to his office assistant. "Get Ambassador Maris on the video pipe, right now!"

Hamilton said, "Mr. President, Perry's got a guy on the scene, but we can't get a hold of him. There's not much that the Dip people can do down there. Give us a few minutes."

Dalukis said, "The Cubans won't release the news until they're 100% ready to. I can check with the Canucks. They gave us one of their guys to work for us down there. He might be able to get us something..."

The President said, "Then, just effin do it... Doesn't anybody in this fucking room have a clue about anything! God Damn it!"

The security team stood, nodded respectfully, and left.

27

WHEN MCCAUL JOINED LARUE TO BEGIN the planning for the raid of the camp in the southeast, Mike was introduced to the rest of the team leaders.

LaRue said, "McCaul, this is Sanchez, his mother's family is from Corea and he knows Sierra Cristal Park like his own palm. We don't only need to get there, we have to find a way of getting our men and the material out and Sanchez can tell us how."

Sanchez shook all the male hands and he also clasped with Kate. Boyd was in his own world, probably worrying about never being able to enjoy another strip of bacon fat.

LaRue had a couple of large hand drawn maps of the southern mountains with different landmarks, villages, roads and valleys penciled in. "Sanchez did up these maps."

He spread out one of them and Kate drew close.

Sanchez pointed out the town of Guantanamo and the highest points of elevation in the mountain range to the north.

Kate said, "Last night we copied the vid to a memory chip. Boyd, set up the playback system, will you?" Boyd unpacked the battery and a little twelve inch Sony video player. He inserted the chip and in a second he had the system operating.

Boyd had taken some footage of them approaching their landing spot and he scanned forward to the spot.

"He is passing by Corea. It is a tiny village near the highest point of land in the area," Sanchez said, and he drew a line on his map below the obviously highest point of elevation. "It is the home of mi Madre."

"There. That's where we flew over the camp," Kate said. The camera showed smoke rising from a mountainous jungle and when Boyd still-framed, tiny tents could be seen. "The camp's on a plateau right... there." She pointed to a spot on the map and Sanchez drew an X there. Larger this time.

"We parked the helicopter about a kilometer from there, on another plateau a little less elevated." Boyd scanned to their landing point.

"Ronaldo. You okay to get us there?"

"Si, for sure, ees like ice cream. I been there, McCaul, and I got GPS anywhere now."

"Do you have the coordinates?"

"Si." Ronaldo reached in his pocket and pulled out a palm sized GPS. He thumbed around the unit until he found the camp and passed it to Sanchez who jotted down the coordinates.

LaRue spoke, "Sanchez, can we get our men out of there carrying material?"

Sanchez nodded. "It will not be easy. Is about a ten kilometre downhill march and the armaments are heavy. We will need to have our men meet a truck near the town of Margot and the men will need to make several trips, I think."

LaRue said, "Do you have trusted friends who can help them?"

"Amigo, I have dozens of trusted friends who will help us."

"At about 0400 hours?"

"No problem. They will be there. I will see if we can get a truck closer to the mountain. We will need those special phones, I think."

LaRue said, "You have them. I trust you, Sanchez. Our entire assault depends on this."

McCaul said, "Ronaldo, why don't you let Sanchez take you to the main camp for something to eat and a nap and think about how you can make this happen."

They both rose and walked away. Good. Now they wouldn't have to shoot their only pilot as the guys finished ripping apart his chopper.

Kate and McCaul walked back to the Sikorsky where LaRue's men were at work. All of the Italian leather furnishings were upended on the ground, as was the big screen plasma TV, the titanium end tables, the stylish lamps, the Bose Wave Radio / CD system, the entertainment centre and home theatre system, three cases of Dom Perignon and six cases of red wine. Out came the refrigerator, the fancy chemical toilet, the padded toilet seat.

McCaul heard a ripping sound and out the door came the plush carpets. Then a crash and the shelving fixtures came flying out.

There was a moment of silence so Mike dared look inside. The velour wallpaper was still attached to the wall, but almost nothing else. The interior was gutted. Even the wall between the passenger area and the cockpit had been removed.

A couple of guys showed up with a welding machine and started fitting a high strength metal frame around the door, while another two guys started cutting the door off. Images of 'Apocalypse Now' went through McCaul's mind. They were building a highly mobile killing machine.

Another team arrived with a huge bucket of paint and started smearing it over the orange exterior. Within a half hour, they had the ship olive drab and camouflaged. While it wasn't one of Raul's MIG choppers, it would pass from a distance. While McCaul had been sleeping, these guys had been emptying Havana's Home Depots or Raul's storage depots of paint.

Things seemed well in hand so McCaul looked up LaRue to nail down the details. He figured they had a little more than thirty-six hours to overthrow a government.

LaRue was around the corner behind and sitting under some well foliaged trees. He was poring over a pad of white paper.

Sounds of the re-construction of the chopper were almost silenced. It sounded to McCaul like the refit team was rustling around, probably hiding the remains.

He looked up and nodded.

"Lucien... Can we talk away from here? Privately?"

"Sure."

LaRue passed him a panatela and they lit up and walked away from the crowd. "What's up?"

"I just got word from my boss. Fidel just croaked."

"You sure? Fidel's croaked quite often in the last ten years or so."

"This comes from inside the Castro's H.Q. He had a stroke or something and died a couple of hours ago. That's all the intell we have."

"Hmmp." Larue took off his hat and rubbed his forehead. "No word on whether he had any help croaking or not?"

"You know what I know. You know Duarte's men went to arrest Kate this morning, and she and Boyd narrowly escaped. That might or might not be connected. They'll sure as hell be on high alert. And I suspect that they are gonna keep the news sealed."

"They are always on alert, Mike, just not always able to do anything about it. We have to hope for that. It's our fate and not everything is in our control. As far as Fidel being dead? He's been dead for a decade, only barely breathing and thinking. The good news is that the politburo will probably lock everything down and not let any panic erupt. That is if Fidel didn't get any help in dying. Otherwise, it will be total lock down."

LaRue sat and Mike squatted down near him for a few seconds but his knees started growling so he sat and crossed his legs at the ankles.

LaRue said, "I think we stay on plan. We need to wait until early morning the day after tomorrow to launch our offensive. We also have to worry about refuelling," he said.

"I've got fuel arranged in Guantanamo and for a fuelling truck to show up here tomorrow morning," McCaul said.

He said. "Perfect. Thank you."

McCaul looked across the horizon and took a long draw on his cigar. A quick trip to Guantanamo, a fill up, defeat the mysterious mountain beasts in an hour or so, load the weapons, another fill up at Gitmo, drop the goodies off and get back early morning, day after tomorrow. If everything went perfectly.

McCaul thought that if they could do this they'd have lots of time to deploy units as needed with the chopper over the course of tomorrow.

McCaul was sure that their only hope was that the Castro Regime had let their defense capability almost totally fade away during the last two decades of grinding poverty. Hopefully, just maybe, one or more of the brutally vicious recent hurricanes had caused damage to their response capability. Or there was someone working inside to cause the turmoil and regime change.

And hopefully, the Cubans had their best equipment and pilots on rental in some other global hotspot in return for hard currency.

McCaul had heard through the airline grapevine their air traffic control capabilities were hooked together with bailing twine and Globalair pilots never fully depended on them. The Cubans likely could never know if a strange aircraft was going to suspicious places.

If this wasn't so, and their defensive utility was in decent shape, then the rebels likely wouldn't have a chance.

There were about twenty men lounging around under covered areas who would travel to the encampment at Sierra Cristal Park to look after the terrorists, whoever they were. The guys were showing varying signs of stress. Some were telling old and tired jokes, some yukking it up, others were just silent and grim. Like every assault team McCaul had ever been a part of. All had their weapons, mostly AKs, within arms reach.

McCaul and LaRue stood and wandered back toward the other group leaders. Mike noticed Kate hanging around on the fringes and Machado walking back toward her.

They both had selfish reasons for a get together. She, to add more bricks to her Pulitzer application. He, to begin the PR campaign that would gain early positive response to the new government. She didn't notice Mike until he sat down next to her and she turned and gave him a million watt smile. Boyd was wandering around shooting footage.

"Hi."

"Hi back."

There was a plate of mangos on the ground between her and Machado and the future First Minister was slicing off bite-sized pieces and sharing them stuck on the end of his knife. Mike accepted a slice and it was delicious.

"Mike, this ... is ... the ... story of a generation. This is jaw dropping." She smiled again. She glanced at the New-Boss-In-Waiting and he humbly nodded his appreciation to her.

"Nobody. Not Cronkite. Not Wallace. Not even Arthur Kent or Peter Arnett ever got in the middle of a bloody revolution before it started."

Mike said, "Well, I hope it's not that bloody."

"Just a figure of speech. Have you HEARD what they're going to do? The Pope's support? A whole country based on religion and music. Unbelievable. I'm not gonna release the story until it's all done, but I can't wait."

She wiggled her bum and nuzzled her shoulder against Mike and he could feel myself blush.

Mike umhummed, breathlessly, "Yep, I know."

"So what do you think of our plan, Señor McCaul?" said Machado in English without an accent.

McCaul managed to recede his blush and regain his breath and spoke. "I think we've got a team good enough to cause a lot of mayhem, Comandante Machado. But we've got a lot to do and only a little time."

He nodded seriously. "What are we missing?"

"A break. There's something you need to know."

"I'm not worried too much about Raul. Duarte is our adversary."

"I agree. But for different reasons than you think. Kate, can you give us a minute or two alone? Military stuff."

"Don't you keep secrets, McCaul."

"Kate, I just can't have you know some things that they would torture you to find out."

"Okay."

McCaul said, "Comandante, Lucien, let's talk."

The three men gathered several yards away from the others.

McCaul said, "Senor Machado, I have just received word that Fidel has died in the last few hours. Word has come from inside of the Castro's HQ."

"Does this change anything?"

LaRue said, "Doesn't matter. If anything it's good for us. They'll be looking inside for threats, not outside."

Machado said, "But... who's inside? What if Duarte had something to do with this? He will be the winner if the Castros both disappear. And he will control all the armed forces and security. I say, we stay on plan. You?"

LaRue and McCaul both nodded and the three walked away in different directions.

After getting about ten yards away a burly guy in fatigues and a Yankees baseball cap came strolling toward McCaul. It was Manuel. "Amigo," he said with a broad smile. Manuel gave McCaul a bear hug.

The two warriors released from the hug, but Manuel still held both of McCaul's shoulders. Mike said, "I thought you were in the management end of the business."

"Señor, I'm never one to miss a good party. And if this works, I'll be a really big banker". Mike wondered if he knew about the Pope agreement. Of course, the Pope hadn't said no casinos and Catholics do love their bingos.

"Comandante. Amigos. Come. We need to do a final briefing for tonight." LaRue said and waved to a few other guys sitting or standing nearby.

Manuel and Mike sat and soon a few other guys, including Machado, joined them. Kate pulled out her note pad and Boyd his camera.

Machado spoke. "Amigos, tonight we fire our first shots. We kill our first adversaries. We might lose our first heroes." He paused. "We will be assaulting a military camp occupied by unknown adversaries.

"We've looked closely at the video and come up with details for the party tonight. Kate, your guy is a very good cameraman".

LaRue had in a clipboard a collection of satellite photos and maps. A jerry-rigged easel with a chalkboard on it was behind him. A line map of the op zone was drawn in green erasable marker. The encampment was roughly to scale.

"Believe it or not, a friend got us an internet connection on a satellite phone and he printed out some really great maps from Google. He nodded to Cameron."

"This one is a high view of the entire region." He showed it to the group and gave several to McCaul to pass around. He showed another and passed them in the other direction. "This is a close up; amazing detail, though it was taken before the camp was set up.

"We don't know who our adversaries are, how well they are trained, or why they are even here. We don't know if they are supported by the Raulistas or if they wish to replace him like we do. But we need their armaments more than we need them causing trouble. So we will take them down.

"We'll need to come in from southeast of the target and our pilot, Ronaldo, will get us there.

"Each of you will be given four grenades and each of you will have your AK47s along with four extra clips and a KBar. Sanchez," he pointed to the big guy, "is our strongest hombre and he will carry and deploy a light 30 caliber machine gun. I will have a sub-machine gun."

He pointed at the chalkboard and drew three lines leading from the landing zone. "We will be dropped here and have about a kilometre to march over mixed terrain to the target. Of course, we will need to be quiet. I will be at the point and we will approach in three columns approximately ten metres apart."

He drew a circle. "This spot is highlighted on the maps. It is approximately one hundred metres from the target and we will start our assault from there. I'll recce the area and remove sentries. Señor McCaul and Manuel will lead two columns to form two rifle lines that will provide a crossfire from here... and here.

"McCaul and Manuel. You will each flick your flashlights once when your team is in place. Each of you will illuminate your flashlights for one second to ensure that your fields of fire are clear. Ten seconds after the last light-click each of your team members will throw two grenades into the tents and when they explode you will decimate the area with withering fire.

"When we have completed our mission we will immediately begin carrying the munitions to the rotor-craft as rapidly as we can. Once it has reached its capacity, Ernesto, Manuel, McCaul and I will return here to our HQ on the helicopter. Sanchez will assume command and will lead you in securing as many of the armaments for activity in the south as possible. He will remain in command there.

"Are there any questions?

"You're dismissed. We will meet again at the chopper at 1900 hours."

Kate and McCaul offered their respects to Machado and LaRue and wandered away from the camp. Mike had a busy and potentially dangerous night ahead and they both wanted to enjoy a few stolen moments of peace before they separated.

Mike and Kate wandered through tobacco fields and came across a small settlement of huts surrounded by sugar cane with a small group of well tanned men and women and a couple of small children and chickens running around. A guy Mike had seen previously wearing a white golf cap with a maple leaf waved them over. Mike and Kate followed and the guy put a length of cane into a crusher and presented them with a glass of syrup for another tasting of their deadly raw rum. He directed the couple into a hut. He pulled out a clear bottle, poured out three glasses and they drank thirstily expecting more sweetness. They both coughed; it was raw rum that could fuel a tractor. They recovered in response to their new friend's chuckle and toasted, "Viva La Cuba Libre!"

As they finished the toast, white hat's female companion presented them with two freshly made cigars, a robusto for Mike and a panetela for Kate. Mike smelled his and tested it for its firmness; it was perfectly made.

Their new friend said, "Por Favor," and presented a machete. Mike and Kate each in turn offered their cigars and the guy sliced off the ends without effort. He might shave with it. If he ever shaved. Mike suspected the blade might spill fascist blood in a few hours.

They took long draws on their smokes and nodded with appreciation; Kate working diligently to not cough. They were perfect. They held the perfect cigars in front of their faces. They nodded their appreciation and admiration for the fruits of this earth and the talent of the cigar maker but really wanted to be alone. Mike reached in his pocket for his wallet, but his friend waved his hands rapidly and said, "No, Compañero. Somos hermanos en la Guerra."

He thought they might both die together soon. Mike offered his hand, "Mi nombre es Mike. Oh, you're Canto!"

He replied, "Si. Mi espousa es Julida." She smiled and she and Kate hugged.

"Esta Noche, Amigo," Mike said. He laughed and replied.

"Esta Noche."

They left to return toward the camp and enjoy each others company; maybe for the last time. They walked slowly, holding hands while chatting quietly about trivia and remembering some of their times together in between drags on their cigars.

On the way they found a tobacco drying shed a few hundred yards away from the camp and made a bed from leaves that were hanging on wooden racks. The plants weren't yet fully cured and were soft and gently aromatic and provided for a very Cuban experience.

They were desperate people and desperation has been known to channel emotions in desperate ways.

Kate and Mike removed their clothing; she stripped down to a halter shirt and her shorts and Mike to a tee shirt and boxer briefs. She laid down on their tobacco bed facing away from Mike, and he spooned in behind her, surrounding her with his arms.

The sun was peaking through the roughly thatched roof of the shed and cast a warm glow around them. It was an almost surreal place, like they weren't on earth and nowhere near civilization. The aroma of the tobacco was earthy and rich and surrounded and enveloped them.

They stayed spooned for several minutes, each of them feeling their own and each other's warmth. McCaul's face absorbed the fragrance of her hair; Mike luxuriated in it and the silkiness of her shoulder and the soft push of her lower back toward his lower front.

Mike gently kissed her shoulder and could feel a slight shiver. He kissed her on the crook of her neck and felt her tense up and stir her hips toward him. When he kissed her neck she turned her face to almost touch his. He shifted to gently kiss a corner of her lips. She shifted to allow him to.

The night they had shared only a few days before was remembered, then everything was forgotten and reality ignored. She rolled to face him and pulled anxiously on his tee shirt as he did on her halter and they wrapped their legs together and tore each other's tops off.

They hugged and kissed deeply and hungrily and then stared into each other's eyes; hers with the fire and liveliness of a jungle cat. She nipped on his shoulder and dropped her hands to his groin. He responded. A few minutes later they fell asleep in each others arms.

28

AFTER HIS MEETING WITH HIS SECURITY ADVISORS the President called an emergency meeting of the National Security Council to inform its members of the status of the missing, and presumed dead, reporter from the Miami Herald. They were all a little bit anti-social so there wasn't a lot of kibitzing so they nodded or said polite hellos and sat around the Cabinet table.

"People. We have an issue. Yesterday, at about 1500 hours, one of our nationals was shot by security police in Havana. There are varying reports as far as details, who he was, et cetera, but at the end of the day, he was working for us. His cover was as a reporter for the Miami Herald, but he was in deep cover doing odd jobs for us.

"Given the sensitivity of us getting caught spying down there, and with a very vocal response expected from the Castros, we have little choice but to deny that he is anything but a civilian reporter. So that's what we'll do.

"Shortly after we were informed by a private source in the Cuban military headquarters that Fidel Castro has died." There was a rumble round the table.

"We don't know what the status is down there. Perry's got his top guy on the case in Havana and Lucas is arranging to present the type of response that would be expected from us on something like this. We've got a Delta Team and a couple of squads of Navy Seals that can drop in for breakfast down there on our orders, but we really, really hope that we don't have to use them.

"Our worst case scenario is to have this guy found out. He has a highly plausible back story as a reporter for the Miami Herald and we aspire that this will be the obvious conclusion of any third party observer.

"The timing with Former First Secretary Castro's death might have the death of our agent be ignored. We hope so.

"Second, you all need to understand that it will be my decision, and my decision alone, to take any action against what can be made to seem to be a premeditated and unprovoked act of violence against an innocent citizen, more critically a reporter, of the United States. I am informing you, as well as the Senate and Congress, by having their respective minority and majority leaders here, of this situation only as a requirement for oversight as is called for in our constitution. Are there any comments or guidance that any of you wish to provide at this time?"

As expected, the Senate Minority Leader, who had his eyes on a higher prize, had an opinion. "Mr. President, I am personally offended by your actions in this matter. This is NOT the way we do things in the United States of America. We not only need to be seen to be doing the right thing, we need to DO the right thing. At this time I will withhold comments except to advise you that you will, indeed, be held responsible for any negative outcome of this event."

"I will accept that burden, Senator Beauregard, providing, of course, that if it works out well, that you will publicly provide this office with appropriate credit. Any more discussion?"

There was none so the President moved on. "Staff? Status."

Perry Dalukis responded, "We're awaiting any minute now for a report from Agent Felix in Havana. We have two issues here. One is what damage can be done by having the decedent identified as our intelligence agent. Is there any detritus or documentation that he had in his possession that can be pointed back to us? If there is nothing, then, frankly, we have no downside whatsoever. It's a pure case of a foreign, and unfriendly, government killing one of our citizens.

"Better, or, I suppose worse for them, is that he is a representative of a newspaper that is often critical of the regime in place there. If there is something, say documents, that prove his attachment, well, then, that is a different matter entirely.

"As far as Castro's situation? Well... as far as we are concerned, it is none of our concern. We had nothing to do with it."

The President said, "So, Director Dalukis, what do you suggest we do?"

"Mr. President, I suggest we pull out decks of cards and wait."

- # -

Felix had a pretty good idea where Don Hughes kept his place. Plaza de Armas was the old military square and served as a place for Cubans to sell books. They were mostly antiques from around the time of the revolution, especially biographies of those whom Fidel had decided were heroes. And he had met Pedro at La Dominica restaurant a block away a few months before.

Felix jumped in a Panataxi which took him down the Malecon and ended up next to the Hotel Santa Isabel and the Plaza in a few minutes.

He passed the driver a fiver and exited the car. The Plaza was covered in broad leafed trees and as always was almost fully in the shade. The book sellers were taking down their stalls and stands and kibitzing with each other.

Felix wandered down the rows of book shelves, hoping to look like a turista shopper, stopping to look at books that caught his eye. He thought he might get into a conversation with one of the vendors and pop the Pedro question.

That was until the police cars arrived. Three official cars pulled up to the building just past and to the right of Felix's book browsing. He watched out of the corners of his eyes.

The three cars unloaded about ten grey suited National Revolutionary Police who all rushed up a staircase. In a minute two of them were half dragging a white-haired, gap-toothed, old guy while the others started throwing things over the balcony or carried boxes downstairs.

Felix knew the gig was up. If Hughes had kept notes, then Duarte had them to do with as he would. Nothing Felix could do about it.

He bought an antique Life Magazine, showcasing Fidel's triumphant visit to New York City just after the revolution. He started reading it as he walked away a few yards from his original destination toward the Malecon.

When he felt safe he turned on his Blackberry. He sent a simple text to his contact at the US Embassy. "XOX". He kept an eye on the proceedings.

Felix had to assume that somewhere in Hughes' notes there was a record of his name and CIA connection. This was not, in itself, fatal. Chances were that Duarte and his spooks knew who he was and who he worked for.

The difference was that now they might have material that would provide evidence to arrest him as a foreign agent, exploit it for all that it might be worth and make him the subject of a show trial and a high profile deportation.

Or ... they could have an accident, lose their evidence and have no story at all.

Felix kept a lot of cash on hand for just such occasions. He also kept a few useful tools in his pocket, just in the event that something might be needed. He had learned this from his father, a legend in USA intelligence circles.

The PNRs that were collecting all the paper from Don Hughes' apartment were putting it all into the trunk of a grey Lada.

One of items in Felix's tickle trunk was a ring of universal skeleton keys for all models of cars made from 1950 to 2000. Interestingly, for cars in Cuba, there were only thirty. The old jalopies made up a dozen and the Japanese and Eastern Euro cars imported since the Soviet times were another dozen and a half.

Felix walked a few hundred yards to the parking lot near the harbor and looked for a suitable vehicle. He saw one. It was a mid-fifties blue Chevy van; probably someone's pride and joy.

He walked up and tried a couple of keys until one fit. He opened the door, got in and drove it away as if it was his own back to a place that allowed him to surveil the apartment. He saw the Lada that the boxes had been loaded into start to move. The remaining detachment either walked or drove in other directions.

Felix waited and lit up a Robusto.

One young PNR cop got into the Lada and started driving toward the Malecon, with Felix following. The Lada entered a long unpopulated alley, a shortcut to the thoroughfare.

Felix sped up, drove down the same street, pulled alongside the Lada and violently turned his wheel forcing the Lada into a wall. He jumped out of the Chevy, rushed toward the young PNR officer and shot him in the head with a silenced sidearm. He quickly moved the boxes into the Chevy and took off. In five minutes he was at the Embassy, passed through security and parked the Chevy van out of sight. He told the guards to secure the contents. He pulled out his mobile and sent out a short message in code to report on the latest event. His job was done for now.

In Washington, Perry Salukis felt a buzz on his Blackberry and checked it. He held up his hand to get the attention of his boss. "Mr. President, we're off the hook."

29

KATE AND MIKE AWOKE. He hadn't thought either of them would nod off. But, they had lain in each other's arms, sharing each other's breath, in the peaceful shade and gentle aroma for twenty minutes after the big event and then drifted away.

An hour or more of deep sleep later the turn of the helicopter rotors stirred them and they stretched and rose. Mike looked at his watch. It was time to move.

They reassembled their clothing as best as they could without speaking and started to leave the shed, but not before exchanging one last, for now, deep and soulful kiss. Reality beckoned and they returned to it. They strolled back to the ground camp as the skies were turning a deep purple and stars were just starting to poke through the darkness.

The attack group was armed and was lining up by the Sikorsky. There were eighteen of them; LaRue and McCaul made twenty, Manuel twenty-one. It would be a tight fit.

Boyd was grunting around the scene taking shots. Mike told Kate there wasn't room for her and Boyd and she only put up a token argument. She recognized there was lifting to be done this night that was too heavy for a tiny perfect reporter and her hefty sidekick.

LaRue and McCaul boarded last, after Mike had given Kate a long hug and a short kiss. The inside of the chopper was Spartan. The three-hour trip would not be particularly comfortable, and there was sure to be grumbling on the way down.

A minute later they were in the air, flying due north before turning southeast to travel feet wet for the balance of the trip. To provide the team more space LaRue and McCaul joined Ronaldo in what remained of the control cockpit. They queried Ronaldo on their destination; he knew exactly the best route to get to their destination. He had ferried Gant many times to Santiago de Cuba, and had landed at Gitmo a couple of times as well as taken Kate to the specific site only a day before.

Ronaldo took a route just out of eyesight of shore at little more than six hundred feet. The flight didn't seem to last as long as McCaul expected. There was lots to talk with LaRue about, and every now and again they would over-fly moon-lit groups of huge sea turtles, schools of dolphins and porpoises and pods of whales. After a couple of hours Ronaldo made a turn to the south and they over-flew a mountain range.

Soon enough, they heard their greeters before they saw them. "Sikorsky Rotor Craft. This is USN Guantanamo Naval Base Security. You are about to enter airspace of the United States of America. Identify yourself."

McCaul took the communicator. "Sir, code name is Zulu-Zulu-Tango-Bravo-Seven-Zero."

"Sikorsky Rotor Craft, continue your current flight settings. Follow me in, Sir." A second later the Sikorsky was book-ended by Cobra attack helicopters on either side. Then one of the Cobras moved ahead, while the other stayed on their tail and to one side.

Three minutes later they noticed a flashing red light and were ushered toward the landing zone. Within a couple more they were feet dry on land and watching a fuelling tanker drive toward them.

Ronaldo didn't mess around. He pulled on a blue baseball cap with a "C" for Cuba emblem and stayed put to be the last man off. The men deplaned for a good stretch, a few to light up stogies or to take a leak, in both cases safely removed from the fuelling station.

McCaul stepped out and was joined by a pilot Major from one of the Cobras. He was still wearing his flight helmet, with his head-up display device and monocle bent back out of the way. "I'm Simpson. Your boy knows how to fly that thing."

"McCaul. I'll pass on your compliments. You gonna be around here for a while?"

"Until you don't need us any more, Sir."

"We should be back in about three or four hours if all goes well. There any unfriendlies around?"

"Not in this sector, Sir. Lots of green shirts about twenty miles away, but none with wings."

"You have any message for me?"

"Your friend told me to tell you your other supplies of fuel are on their way to your destination and will be there before you are."

"Thanks for your help, Major Simpson."

"Our pleasure, Sir. Godspeed."

They were fuelled, armed and dangerous. McCaul hoped they were lucky.

Once the tanker uncoupled and retired the gang had returned and were reboarding. McCaul joined them and they were off.

Knowing the area, Ronaldo took a big circle away from the base well into the Caribbean and to the east, wanting to avoid sightseers on the Cuban side of the bay. As far as any nosy Cubans would be concerned, McCaul thought, they would likely think that they were visiting from a ship off-shore to load up on Coors.

About twenty minutes later they were back in sight of land and Ronaldo went up high and fast, likely two thousand feet at 300 miles per hour. He'd been there before and came in the back way, out of sight of the encampment.

McCaul was tense and he looked over at LaRue and his lips were tightly pressed together. It was pitch dark with only a slim sliver of a moon to light up the surface.

Mike took a look down and saw that they were flying over the Sierra Cristal mountain range: incredibly verdant valleys surrounded by extremely lush mountain ranges with some peaks topped by cotton candy and others interrupted by deep ravines. It had been not too far from here that Fidel and his friends had launched the revolution with 80 people and where he had hidden after almost being annihilated.

Looking over to the right Mike could see the profile of a huge flat-topped mountain in the dark and Ronaldo started to descend. For the last few minutes it had been lightly raining and McCaul could barely make out that they were flying along a valley and starting to move toward the peak. Just as he thought Ronaldo had lost his way and was about to crash, he turned on two incredibly bright landing lights, did a breathtakingly fast descent and they landed. Mike replaced his stomach and his decorum. He could hear retching from behind. He glanced at LaRue and he was as calm as if he had his feet up watching Les Canadiens.

Ronaldo had gotten the assault team to their destination. Like many things on this confused island Ronaldo was much more than could be seen on first glance.

LaRue had a chat with Ronaldo and gave him his satellite phone. McCaul still had his. He didn't want it to ring in the next half hour or so, so he put it on mute. Ronaldo was drawing directions for LaRue.

The men had left the rotorcraft. It was serving the group well, this night. LaRue joined them and McCaul went to shake hands with Ronaldo. He reacted with fear at first and then broke into a huge smile and gave Mike the warmest hug he had received all week while fully clothed.

His piloting skills were tremendous, but his English still needed some work, "Señor, you go and bring back the womens. I mean bring back the weapons, Señor. Mañana, Cuba be free!!"

He gave McCaul a drab green forage hat and he put it on. A little large, but comfy. It made him feel more sinister.

McCaul smiled; while he was a pro at these things, he was always tense until the shooting started. But Ronaldo had relaxed him, which was good. Mike thanked him and told him he was an excellent pilot.

"My Seek is an excellente aircraft, Señor. I just try hard. I stay with my Seek, Señor McCaul. High Cinco." McCaul held up his hand and Ronaldo gave him a high five and Mike exitted.

He met LaRue outside. It was misting a little, which was perfect for the mission. Small noises wouldn't travel very far; sentries, if they had any, would be hunkered down and not paying much attention. It was highly unlikely Raul would have any surveillance within earshot.

LaRue met the men and gave them a last minute briefing. Each had a rucksack that doubled as a seat and they dropped them next to the chopper. Each stripped down to their forage caps, basic battle dress and an ammo pouch. Sanchez had the single thirty calibre General Purpose Machine Gun. The remaining team members and McCaul had their grenades and five full magazines of 7.62 Calibre rounds for the AK47s. They also each had a Bowie knife if they had to cut any ropes, bushes or throats. LaRue, Manuel and McCaul had small radio communicators. A few of the men had homemade wire garrotes.

LaRue sent Manuel and Garza each about twenty yards to each flank; he took the point and told Sanchez to take the rear. McCaul was happy to commune somewhere in the middle with the main force. The flank always had the toughest job; they had to keep their positions even when the main column veered in one direction or another. The men knew enough to spread out as LaRue gave the arm signal and the team started silent marching, testing every step for a noise-maker before they put their full weight to the ground.

They were quiet enough in the rain to hear leaves falling, birds chirping and snakes slithering above any noise they made. McCaul kept his eyes on the back ahead of him and his weapon on safe and pointed down. The trees were festooned with beautifully coloured birds and gigantic fluorescent snails. There were even bright red land crabs McCaul had no immediate urge to boil and feast on.

They moved for about forty minutes, not because of the distance but because LaRue was being very careful. Suddenly the back ahead of McCaul slowed down and stopped and they had caught up with Cien. The flanks joined them and he asked them if they had seen anything. They all shook their heads. LaRue spoke silently in Spanish and McCaul tried to follow along. LaRue pointed to Manuel and Mike to come forward and they moved ahead of the rest of the platoon. He was very silent, invisible, and McCaul tried his best to be ghost-like without scaring anyone.

LaRue held up his hand and motioned Manuel and McCaul forward. They had reached the target. Their eyes were night conditioned and they could almost see across the clearing. There was a sentry, seemingly asleep with a poncho of some sort covering him about twenty feet to the right. LaRue made short work of him, and came back wiping his knife on his pants. He told Manuel and McCaul to wait and in about ten minutes returned.

"There were three others," he whispered. In ten minutes LaRue had killed four men without as much as a whimper. "There is no other movement in the camp. There are four tents, likely capacity four to six men per tent."

They went back to join the column.

The three leaders huddled with the rest of the platoon back about a hundred meters. LaRue explained to the men how they would break the unit into two groups of eight men each. Their tasking was simple; three grenades in each of the tents. Sanchez would set up his GPMG to cover the field with withering fire, after the grenades detonated. All fire was to be directed toward the lowest point of elevation in the camp where their own men wouldn't be. He drew a small map in the dirt to show the layout of the tents and their positions. Their retreat, if needed, would be covered by Sanchez who would decimate the camp with the support of the rest of the team when they retreated.

McCaul had a sharpshooter badge from both Airborne and the Mounties and he was appointed to take the position furthest from their starting point. LaRue appointed four likely Latin American Baseball League fans to toss the pineapples. They moved silently out to their positions.

Mike saw the flash from the other side of the camp.

The appointed grenadiers threw their tools of death.

And nothing happened.

It was quiet for a second until a single terrorist, unknowing of his new fate, poked his head through the flap of tent four and exited scratching his beard and pulling up his gotch. He wandered around his shelter looked down and saw the dud grenade lying on the ground. He showed surprise and straightened up and McCaul shot him in the head and spent a magazine turning his tent into fishnet. In a second all the fifteen other riflemen and the GPMG opened up.

Then a Cuban shouted loudly in Spanish. It was Duarte. The Cuban general loudly ordered his men to seek cover.

Things could still have worked out fine if the Islamists didn't have light arms in their tents. But they did. Before they had cleaned them out, the Cubans disappeared over the edge of the cliff and started returning fire and LaRue's guys fired back. This wasn't in the playbook. But not all things that could ever happen ever are.

They had no targets and neither did the assault team, so after about a minute they all stopped firing. Manuel on the other side and McCaul were closest to the drop-off that provided their remaining adversaries safety. McCaul had no idea if Manuel thought like he did, but Mike knew the longer they waited, the more likely the opponents would prepare an offensive or escape maneuver. Mike patted his nearest fellow rifleman on the shoulder and indicated to him to follow.

Silently they worked their way through the jungle, careful of the drop off before them, often holding on to thick needled vines as they moved. McCaul came to the edge and almost rolled about six hundred feet down a steep incline.

Between them, Mike thought, they had enough, but not excess, rounds of ammo. He figured they had to hope that Manuel had at least two comrades flanking from the other side.

Walking was treacherous; a wrong step would lose half of his unit; McCaul was careful not to be one. All members of his team were extremely careful, and in about two minutes could hear rumbles of humanity just ahead.

Just before they launched the strike on their side, a firefight erupted away from them. Manuel was in the battle and McCaul and his team all of a sudden had their adversaries in a crossfire. With the sound from the other side covering their movements, and with the opponents focusing on Manuel's team, McCaul and his guys were free to take any firing positions they wanted, providing they didn't get hit by Manuel and his guys. They stayed low and took prone sniper positions.

It was a killing ground. With Manuel's AK rounds flying five metres above their heads, McCaul's men were twenty metres from the Islamists. They couldn't hear the McCauls' shots. They took them with patience. One at a time. In the back, as they tried to respond to the only attack they were aware of. They never knew what hit them. In a minute, and with two new mags each, all but a few were dead, most tumbling down the mountainside. A white rag was waved and a single figure rose, his hands in the air.

"Amigos, I am your prisoner!" It was Duarte, his hands in the air.

Manuel stopped shooting and he and his partner joined McCaul walking toward the lone survivor, their guns all on the target. Manuel gave Mike a big smile then leaned over and reached into a dead body at his feet, grabbed a handful of brain matter and rubbed it onto his battle shirt. And then smeared some on McCaul's.

Duarte spoke, "Cardenas," he looked at Manuel, "you are a traitor to the Revolution. You were to be my lieutenant."

Manuel took out his sidearm, "You, you slime, you are an asshole." He raised his 9mm, pointed it at Duarte's face and pulled the trigger, exploding the man's head.

Manuel cleaned his bloody hands on his face and he and Mike started climbing back up into the encampment, both of them holding their forage caps well over their heads on the top of their rifles and yelling in English at the top of their lungs.

LaRue and the rest of the crew were waiting for them at the top of the hill and they had a group hug. The only thing missing was a photographer. LaRue grabbed McCaul by both shoulders with a broad smile. "So how do you like killing, amigo?" He hugged McCaul, who hugged him back.

McCaul said, "Amigo, I do it lots. It's not bad. But I don't love it."

LaRue's men walked through the battle theatre. A few handgun shots finished off the wounded.

The hooches Kate had filmed were where they expected, away from the main barracks tents. They were filled with munitions. Much more than McCaul expected. There were at least two dozen Russian RPGs and dozens of SMAWs, along with a crate of missiles. There were stacks of ammo boxes for AKs and other weapons favoured by Stalinists and various other malcontents.

Eight men were assigned to secure the camp. McCaul joined them and they hunkered around smoking cigars. The remainder were assigned to carry weapons back to the chopper. Each could carry about half a dozen RPGs or a couple of SMAWs, so the pile of death makers got smaller by the minute.

LaRue directed the operation, and when word got back that a full load had been moved, LaRue gathered the men around. He lit up a cigar, walked around shaking hands and signalled to Ernesto who passed around bottles of rum.

LaRue came to Manuel and started laughing, "Amigo, you look like you were in a war!" Manuel looked a little embarrassed but laughed back and accepted a slap on the back with one in return.

Once everyone had enjoyed a good haul on the rum, LaRue said loudly, "Amigos, this is good work. But our job has just begun. Ernesto, Manuel and McCaul will return with me. The rest of you will carry as much as you can down the mountain for your diversionary attacks in Santiago de Cuba and Guantanamo. You will all report to Sargento Sanchez.

"What you cannot carry, throw over the cliff along with the bodies of terrorists and the remains of their camp.

"We leave you now to take the revolution to Castro."

The leader team went back to the chopper, now filled with firepower. Ronaldo took control, and they moved.

30

THE SHORT RIDE BACK TO GITMO didn't give the leadership team much time to talk. But they didn't have much to say. They were all subdued by the violence behind them and whipped by the adrenaline filled hour before. Even Ronaldo was quiet for once.

They went through the security routine and landed at McCalla in Gitmo. Simpson was waiting for them on the ground when then deplaned. He looked Manuel and McCaul up and down and shook his head at the gore on their fatigues.

"Come on out, Fellas. I suspect you might like a coffee or something." He shook all their hands and started chatting with Ronaldo in Spanish while the three others went ahead. They entered the mess and visited the latrine while the two rotorcraft jockeys waited outside trading secrets.

Simpson and Ronaldo joined them.

"How'd it go, Comandante?" Simpson was looking at McCaul.

"I kinda like this kinda adventure, Major."

"I did in my day, but I kinda like this babysittin' postin' now. I get a week a month back in civilization."

"You guys always ready?"

"Ready for anything, McCaul. W W Three if it happens. We got some big goodies down here if we need 'em."

McCaul asked, "What about the terrorists you're baby sitting?"

"They actually seem to like it here. First time in their lives they got three squares a day and a library and they got no fleshly temptations. To be honest, not many of them seem to be all that anxious to leave."

McCaul suspected the feeling was mutual and the USA was happy to see them stay put. More than half the internees that had been released had ended up in Iraq or Afstan fighting for the bad guys.

"Have a seat guys. Cookie brought you some treats for the trip home." A steward arrived and presented a platter of steaming Big Macs and fries and an icy cooler heaping with Red Bulls and Coors.

"I'm getting a couple of cases of the Red Bulls put in your chopper for the rest of your guys tomorrow night."

The guys dove into the burgers and fries.

Ronaldo took one bite of his Big Mac and his head appeared to almost explode. "Señor, Señor, theese is amazing. What you call it?"

It was a gas for the Canadians to see the kid have his first Big Mac. Ronaldo grabbed a handful of fries and stuffed them in his mouth smiling and talking while he was chewing. "Santa Maria!"

Manuel seemed to enjoy his first truly American experience just as much as Ronaldo, but with a little more decorum. He didn't let a fry go uneaten though.

Simpson pointed to Ronaldo, "Amigo, you might want to pour one a these down your gullet before you take off; it'll make your trip go faster and keep your plane from going for a swim." He passed Ronaldo a 500 ml can of frosty Red Bull.

Once the burger wrappings were tossed aside and the fry cartons crushed Simpson brought the team back on schedule. "Okay guys, you better get

247

a move on. Far as we can see, no storm clouds or adversaries between here and home."

They all stood and followed the Major out of the mess and back to the helipad.

McCaul said, "We owe you, Major."

"Buddy, my life ain't at risk in this mission. We owe you a helluva lot more.

"Ronaldo, here's a present for you to open when you get back to Pinar del Rio."

He gave the little guy a duffle bag with something a little bigger than a head and Ronaldo offered his thanks, "Gracias, Major, for this and the wonderful Big Max. I come back sometime, okay?"

"Anytime, Amigo."

The Sikorsky was gassed and checked out, the three warriors got aboard, Ronaldo took them up and they spent four hours fighting a mean head wind before they arrived back in Pinar del Rio to a camp arming for bear.

Once Ronaldo's "Seek" became audible, paint-pot fires were lit to guide him in and they were soon on the ground. It was just before dawn and men were moving around more by natural light than torches.

Machado and a group of his strongest met the conquering heroes. The second they were out of the gunship his gang began unloading the armaments. They appeared to have already uncrated an unwieldy object from another source. It was lying a few metres from their landing spot, wrapped in heavy industrial, Camo olive drab plastic and indistinguishable. Surely a gift from McCaul's newest best friend forever, Harry Felix.

LaRue, Ronaldo, Manuel and McCaul exited. Machado had a broad smile, rushed forward and ambitiously offered his hand. Mike grabbed it and Machado used his leverage to push McCaul slightly back and then pull him back into a firm hug.

"The mission went well, Comandante McCaul." Mike recognized that he had received a battlefield promotion. He released McCaul and shook hands with and hugged LaRue.

Machado looked at Manuel, started to laugh, and said, "Manuel! How did you get all that blood and gore all over you?"

Manuel looked embarrassed for the second time in the day and maybe his life. He slapped Manuel on the back and said, "I'd hug you, Amigo, but I am wearing my last clean shirt."

LaRue told Machado about their adventure as they walked away from the chopper, "No casualties for us. Total for them. We took as much materiel as we could carry."

Machado asked, "Who were they, Cien."

"Well, you won't have to worry about Duarte any more. I don't know the rest, Amigo. They were dark complexioned. I think Arabs, but we didn't have time to interview them."

Machado offered Mike a cigar and he accepted and lit it. Like the hand-made one of a few hours previous, it was better than anything made in factories.

McCaul hadn't shaved for a few days and with his forage hat on, with the Cohiba, and in the company of Machado and LaRue, he felt kind of like a less loco Che or a less bearded Camilo. He kind of liked the feeling.

Mike looked back at the chopper and saw the welder back at work. He had no idea what renovations they were making, but he'd bet they weren't cosmetic.

Mike was approached by a Martian. At least, he thought it was a Martian until the E.T. moved aside his targeting monocle and removed his combat helmet. It was Ronaldo, of course, smiling from ear to ear.

"Major Simpson gib me his hat, Señor McCaul!"

"Ronaldo, mi amigo, he told me you deserve it."

"McCaul, come wid me, see my Seek."

Mike followed. The welders had unwrapped the mysterious gift from Felix and were attaching a Gatling gun and gunnery platform to the helicopter. Others seemed to be installing new floors, sure to be armour. Ronaldo's Seek was being converted into a terrifying killer of men.

"Ronaldo, you okay?"

"Señor, we win the free Cuba, then I get rich. I muy, muy okay, Señor."

McCaul offered a knuckle tap, Ronaldo responded and Mike left to find Machado and LaRue. They were sitting alone, smoking long Esplendidos, and seeming to be deep in casual conversation under a cluster of coconut palms.

Machado said, "Join us, Comandante McCaul. You know there was an Americano who served with Fidel and Guevara."

"I didn't."

"Comandante William Morgan. He was a friend of Cubans, and he fought fiercely for Cubano Libre. The event, not the cocktail..." They all laughed. "But when he saw that the Castros intended to imprison the Cuban people, not free them, he protested. And Fidel had him executed. Now we strike back for all the true fighters on behalf of Cubano Libre who were imprisoned and executed by Castro criminales."

He led the men to a board nailed to one of the trees with a large tourist map of Havana attached to it decorated with various circles and arrows.

Machado inhaled from his cigar and exhaled for several seconds. LaRue was looking at smaller maps. He had a full beard now and he definitely reminded Mike of the pictures McCaul had seen of his famous father.

"Michael, enjoy some of our fine tobacco before we start worrying about our future, and join me in the shade for a moment of peace." Mike followed him to join LaRue under his shade tree and they sat on roughly hewn stools. Machado looked alive, his eyes were sparkling and it was easy to sense his level of excitement.

"It is really going to happen, Michael."

Mike smiled and nodded.

Machado said, "When I was exiled in New York City I wondered if this day would ever come. It never would have, of course, except for you and Cien, and maybe your friends in the CIA, of course."

"Maybe it is just your destiny."

"Quizas. Perhaps."

"Why did you do this?"

"Decide to replace Fidel. Now Raul?"

Mike nodded.

"My family was not opposed to the revolucion, at the start. My father's cousin, Camilo, of course, was one of Fidel's strongest supporters."

He leaned back and almost tipped his stool but caught himself. "It all went bad when Che started to murder innocents; students and professors and the naïve who falsely believed that the revolution was designed to set people free.

"My father was discouraged, but he never dared to let anyone know of his disappointment.

"I left on the last flight of the Pedro Pan exodus. You know of this?"

Mike shook his head.

"When it was obvious that the revolucion was going bad, the Catholic Church in Miami arranged with worried Cubano parents to send their children to the USA for visits. Of course, these children never returned."

"I've never heard of this."

"It was kept secret for over two decades. Fourteen thousand children were resettled in just over a year. Many never saw their parents again, but many are multi-millionaires, some are senators. One is trying to take Cuba back for Cubans."

"What happened to you?"

"My father died in prison and my mother lives in a small village not too far from here. I never saw him before he died and my mother, not until I came here only a few months ago.

"I was raised in a Catholic orphanage, but educated in excellent schools. I was fortunate to receive scholarships and graduated as a lawyer from Fordham."

"How did you get here?"

"There are speedboats that take Cubans to Florida for ten thousand dollars. They bring people in for much less.

"My cigar is starting to extinguish because I am talking too much." He stood up.

"Cien, wake up!"

LaRue had been napping, still recovering from his late night. He rubbed his eyes. "Sorry, Amigos. Killing people is tiring work."

All three men laughed.

"McCaul, so you want to know what we have to face with our opponents tonight. Your friend, Mr. Felix, has been helpful with this.

"The opponents have three military command centers in Havana, Santiago de Cuba and Matanzas. Each HQ has armouries of light arms but none of the members of the Cuban army have access to automatic weapons without the written approval of either Fidel or Raul. If we remove their communications, then we don't need to fear them to raise a significant military response. In any case, we will have missile crews prepared to respond to any attempt to enter these armouries."

He relit his enormous cigar and emitted a huge cloud of rich aromatic smoke.

"They also have light arms supplies in Managua and Camilitos military bases in Havana. There are many soldiers barracksed there, but they too have their arms secured and they can't get them without written orders. And two of the three officials with authority are now dead. We'll have missile teams at both these armories that will not allow weapons to be removed.

"Their remaining troops are based near here in San Luis, Pinar del Rio, Santa Clara, Holguin and Camagüey, but they have no means of transporting any significant number of troops to Havana. We already have men in place to block these roads from each of these bases to Havana, and they have too few troop transports and rotorcraft to respond with any effect in Havana. In any case, after we distribute and use the missiles, these will not leave their staging areas anyway."

LaRue joined in, "Duarte's Secret Police is supposed to have about thirty thousand security policemen across the country, but they're conscripted, poorly armed and not very motivated. And our banker friend, Manuel, has corrupted almost all their leaders. The National Revolutionary Police are everywhere, but only have batons or sidearms. We would count on them to move to our side after the Castro regime is retired.

"He does have two thousand Special Ops forces, but they're now almost all deployed in other countries doing security or creating mischief on contract. There are less than a hundred stationed at Castro's HQ at the Plaza and these are on shift work. We should need to only deal with less than fifty."

Machado said, "There is a joke, Mr. McCaul, that Havana has one million people and one million policemen. But these policias are all spies, paramilitaries with batons and a few hundred with side arms. Their purpose is to stop rebellion before it begins, not to do anything after it does. And they're dependant on the government to eat, but not necessarily Raul's government. They have limited if any loyalty.

"None of the military aircraft are armed and they only have a few that they could get in the air even with twenty-four hour notice. None that can they respond with immediately. The Castros have always been paranoid, Mike. They do not trust their own military and keep their shoulder mounted and air-to-ground missiles in three cave bunkers. We know where they are and they will be closed by our own missiles as our first action."

Machado dropped his cigar and stepped on it and rose.

"Let's go get our other leaders and start the ball going." He stood, LaRue gathered the maps and the three men walked purposefully over to where the team leaders had gathered.

A few of the guys were playing dominos and laughing and kibitzing. Piles of Cuban pesos were in play and piled up. Some others were playing solitaire. A couple had bottles of moonshine and were sitting by themselves on recycled leather sofas rescued from the chopper. Others were sleeping under trees on the Sik's ripped out carpets.

Fidel had landed in Cuba in 1956 on his commandeered yacht 'Granma' with eighty men, had lost almost all in the first skirmish, and then had started his revolution with eighteen guys and seven rifles. McCaul suspected that Machado had a lot more men and they were a lot better armed and probably better led and they didn't have to fight mosquitoes and walk through swamps and over mountains for two years. It would only take them an hour to get to Havana not months. So McCaul almost liked their chances.

"Mis Hermanos y Caballeros," Machado said loudly in Spanish and continued. After McCaul's Spanish immersion of the last week he didn't even notice that Machado wasn't speaking in English.

The men gave up their distractions, the nappers woke up with a start, and all paid attention.

"This night we take the next step to create a New Cuba, a free Cuba. Our compañeros in other parts of Cuba have been instructed, accepted their missions, and have been armed and are being deployed. But this war for our democratic independence will be won in Havana, and by the men here with us today."

He drew strongly from a new long cigar, looked at the burning ember and spit a spot of tobacco.

"We have three main targets and two individual takedowns. You know who the takedowns will be and you all know Havana well." He pointed at a large map of the City and tapped on the map to point at key places as he spoke.

"The National Communications centre near the Hotel Nacional, buildings at the Plaza de la Revolucion and la Villa Marista are the big three targets which offer us the most value and will take most of our resources."

He pointed to the smallest member of the briefing group, who was about the size of a pit bull and had just as daunting a visage. "Gomez, your team will assault the Plaza de la Revolucion.

"You will destroy the communications infrastructure and towers at the Ministry of the Interior, at the Havana Barracks and at the party headquarters at Plaza de Revolucion starting at oh one hundred hours and be completed by oh one thirty hours. You will be reinforced by Garza's group and will then destroy the Havana Barracks and all its occupants. You will have benefit of the gunship for overwhelming the barracks.

"Expect strong resistance and you must attack with devastating force. Have at least six rocket launcher teams with at least four RPGs each. Do not take prisoners; if men offer to come willingly to our side, then gladly accept their support. If they are obviously Raulistas, then treat them as you would Raul. Kill them. You will stay at the Barracks to ensure no one escapes to issue an alarm.

"Colonel Garza, your platoon will accompany my crew to central Havana to the National Television and Radio Centre. We will occupy this facility. This will be started at 0200 hours and finished shortly after. There should be very little, if any, opposition. Once this is accomplished and the facility is secured, you will take most of your men and join Gomez at the Main Barracks and Ministry of Interior at La Plaza to complete the destruction of those targets.

"Comandante Cien Camilo LaRue will lead our largest force and eliminate our dead friend Duarte's secret police at Villa Marista.

"Cien." Machado became even more intense than normal, "You will lead our vanguard and capture our most vital target. Mi amigo, you have our strongest fighters with you. And you will need to have a very excellent night for us to be successful. It is you we have chosen to capture and kill all command forces at Villa Marista. Fidel is dead and Raul a pervert; they cannot stop us. But it is Duarte's secret police who carry the sticks in this corrupted revolucion.

"With Duarte gone his second in command, Eugenio Famosa, will be more difficult, especially if he is alerted by what happened today with your television friends. He is as mean as a starving dog and likes to spend time at Villa Marista, the main prison. There he is able to exercise his enjoyment of giving pain to others."

McCaul knew about Villa Marista, an old boys school that Fidel had converted to Cuba's Lubianka Prison equivalent.

Machado pointed at a map location near the Airport. "Cien, you know of the secure communications facility outside of the prison. This must be disabled before the attack. His quarters are outside the prison facility and he will likely be well guarded. Famosa will be a fox. Be ready for anything. You will have benefit of the gunship before it assists in the destruction of the Havana Barracks. Take down his communications, destroy his residence with RPGs and clean up what remains. You will need to secure him or our night will continue into another day or more. This mission will start at 0045 hours and must be completed by 0230."

"You will have no aerial resistance and no advanced weaponry to face in your missions. We have teams in place now to prohibit access to these by Raul's people. Anyone who attempts to arm or fly an aircraft will be destroyed on the ground.

"And our most critical and silent mission will be to meet with Raul Castro." Machado said this last word with contempt.

"Ernesto, you and Manuel and our new friend Comandante McCaul will join another assault team and visit the pervert Raul at his compound in Playa by 0200. By the time you capture them, they will have no friends left on the island. If they resist, you have permission to execute them. At your zero minute, if any vehicles leave the compounds, eliminate them with RPGs.

"But if they surrender and offer no resistance, you might transfer them to a small raft in the Florida Strait. Perhaps they will be able to find their way to safety in Miami Beach, or into the belly of a shark."

The men all laughed, slapping each other's shoulders."

Machado reached down for a new bottle of Havana Club. He took a swig and passed it on to LaRue who did the same and passed it to Manuel. It went around the circle and came to McCaul. He finished the bottle.

"Once everything is secure, I will make a national broadcast, scheduled for 0800. All hostilities are to be completed by four in the morning. Are there any questions."

McCaul asked, "What about getting to Raul."

Machado said, "We follow Raul every night. He is much less careful than he used to be as far as rotating sleeping places.

"He and his dead brother have a compound near the Jaimanitas River in West Havana six or seven miles from the Hotel Nacional."

McCaul thought, if these guys, with a little bit of help from their friends, could pull off a handful of skirmishes, with the right weapons given the right scenario, there would be a new Cuba before the bars and bodegas opened in less than twenty four hours.

The men rose and went their separate ways. McCaul jogged back to the helicopter.

The next part of the founding of La Nueva Cuba was for Ronaldo to get killing devices to all those who weren't already armed from their earlier escapade in the southeast part of the island to any centers of police or military within a few hours drive of Havana. This would be a long day for the young guy, but with his energy, a streak of his Gant inherited tenacity and his love of flying his Seek in new ways, McCaul suspected he could handle it.

Machado's men carefully loaded uncrated RPGs and crated missiles. The outbound weaponry took up about a third of the available space. After the chopper was loaded, a swarthy Machadoist with his campaign hat tied to his chin followed, linking himself by a belt to both the Gatling gun and the support beams. Then Ronaldo rose and left with an airborne flourish for parts unknown.

McCaul saw several dilapidated two-ton trucks with canvas tops start to leave, all with a dozen or so men and a large store of RPGs and SMAWs and a case of Red Bull. They were most likely to cover off Raul's Pinar del Rio depot and the rural bases near Havana to prevent counterattacks forming and arming.

Once the weapons were deployed as needed Ronaldo would continue to shuttle weapons and return to rest and refuel. That would all be completed in about six or eight hours if everything went right.

Kate arrived, slight dark circles under her eyes, but still ravishing.

"Mike, what happened? Where'd you get the blood on your shirt. You get hit?"

McCaul hugged her briefly and carefully, not to pass on brain stains, and said, "I'll tell ya later." Mike looked around.

"Mike..."

"Have a seat." She did and crossed her legs and pulled out a reporter's notepad.

"No notes, Babe. If they get found then we're all dead. We took down a terrorist camp in the southern mountains last night."

"Really?"

"Really. I'm okay, Manuel's a little enthusiastic but he is one scary hombre. He smeared me with a handful of brain matter. They're gone. There were a couple of dozen of them. Not sure, but it looks like they were Islamists, but they might have been drug dealers or even Raul's Florida invasion task force. But Generalisimo Duarte, was among them. So he was up to something.

"What did you get?"

"Enough armament to take down a middle eastern dictatorship with enough left over to clean up Venezuela and Puerto Rico if we get on a roll."

Even though it was still morning, men were finding soft places to lay their heads and cover their eyes, their first time as heroes, perhaps for the last time as living entities. Some took bottles of Havana Club with them to their hooches. Many were again playing dominos.

"But I don't want to talk about stage one, Kate. I'm worn out and I want to relax for a little while before stage two and I'd kind of like to relax with you for a few hours."

They wandered back to their secret hiding place in the tobacco shed and cuddled. Passion wasn't on the agenda this time like it had been before. Mike was tired and nervous and needed the warmth and comfort of the only woman in the world he cared about.

They slept for hours. When Mike awoke, the sun was hidden behind the mountains and he was restless and rose reluctantly. Kate was gone, no doubt following her story. The camp was quiet, almost dark, except for a few paint bucket lights, and most of the men had already left and mostly only the commanders and their immediate aides remained. McCaul wondered if Ronaldo would soon give him his last flight on his famous Seek.

Machado had advised earlier that they would meet up with their fellow marauders at 2300 hours in Havana, so they had to get prepped to leave.

Mike heard a young voice speaking urgently and chuckled; Joel had made his presence known. He was effusively speaking with LaRue, waving his arms and gesticulating.

McCaul listened in from a dozen meters away and it was soon obvious Joel urgently wanted to participate in the night's adventures and that LaRue just as urgently didn't want him to.

As Mike expected he would, Joel anxiously rushed toward him. He was speaking Spanish at a speed far beyond McCaul's humble comprehension, but Mike had a pretty good idea of his intent.

"Whoa, amigo. Hable más lento."

"Señor McCaul. You must order Señor Cien to allow me to fight with you. I am a fierce fighter for freedom for Cubanos and I will follow all your orders."

McCaul didn't doubt his sincerity, but did have a few questions about his capability, fierceness and ability to follow anyone's orders. But without Joel, Mike thought, he wouldn't be here, nor would the assault force have the chopper and weapons, and maybe this little soiree wouldn't have a prayer. "LaRue, Joel will ride with me tonight, okay?"

LaRue nodded his head several times vigorously and said, "McCaul, you have about as much authority on our force as anyone but Machado. You say he comes, then he comes."

Kate said, "Mike, what about me? I'm going with you too."

Mike needed to try to stop her, but he knew his resistance would be difficult if not futile, so he decided to try logic. "Kate, there's a truck going back to Havana, I'm sorry. There ain't a chance in the world you can come with us, but maybe I can get you word on where the best action is once it starts. Besides, your story's no good without pictures so you have to stay with Boyd anyway."

She set her lips, "Mike, if you let me down on this, I'll bloody well have your balls for bookends." She paused. "Just kidding. I like your balls."

"Kate, I promise. Here's my sat phone, I'll get another and call you the minute things have begun happening."

"Mike!"

"Kate, the truck's leaving, go now or stay here."

She shook her lovely head angrily, but grabbed her bundle, shoved the phone in her backpack and ran down the hill to join Boyd and jumped on the back of the two-ton. She was off.

Ronaldo had returned and was standing by his rotor craft sucking on a Red Bull. Mike wondered for a second how middle of the night assaults had ever worked before the high potency liquid was invented. They had had caffeine pills in his younger days but they didn't work all that well and weren't nearly as chic.

Machado was martialling his men and Ronaldo and McCaul followed LaRue to the chopper. Manuel, Gomez, Garza and Ernesto were already there with the soon to be new Jefe.

Machado followed them into the Sikorsky, "Hombres, Let's go! Vayamos."

When they boarded there were already a dozen stalwarts aboard including the gunner with his forage cap ready to man the Gatling gun and another, obviously his loader.

Ronaldo, wearing his gaudy chopper helmet got them off the ground in about a half-minute and they soared into storm clouds forming over the Pinar del Rio mountain range and around various collections of mogotes until they levelled off and headed to Havana.

The trip was bumpy but short; maybe only thirty minutes, but there was considerable turbulence. Except for the sound of the rotors, a pin could have been dropped and maybe spooked the team members. The feeling of anticipation and smell of sweat and adrenaline with a tinge of fear filled the cabin.

Before they could see any of what passed for the lights of Havana they were on the ground in what seemed to be a pineapple field. They exited quickly into a cleared patch, trying their best to stay dry in a steady drizzle.

As soon as they were free of the rotors Ronaldo was gone again, his gunner ready to defend Cuban liberty at a rate of 120 fifty-calibre rounds a minute. An ancient blue panel truck awaited them on the ground. Not a chariot to paradise, more like a jalopy to no man's land, but whatever it was, it was their next ride to immortality. But hardly a suitable steed for a conquering collection of heroes.

They crammed into the truck and bumped over the pineapple farm for about twenty minutes, up an incline and onto what seemed from the back of the truck to be a road, of sorts. A couple of Mike's compañeros smoked cigars while a bottle of rum was passed around. It was finished and another took its place.

Before long the road got smooth and they pulled to a stop and disembarked. They were in a grove of trees and there were a couple of different coloured Ladas parked there.

Machado explained the order in which each commander would travel to their meeting places. Ernesto, Joel, Manuel, Sanchez and McCaul were to be transported last and he told them to wait. Garza and Gomez got in the blue jalopy and left. Machado and Lopez stayed in the panel truck and it took off, then LaRue jumped in the red Lada and roared away in a cloud of fumes.

Ernesto still had a bottle of Havana Club, and the four members of McCaul's team swapped it back and forth and they all opened Red Bulls. They didn't talk. They all had cigars, Ernesto and Joel's were both lit; Mike was about smoked out so he chewed on his.

McCaul looked at the ground and thought about what he had gotten himself into. He realized he hadn't gotten another phone from LaRue, so he couldn't call Kate and she'd be steamed at him, if he was still around to be steamed at. Mike kind of hoped she yelled and screamed at him and called him nasty things when they got together again. He hoped they got together again.

When he was a kid in Airborne, the times that he had been at risk in the Balkans, he hadn't cared. He had been looking for adventure and he'd found it. Now he was really, really hoping he lived to love another day.

Ernesto was praying.

Mike wasn't very religious. He'd gone to Sunday school when he was a kid, but it hadn't stuck.

In Regina, at the RCMP Training School, one of his fellow cadets had taken him to a Pentecostal service one time and he had marvelled at the light that shone from the faces of the members of the congregation. He remembered how the hymns had inspired him, although he didn't know the words, and how some of the older women, all in hats, had been in a kind of rapture; waving arms above their hats to heaven, some on their knees, others prostrate at the altar.

Mike realized he didn't know how to pray.

Mike thought of saying the Lord's Prayer. He knew most of the words, but didn't feel at ease reciting them. He wasn't sure if the version he would use was the Catholic version of not.

Mike gave up. If there was a higher power, McCaul put his future in His, or Her, hands.

Mike rationalized what he was doing; he thought that since he was to some day die, this was as good a night and place as any. And if not, then it would be at another time, in another place.

But he also knew that his fate was not entirely his own, unless he decided to cut and run. And Canadians don't do that. But he still didn't want to die.

The panel truck returned and Ernesto, Manuel, Canto, Joel and McCaul rose. Mike tossed the empty rum bottle away and they got aboard.

Their roles were about to be played. If all worked well, in about an hour or two Mike thought, 'I'll meet Raul again'.

31

THEY HAD BEEN, UNBEKNOWNST TO MCCAUL, in a heavily wooded area not far from the Havana airport. They puttered along Boyeros through a dark and, except for the invaders, silent, Havana. They were still weaponless, so if they had been stopped by the PNR they would have been bothered but quickly released; they looked and smelled like four drunks returning from an evening Cuban fiesta.

Soon they veered west onto San Francisco and were driving past the opulent diplomat occupied homes in Miramar. This was better lit than most of the city and once they got onto 5th Avenue Mike was able to make out the string of beautiful ambassadorial residences and fairly modern hotels. But with a storm coming in, the streets were empty and almost all the lights were off.

McCaul hadn't spent much time in this part of the city since he had re-located to Havana. He had visited the Canuck embassy a few times for paperwork; that was about it.

Fifth Avenue through Playa Miramar reminded him of Miami except for the lack of drunken and stylish revellers. Plus, Miami would be hopping at midnight and this place was quiet with little traffic.

The palm trees were blowing almost sideways in the wind and little drops of rain were starting to splash the windshield. Mike thought back to the Santerian priestess who had warned him of the weather.

Mike thought that a big tropical storm worthy of a name wouldn't hurt their chances. If the defenders of the Castro regime were hunkered down and trying to protect their lawn furniture, then they wouldn't have a lot of time and energy to repel revolutions.

A few miles later they turned north and drove along a narrow dirt road and stopped. McCaul checked his watch; it was 1150. They had just over an hour to begin their part of the scheme. They left the panel truck and walked about 100 meters. Then McCaul almost fainted; there was a camo-painted and combat dressed Hadrian Felix.

"Compañero!" he said flatly with a Texan accent and without emotion.

Mike had to laugh and did.

"Felix, what in Christ's name are you doing here?"

"McCaul, you're allowed to call me Harry. You didn't think I was gonna let you have all the fun?" Not a hint of emotion. McCaul doubted that he and Felix shared the same definition of fun.

"Are you that deep inside this?"

"Comandante Machado and I go back a ways, McCaul. He even stayed in my apartment in New York for a while. He thought I might be able to help out a little. So I'm here on my own account, with my Canuck passport, so I'm your paisan tonight if I get caught."

"So what are we gonna do?"

"I'd like to be there to take down Raul. He's hurt some friends of mine so it's personal." He pointed down the path.

"It's my gig now, Felix. You're welcome to come along. But whoever gets the best shot takes it. What's Raul got in there?"

"He's got motion sensors around the boundary of his estate, so we have to go in the front door, but we're going through the jungle in the back way. I've got little gadgets with me that will disable the ones in front of the place.

"Raul usually keeps two guys at the front gate, and three guys in two command posts at both ends of his side street. He doesn't allow any guards in his hacienda so as far as we know he's only got his valet and maid in there with him tonight.."

McCaul's team was now five and a half guys, including Joel. Felix pointed them to a weapons cache and they each took Ka-Bar knives, silenced Tokarev sidearms, stockless AK-47 variants and two extra thirty-round magazines. There was camo grease paint in tubes and they all applied it liberally.

McCaul pulled Joel aside, "Joel, we're giving you the most important job."

"Yo, Comandante?"

"Si, Joel, usted, amigo. We need you to be our last chance to save us if we need to escape. When we finish our recon and start our assault you have to stay and cover our retreat. But you can't make any noise, and you can't use your gun unless someone is shooting at you. Entiende?"

"Entiendo, Comandante." McCaul helped Joel back toward their team. The Felix gang was gone and had left without a whisper.

Ernesto was their reconnaissance master, and he had a rough map for them to look at to have an idea of their route. They had to silently approach from about two hundred fifty meters and would come in behind the command post at the entrance to the street on which the Castro compound was located. Manuel, for a change, was quiet and looked serious.

Felix shoved an unlit stogie in his face, shouldered his weapon and led off. He was silent as a cat burglar, and the rest went in single file behind him. The wind and rain helped.

If Raul's famous Rottweilers were still alive and around, McCaul hoped they had colds because, even in the rain and wind, the men surely smelled to high heaven.

But every step they took had to be silent. Not just quiet; completely without sound. So they advanced at a speed that would see them overtaken by glaciers, once global cooling catches up with the world.

Every step they took came only after they had examined the ground ahead. They tried as best as they could to step exactly where their predecessors did and tested their footing before they applied their weight. They were careful to not spring a branch and snap their followers in the kisser.

After thirty minutes, Felix raised his arm and they stopped. McCaul turned to Joel, pointed at him and pointed at the ground and then held his finger to his lips. He nodded that he understood.

All the effort to conceal themselves was probably unnecessary; if there was anything to hear, short of a siren or alarm, Raul's guards wouldn't be able to hear it. The wind was howling.

Felix held up his hand to direct them to stop again and moved on by himself. He returned 5 minutes later and pulled out a hand drawn map. He drew the positions of the three guards and quietly told his comrades how they would each participate in the take down.

Felix, Manuel and McCaul pulled out their knives and crawled to within twenty meters of the eight by eight guard shelter. The wind gusted from the south and blew sheets of rain sideways. There were two guards in ponchos facing away from the wind, holding on to their hats. Ernesto turned around, pointed at his watch, and held up ten fingers and began counting down, finger by finger stopping at five. He touched Manuel and in five seconds they had crossed the road and finished the two Raulistas without a sound. Ernesto and Manuel looked through the shelter window and turned around looking confused. They ranged their sidearms side to side to look for the third guard. Felix shrugged.

At that moment there was a thrashing in the bushes, a cry and the sounds of a struggle to McCaul's left. He moved toward the sound and found Joel wrestling on the ground with the missing sentry, the guard's pants around his knees and Joel at risk of losing his knife to his victim. Mike charged in, finished Joel's adversary and pulled Joel to his feet. He was sweating and dirty and the rain was pouring down his face.

"Comandante, lo siento. I sorry, Comandante. I see him come into bushes to use tocador. I think it best I get him and not let him go back out."

Joel had saved the first part of their night, if the guard had had a chance to wipe, return to his post and sound an alarm, they might have been done for.

"You did real good, Joel, muy bien, amigo. Gracias, Muchos gracias, mi Compañero." McCaul slapped his back and returned his high five. They rejoined the men. "Joel, you have to defend the command post and protect our retreat with your life, okay?"

"Hokay, Comandante." McCaul shook his hand and the kid disappeared back into the bushes.

The team had another ten minutes of stealth ahead of them and moved back into the bushes. Their next time check was 0040. All of them listened intently as they moved; especially for gunshots, which would cause a drastic change in their strategy. If there was gunfire from either of their incursions, they were to launch an immediate assault. Not having had the chance to destroy the comm systems, this would almost certainly mean the end for all of them.

They came to their second destination and were about fifty meters from the main gates and its two green ponchoed army guards. It was an easy sniper shot, but a very long pistol shot especially with a silenced weapon and the weather.

They were on the other side of the road and the terrain on their side of the road was covered by huge trees. The shots wouldn't be easy with the rain and wind, but given two taps of a trigger fairly certain.

Felix and McCaul carefully moved ahead of the team to a place just across the road from the guards. Both guards were obviously distracted by the weather. Their ponchos were high on their necks, their helmets pulled low and their rifles hidden underneath their weather gear.

Felix pointed at McCaul to take the lead. He crawled to as close as he could and carefully aimed.

They were candy; down before they knew what was happening. Once they dropped, Manuel and Canto left the trees and pulled the bodies under cover and took their places with ponchos borrowed from their previous adventure only a few seconds before.

The way was clear. Felix dug through one of the dead guards pockets and failed to find a key, but he was prepared. He had bolt cutters and in a minute had sliced through a section of the fence about twenty meters from the gate that was partially covered by low palms. McCaul rushed across the road to join him and they hurried through the gap in the fence and were inside.

They were about thirty yards from the house and ran to the front door. Three shots from McCaul's silenced Tokarev, a side kick, and the door opened to silence. Not a peep.

One map they didn't have was the inside of Raul's house, but it wasn't a big place; probably go for about five million in Rosedale, which would position it as a nice home on a nice cul de sac. He couldn't be far away, and he must have earplugs; or he was calling in air cover from a panic room while he prepared his escape.

Within the silence was the smell of a cigar. None of McCaul's guys had one lighted up and he'd read somewhere Raul had quit years ago. McCaul wondered what was up. He shrugged at Felix.

They wandered through a wide hallway toward the source of the smoke. McCaul signalled to Felix to wait. Mike entered a library, and there was a trail of smoke arising from in front of a high armchair the back of which he was facing.

"Entrez-vous, mon ami."

269

It couldn't be. McCaul hoped it wasn't; but he knew it was.

"Asseyez-vous, Monsieur McCaul."

McCaul turned to Felix and gave him a 'what the fuck' expression. He walked carefully around the chair to face he who had been McCaul's friend and brother in arms.

LaRue was dressed civvy; once more a young Trudeau. A glass of red wine in hand, with the bottle on a table in front of him, along with an extra glass. "Have a glass of wine with me, Mike, as comrades."

McCaul ignored him; thought for a second of plugging him with a 9 mm round. He holstered his weapon.

"Your men can leave peacefully, we know who they are and where they live." He took a sip and poured another glass and topped up his own.

"Please join me, it's an excellent Bordeaux. Raul doesn't drink, but he keeps an excellent cellar." He passed to McCaul the other glass of wine and Mike accepted it. He couldn't believe the treachery he was witnessing first hand.

"Don't worry, Mike, you will be safely returned to Rosedale, and Señor Gant's son will be allowed to expatriate safely. And your friend, Felix, will be offered a speedboat to travel to the Keys if he wants, as we enjoy a glass of wine together. We can't afford to have him arrested as a CIA agent." He drank.

"Mike, have a seat. I have a story."

Mike sat and he listened, wine untasted.

"My cousin, Machado, is now on his way to Villa Marista for an examination with Eugenio Famosa. Most of the rest of Machado's men are dead, captured or soon will be."

McCaul finally gave in and swallowed a large mouthful of the Bordeaux and said, "Why, LaRue? Where did your lies start? What's real and what isn't?"

"Mike, I was in the Canadian Army for fourteen years. I served my adopted country loyally and with bravery in Yugoslavia, in the Arabian Gulf and in Afghanistan. But my home is Cuba, and my future is here."

"But, why wouldn't you have had that with Machado? With a free government?"

"This whole affair wasn't mine, McCaul, and it wasn't Machado's. It was Fidel's as much as anyone else's. Every five or ten years he starts a counter-revolution to smoke out all of his enemies. So he actually started this off and we took it over. This little adventure was particularly useful as it also cleansed the island of the Arab scum who were using Cuba to cause trouble with the USA, which would cause more trouble for Fidel and Raul. And it revealed Machado as a traitor.

"This way Fidel got the Arab money without having to supply merchandise in return. Fidel is dead, Mike. And he might have been loco, but he wasn't stupid."

"What's the connection, LaRue? How did you get tied up in this?"

"Simple, Fidel called me when he was in Montreal for a diplomatic mission. He told me he knew of me and wanted to explain about my father's death sentence and offer his apologies personally.

"I was honoured, so we visited and he was immensely charming. He told me his own children were failures or traitors and asked if I might be a son to him.

"Fidel told me Che had demanded Camilo's death and arranged it. Fidel told my father about this and arranged for him to leave Cuba.

"This showed Fidel how crazy Che was, so Fidel sent him to Bolivia to get him out of the way. He leaked Che's location so that the CIA could have Che's blood on their hands, instead of his own. Fidel even wrote Che's farewell letter to the Cuban people."

McCaul nodded, "and he offered to make you his successor."

"Eventually. After we met many times. Like many French Canadians I vacationed in Cuba frequently and I would drop in to renew our acquaintance when I did.

"I don't believe for a second that Fidel has ever done a single good thing for the Cuban people. I think he refuses to admit he has ever made a mistake and always blames someone else for every problem. Raul will be no different.

"I think my father, if he had lived, would have been a good advisor to Fidel and have helped him evolve the revolution into a form beneficial to Cubans. Fidel, on his own, has been a complete disaster. Perhaps I can help change things."

"How did you manage to prevent the Machado raids from succeeding at least a little?"

"McCaul, none of the rockets were armed. His men were almost unarmed. All were met by Cuban Special Forces troops when they reached their destinations. We knew where they were going and their way of getting there so they were all arrested."

"Tell me the truth, LaRue, don't you have the blood of Machado's men on your hands? And if you love Cuba so much, why not give Machado a chance?"

"McCaul, he and they would be no better than Fidel's motley band back in the fifties. They would have been spoiled by the power as Fidel's men were, and done nothing for the Cuban people. They too would have fed themselves and their own instead of the peasants. And in four or forty years someone would have to have another revolution to remove them. The last thing Cuba ever needs is another revolution."

"And you think you'll be different?"

"McCaul, I am not the narcissist that Fidel was. His glorious revolution will end with him. Raul will be retired soon enough and I will succeed him, and within thirty days I will begin negotiations to restore full diplomatic relations with the United States of America. I will restore the US dollar as our only currency and invite the US and other western countries to propose investments in Cuba that will provide profits for them and economic development for Cubans. I will even allow the American Cubans to take back their properties. Who knows? Perhaps I will be the first state governor someday."

McCaul sat back in his chair, emptied his glass and savoured the deep flavour of Raul's wine. He thought of Ernesto and his quiet intelligence, his efficiency in leading their way through the woods and his ability to quickly kill. And Machado's charisma and his unyielding dedication to building a new Cuba based on religion, music and culture with Brother Francisco Juan Lopez.

He thought of Joel, his wife, his baby and the dirt which their father's body would almost certainly soon be staining with blood. He wondered what the Pope would think and whether he could save any lives here.

McCaul reached to his side, pulled out his sidearm, released the safety and pointed it directly at LaRue's nose.

"Oh, McCaul, you can kill me if you wish. It will mean your death, of course. And Raul, when he dies, will pass on full authority to Famosa the butcher, Accardo the idiot or the Venezuelan Marxists will take over and make things worse. I don't think if you have developed any love for Cuba or Cubans during your stay here you will want me to die. I think you might even volunteer to be my bodyguard. But I leave that up to you. You can decide my destiny at this moment."

McCaul did.

He clicked his safety, reholstered his sidearm and left the room without a word or a look back to LaRue. He found Felix by the door and they exited the mansion to enter a maelstrom.

32

THEY WERE IN THE MIDDLE OF A HURRICANE he learned later was called Diane. Palms were bending sideways.

Manuel and Canto were still serving as doormen when Felix and McCaul left the house. They collected them and they all double timed back the way they had come an hour before.

The winds were probably a hundred klicks an hour and the rain was a solid wall before them. They should have checked the Weather Network before they started their revolution to at least be able to swear at the storm by name.

McCaul staggered and they had to slow up and walk head down to make any progress. Right at the place they had taken down the guards Mike saw movement in the bushes and raised his sidearm and saw Joel stagger out. He was dirty and his combats were soaked and he looked like a drowned rat.

"Señor, Comandante!"

"Hola, Amigo."

"Cómo se? How it go?"

"No asi, Amigo. Very bad."

He had no sign of injury, but his eyes went dead. He had enough savvy to know that if they had done their job that there would have been fireworks and signs of a celebration. McCaul thought that he was thinking his life would soon end and his wife and baby would be treated as traitors to the revolution and never rise from Cuba's lowest level of poverty.

"Señor, it is then all over." McCaul put his arm around him and they hugged. He was crying.

Mike said, "Amigo, everything will be all right," but McCaul knew that it wouldn't be.

"Hermanos, let us pray for our souls." Manuel had taken it on his shoulders to bring a little hope to the squad.

Mike still didn't know how, but he kneeled beside Manuel and the others followed his lead, and together they made separate peace with their higher powers. Mike stood and Felix and he looked at each other and nodded. They muttered goodbyes to each other and Felix left.

Ernesto had recovered a military poncho and plain green baseball cap of one of the dead sentries and would play the role of his life for his own survival for the next few days. He nodded at Manuel and Joel, and beckoned to Canto, to come with him and they started off on their own.

Manuel was still wearing his Cuban army weather gear from serving as a fill-in sentry at Raul's. Joel and McCaul collected the hats and the remaining poncho from the dead guards in the bushes and along with Manuel started a trek to what they hoped might be safe ground.

McCaul followed Manuel and he headed what Mike thought was east and a little south, using any cover and foliage they could, not that caution was needed; the storm absorbed them and they were totally wrapped up in it, unable to perceive any event or activity outside. If they were mere feet from a machine gun nest they couldn't have been noticed.

Fronds from royal palms were flying past their heads and sheet metal, torn off of Miramar's relatively chic residences, were loudly flapping against the structures they were attached to before flying off and smashing into trees. There wasn't a light to be seen; Havana's electric system failed often enough in good weather, it didn't have a chance in bad.

They also didn't see any people. McCaul had heard that Cuba was world class when it came to evacuating people during a hurricane. He had always figured it was an easy thing to accomplish with as many cops in a place as non-cops and a population with nothing to have looted. But whatever the case, the streets of this part of Havana were empty.

McCaul's own place wasn't too far away from where they started and Mike thought he'd follow these guys as far as the Hotel Nacional and get cleaned up before he went to find Kate.

It took them over two hours of slogging to make it through the storm to get near the Nacional. It was exhausting, but there was still much to do. Although they saw no one, on foot or in cars, they tried to be hidden as best as they could.

"Amigos, I am going to leave you to clean up and change. Joel, I can see you at Parque Centrale in two hours. Manuel."

"Señor, I'll be there."

McCaul removed as much of his combat clothing as he could and tossed it under foliage. They all hugged and Mike left them to carry on. He scrubbed the camo paint from his face on the way up the hill to his place. Wouldn't do to have his neighbours see him in his commando persona.

No one was on the street so it was easy for McCaul to sneak into his building. The exterior shutters were closed; Janisleyda would have made sure nothing in his place was damaged. Mike noticed the hum from his noise suppressed battery operated generator and he turned on a table lamp. He poured a water glass of aged rum, drank it down and stripped. He refilled the glass of rum and then his belly with the contents.

He started the shower and sat under it for a half hour. He washed off what remained of his camo paint and shaved. For a time, with the water dousing the top of his head and the rum taking effect, he forgot about the predicament he had gotten into, but then he returned to reality. After he finished towelling off he thought about calling Webster but realized he wasn't yet ready for that conversation.

McCaul dried off and threw on a tee shirt, cargo pants and hiking boots; he wasn't likely to find a cab to go to the Telegrafo. He was thinking that he might not be back, so he went through his place looking for anything that might cause him or anyone else trouble. There were a few slips of paper with notes that he burned in the sink. He smashed his laptop.

He filled a knapsack with anything that might be useful to Joel and his family: clothing, a couple of watches, a bag of medications and other commodities and clothing.

He filled his pockets with granola bars, cigars, matches and the bottle of rum, pocketed his passport, locked the place up and went down the stairs and into the street.

Dawn was breaking, but it had no effect on the power of the storm that was assaulting Havana. The only relief was that anything that the winds could pull off had been pulled off and blown into the sea. The landscape, which only a day before was plush, now looked mostly nude. But like Cubans, the palm trees had bent rather than broke.

He pulled the knapsack over his shoulder and started the trek east on Neptuno which was mostly sheltered from the wind. All the windows were boarded up and the doors were barred shut so there wasn't yet a sign of life.

Protected from the wind, except when he crossed avenues, he had lots of time to ponder what had just happened and what was likely to occur. He wasn't very optimistic.

Fidel and Raul had publicly softened their public positions on almost everything in the last few years. But even a little bit of examination revealed the truth. They were still jailing dissidents, but mostly those without the constituency, numbers and energy to cause problems. Women in White were harmless, just bad press. The hip-hopping black kids were being left alone.

And the new economic opportunities they were offering to people in opening restaurants, B&Bs and small businesses were just designed to take people off their government payroll and make more black market hustlers into tax payers. If Manuel made it through the next few days, he'd have a lot more competition.

Mike thought he'd see what he could do for Joel; he had no doubt that Manuel had already maneuvered himself to safety. For now he needed to find Kate and make sure she was okay.

As he approached Parque Centrale and left shelter, the storm became more apparent. He staggered along the Prado against the wind to the hotel.

He had to come up with a scheme that might save at least the lives of Joel and his family, not to mention another to rescue Kate and get his own ass to safety.

McCaul was almost blown toward the Telegrafo but managed to find his feet, regain his composure and enter the hotel.

There wasn't a bellman in sight, which was good because McCaul looked like a drowned rat. Lobby staff were nowhere to be found, maybe in the back room playing high stakes poker, drinking Moet Chandon or something. More likely just somewhere that they couldn't get blown into a wall. But the Telegrafo was safe; it had survived a hundred or so big storms in its day. Its reno was water-tight and it was likely as safe as Fidel's bunker.

He walked through the bar and crept up the staircase to avoid tell-tale elevator noise and knocked on Kate's door.

"Who is it?"

"Fidel."

"McCaul, you rat. You didn't call; I was up until three a.m. waiting for it," she said.

"I'm sorry."

"Tell me what happened?", she said.

"It didn't go well. LaRue set us up. Most of the men are dead, the rest soon will be. I think Machado will be publicly hung. I can't tell you more, but will when we're out of here. Let me in."

"Sorry, yeah, yeah, come in." She opened the door.

Kate's hair was tousled; she was wearing pajama bottoms and a halter-top. She looked stunning and reached up to Mike and hugged. He hugged back. She held him close.

"What are you going to do?" She said.

"I'm going back to Toronto." He talked quietly to her. "You have any cash?"

She said, "Do you need it?"

"A friend of ours does. Do you have a way out yet?" He said.

She said, "I was just told to stay in here until things got settled down. I got a week's supply of ham sandwiches and a case of Cristal beer. I suspect Boyd has got a bigger cache. We're supposed to meet at oh nine hundred to get some video of the hurricane."

"You got a bigger story, now. But probably best that you don't tell it."

"Whaddaya mean?"

"More people will die if the story gets out before said people get out. The story will still be a good one in a day or two. There's nobody else here that will tell it."

She looked skeptical. "Okkkaaaaay... You got forty eight hours."

He said, "Money?"

"I've got a little over seven hundred dollars. Who's it for?"

"A friend has to get himself and his family out."

"Can't you get them out on the chopper?" she said.

He shook his head. "According to LaRue, Ronaldo's safe but his Seek is grounded. I gotta find something else."

"I wish I could do something." She opened her closet door and her safe, pulled out a wad of cash and gave it to him. "Can I make some calls? Maybe I can get your people a haven at the Canadian consulate or at the US Embassy."

"I don't think so, Kate. This thing didn't officially happen, but thanks."

She rose up and kissed his cheek. "Be careful, Mike. I'd kind of like to see you when we get back."

"Me too." He hugged her again, gave her a long wet kiss, and left.

McCaul took the elevator to the lobby. He still had the hotel room that LaRue had arranged and thought about checking out but then thought, 'screw him'. He expected they had LaRue's credit card and he'd get dinged for the room. Good.

For the first time, while the storm was slowing, there wasn't a Panataxi or cyclo-cab in sight. He walked across the Prado to the park benches to try and find Joel. No one was sitting around arguing about baseball.

Joel found Mike first. He'd mostly cleaned his face, and had torn off all his combat clothes except for a risqué pair of green shorts. They found a spot on the leeward side of the Marti statue, but McCaul still had to shout to be heard. Mike opened the knapsack and gave him the clothes he brought him to change into and the kid slipped them on over his shorts.

Mike was about to give him the cash and leave him to his own devices.

"What will you do, Joel?" McCaul said.

He shrugged and replied with the universal unspoken: 'I have no effin idea' expression.

McCaul knew he didn't have money. "Joel, you okay?" He nodded. Mike clasped his hand, pulled him close for a hug and passed him a roll of bills.

McCaul was about to leave; get to the airport, and get to safe ground in Toronto.

But all the money in the world wouldn't solve Joel's problems or save his life. Raul would be looking for scapegoats and people to execute and Joel would certainly be held up as an example to young Cubans who might cast an envious eye across the Strait of Florida.

Mike asked, "Amigo. Where do you live?"

"Yo? I live not far. In Centro with mi Madre."

"Where is your baby and wife?" Mike asked.

"They are with mi wife's Madre," he said. "Next casa to mi casa."

"Let's get them."

They stood and staggered across the Prado and past the Telegrafo down San Rafael where only a few days before Mike had fallen in love with ballet and back in love with Kate.

Mike hoped Joel's families hadn't already been arrested by the PNR and taken to prison. Hopefully Joel had instructed them to wait for his return as a conquering hero. Hopefully they hadn't been evacuated. Hopefully Famosa wasn't there waiting for them.

After about a half hour dodging deadly hurricane powered missiles they turned a corner into the teeth of the gale and up a hill. A door about nine feet tall was held open on one building, its latch broken by the wind, and Joel went inside. McCaul followed and managed to pull the door closed behind him. There was a length of rope attached to its handle and Mike tied it closed as strongly as he could to a spike driven into the door frame for just that purpose.

They were in a dilapidated hall with a beautiful but decaying mosaic floor, a checkerboard wall of ceramic tiles in various states of repair and a cathedral ceiling and a staircase that rose about three stories. The wind was howling and the big door continued to bang in its frame even while secured firmly.

Joel said, "In back, Señor. My baybee ees in back."

He rushed there and McCaul followed.

Joel turned left under the stairs and pounded on one of those amazing 10 foot high doors. He knocked again and it was opened. They went in.

Joel deeply hugged a beautiful young light skinned woman and moved aside to introduce Mike. "Elena, thees is my friend, Señor McCaul. He rescue us now from Raul."

Elena came over and hugged McCaul and thanked him effusively in advance for doing something that he had no idea how he was going to do. "Señor McCaul, you are a hero to us. We thank you in our prayers always."

McCaul wondered how long "always" would be. "I will do what I can, Elena. Can I make a telephone call, Joel?"

"Of course, Señor McCaul, but we have no telephone." Mike showed him his satellite unit, and he motioned toward a room at the back of the apartment. Mike checked for a signal and had three bars; good enough. He dialed the Hotel Nacional and asked for Steve Harper.

He was about to give up when it was answered. "Felix."

"Felix, how ya doing?"

"Call me Harry. I'm okay. Been in worse jams. They let ya live, did they? They told me that, but you can't trust any of them commie bastards." As Mike was growing used to, Felix always spoke with a little more whimsy than his dour appearance suggested he would.

"Felix, how many can I take out with me?"

"You're asking me? I'm the last one down here can give you permission. Call me Harry."

"How you getting out?", McCaul asked.

"Now that would be something that we spooks refer to as a secret, pal."

"Come on, Harry, you guys are behind all this, you've gotta look after some of the collateral damage."

"We can't keep track of each fallen robin, McCaul."

"They're not robins, Harry, they're people and you got them into this."

"Actually, McCaul, you got them into this, if my memory still works," he said.

"Okay, you're right, but you'll get me out, won't ya? Tell ya what, you take a family of three and leave me to find my own way home."

"That isn't part of the deal with them, McCaul. We're not allowed to take any nationals out and we sure as heck don't have permission to bring any back to the States."

Mike tried to think quick to come up with some leverage he could apply. "Felix, here's what I'm going to do. I am going to go live on CNN at noon and reveal that the CIA Bay of Pigs Two to overthrow the Castros was defeated."

"You do that, McCaul, and we ain't friends any more. Everything's off the table."

McCaul was angry. "Felix, exactly what do I have to lose? Be in a show trial in Havana? Be in a show trial in Miami? Ain't worth it."

"You're a stubborn fuck, McCaul. Get your wetbacks to Marina Hemingway in Miramar at 1600 hours. We got safe passage for your friend Ronaldo to fly us across the Strait to Florida. You're on your own," he said.

McCaul said, "You're on and there better be a friendly Immigration and Naturalization geek in Miami."

"Yeah, sure." He hung up.

McCaul walked out into the main room. "Joel, pack your stuff. You're on your way to Florida. You need to be at Hemingway Marina before four o'clock this afternoon and ask for Señor Felix. You know where that is?"

Joel smiled broadly, danced for a moment, and nodded.

Mike gave him his Globalair business card along with all the cash he had left, except for cab fare to the airport, his exit visa and some food. Not enough, but a start.

"I hope I see you and your family in Toronto, Joel. You've got a job offer from my company and my phone number and address is here. I don't know if this will work or not, but if it doesn't maybe there's enough money here to get your family to a safe place. I'll buy you plane tickets to Toronto from anywhere if you get off this island."

"Señor, what can I say?"

"Hasta la vista works, amigo."

They embraced and, with the storm finally starting to moderate, McCaul made his way back to the Telegrafo to get a taxi.

Sitting in Francesa's pastry place next door was Manuel, again dressed for the disco in his black linen suit. "Amigo!" McCaul smiled and nodded. The place was opening for business and the waiter who had served Mike before brought him a Café Americano after he sat down without being asked.

"Was a bad night, Manuel."

"I guess for some, McCaul. For me, it means I wait a while longer." They saluted with their coffees and took long drinks and sat on the couch. Mike signaled for two more and asked for rum on the side.

"Can you help any of the combatants?" McCaul asked.

He said, "I will help some. Most are peasants and I have no real interest in them. Machado will be hung. Those with resources and friends will not be charged."

"You know Joel?"

He nodded, "He is a bright young man. I like him."

McCaul said, "Can you get him a car and a driver and maybe a bodyguard at his place to go to the Marina Hemingway before four this afternoon?"

He mashed his thick lips together and nodded. "I will do that. He's a good boy. I know where he lives."

"What's next?"

The waiter arrived with two more coffees and two good sized shots of dark rum.

"Yo? I keep doing what I do, Comandante. Raul and his top people, even Famosa, will not bother me, I have enough money and power to be protected."

They each swallowed their rums. "They won't be around much longer and their successors will have bigger problems than worrying about how restaurants get their brandy."

McCaul didn't know how to leave it. Manuel had been good company, but everything he did was calculated for his own benefit. It was strange to find capitalism successfully at play in the last remaining Marxist state.

They both stood and the Cuban broke into a huge smile. "Amigo, I want you to know that you will always be my friend and it isn't always about making money. But it's always nice to make money when you're having fun."

McCaul chuckled. "You too, Compañero. I'll be back and buy the next round."

They hugged and slapped each others' backs and Manuel ambled out of the pasty place and across the park. He stuck McCaul with the bill and he gave the waiter a ten CUC bill.

The Prado was getting back to its normal self. There were even a few baseball fans hanging around under the Jose Marti statue.

McCaul wandered out to the street, got in a cab in the tail end of a hurricane and a failed revolution and told the driver to take him to the airport.

Mike paid the cab driver and looked around until he found a lonely passenger agent to check him in for a flight. After getting a boarding pass, he stood in line for a few minutes and hauled out his passport to purchase a resident exit pass and cleared security.

As it worked out, Globalair had had a 737 stuck in Havana before the storm had broken out and had tied it down. Unfortunately, for them, about a hundred and twenty passengers had been stuck in the airport for almost eighteen hours among with a few hundred others.

The mass of travellers had eaten out the entire food rations that the terminal had in stock and looked like refugees. Unmade-up women wearing expensive fashions from Banana Republic were sprawled out on benches with their hair unwashed and stringy; most having given up trying to look glamorous for their return home.

Many of the men were sitting beside stacks of emptied coffee cups and at least a couple of empty duty-free purchased bottles of rum. The smoking section was filled with unrepentant born again smokers hauling on their cigars, many with IPODs blasting in their ears while they drank Havana Club directly from the bottle.

All in all, vacationer hell. But a little over six hours later, the airport was re-opened, they boarded and he returned to Toronto.

33

MIKE HAD ALWAYS LIVED ALONE. He kept his place in Toronto as a safe haven and place of respite as well as an investment. But when he left for Havana he'd gotten a room mate.

Toronto is a world-class movie city, appearing as every possible place but itself and McCaul's place had been rented for filming. The lead actor in the show absolutely had to buy it and after Mike declined, his agent pleaded with him until Mike finally allowed his client-actor to move in and pay rent. He agreed, which gave him a place to stay while filming in Toronto. It also provided a live-in gardener for the grounds: Mike's roommate had a lot of time off, and loved to work around the house. Josh Tanner was stunningly handsome, women always told Mike, and had a starring role in a series filmed in Toronto called "Victim of Fashion". It was about a male model turned private detective. Mike had no idea how they dreamt these ideas up.

Josh wasn't around when Mike got home a little after seven pm and he slept until about noon and then called Webster.

Jud's major domo, Clarence, answered, "Webster residence."

"Clarence, is Jud in?"

"Mr. McCaul, it is so good to hear your voice. Yes, would you like to speak with him?" When Mike replied in the positive Clarence apologized for putting him on hold and he listened to Joni Mitchell singing about paving paradise for about twenty seconds."

"Mike, my boy, you're back?"

"Yes, Boss. It went really bad."

"What do you mean, Son? It almost couldn't have gone any better. You're a bloody hero."

McCaul shoot his head, his eyes shot wide open and his jaw dropped. "Huh?"

"Yes, you're a bloody hero. I just got off the phone with the Minister. Our friend LaRue has positioned himself as Raul's most important confidant and successor. My boy, Cuba will be brought into the community of nations a lot quicker than anyone ever could have expected."

"You mean..."

"Well, I didn't know what was going on, but Earl certainly did. The Secretary of State called him this afternoon with the good news. LaRue has already been in touch with the U.S. Secretary as well. LaRue will be pushing Raul to give amnesty to all the combatants, except Machado, of course. Only a couple of dozen men were killed, an almost peaceful transition, I'd say."

McCaul was awestruck and pissed at the same time. He had been wrung in a ball and hung out to dry by his government even worse than he had been with the Mountie scandal. He had been manipulated and tossed around like a maple leaf in the wind.

"I don't know what to say, Jud."

"Listen, Mike, Manny Gant is over here having a glass of wine and a bite if you'd like to join us. I've never seen the old fart so happy. Oh, and he's looking forward to seeing his son, although I doubt his wife is..."

"I think I'll pass, Jud."

McCaul put on a sweater and walked down Bloor Street to Parliament and south into Cabbagetown until he got to Ben Wicks pub and drank beer with Robert, Mark, Doug, Bruce and his twin Alec until he started to get sleepy and went home to bed.

He started normalizing his life after a couple of days. Josh showed up along with an addition to their family, an eight pound Scottie pup named Henry. Kate had returned to Atlanta and they chatted on the phone, but there was nothing Mike could tell her. They promised to see each other soon, and she blew him a kiss over the phone.

About two weeks after his return home he was flipping through channels, Josh had returned to Los Angeles and McCaul's usual drinking buddy, Mepham, was working nights and he was kind of lonely.

He clicked on CNN for a moment and heard Kate's voice and left the channel there. Boyd's film showed a mass of people and zoomed into Raul Castro on a stage next to LaRue.

"Today the President of Cuba, Raul Castro, announced that he will retire in the next few months to spend more time with his family.

"The President also informed his people that Señor Lucien Camilo Cienfuegos will succeed him in his positions. In the interim, Señor Cienfuegos will act as Commander of the military and of the Interior Ministry.

"In other announcements Señor Castro advised his nation of the successful prosecution by the Cuban courts and the subsequent execution of one Carlos Machado for treasonable actions against the Revolution and that head of security, General Ramon Duarte Borges, was killed by security force for acts of treason.

"Observers do not expect any change to occur in Cuba as a result of these announcements."

She, and they, had no idea.

FINITO

AMERICANS DON'T HAVE A CIVILIAN HONOUR SYSTEM. The Brits hand out Knighthoods at Buckingham Palace. Canadians don't qualify, unless you're Conrad Black and give up your Canadian citizenship. But that comes with other costs.

In Canada, they don't have swords, or stars, or eagles or lions rampant. Canada's highest honour is suitably in the shape of a snowflake.

Their call came just as Mike had finished bowing his tie and making sure his hair, for a change, was correct. He was going to be on CPAC, the Canadian cable industry's sop to the government to get politicians on television and off their backs. He wanted to make sure he looked good for Canadian government archives.

They had only been back from Cuba for a month, and the Government of Canada tends to have a short memory, so Webster and Inglewood had arranged for a special ceremony.

Kate snuggled up next to him and gave him a fresh flute of Hillebrand Trius Brut. "Mike, it's time."

He put on his scarlet serge jacket. He had a new job; really an old job. RCMP Commissioner, Mike Cormier, Mike's former and new boss, had given him special permission, in advance of his re-engagement, to wear the Full Review Order of Dress, the whole kit, as the first Member of "The Force" to be inducted into the Order. He put on his brown leather gloves.

While sitting alone in his house a couple of nights before, Cormier had called him and asked him to come back. He wanted a Deputy Commish experienced in dealing with overseas hotspots. It would be a year or two, but he'd be involved in helping Cuba, Haiti and Jamaica evolve into functioning democracies. Mostly by cleaning out their criminals.

Kate put on her mink stole. She looked stunning: diamond teardrop earrings, her hair up and her gown off the shoulder.

A sharp knock came to the door and Mike walked across their Chateau Laurier suite to answer it.

A smartly uniformed sergeant and infantryman in dress greens saluted: "Michael McCaul. The Queen of Canada in the name of the Governor General of Canada summons you to attendance at Rideau Hall to be recognized for your contribution to Canada. Will you come with me, Sir?"

Mike didn't return his salute, he was hatless. Canadian officers don't salute every chance they get, like Americans do. They reserve it for special occasions and it must be done in certain ways.

"I will," he said. Kate had his Stetson, and he donned it. McCaul then ran his finger around the brim, as he liked to do and honoured his guardsmen with a Mountie salute; palm toward his counterpart. It was perfect.

They followed the sergeant to an open elevator; it was on service. He let them precede him and very smartly stood at attention after pushing the requisite buttons. Again he allowed them to move ahead as they exitted and he followed them to the front door where the Chateau's head doorman held the door for them. All done in absolutely proper carriage and form.

In front of the Chateau was a black stretch Cadillac and a requisitely correct driver, a lance corporal, holding the door for them. Kate entered first and Mike followed. The Sergeant sat in the "shotgun" seat up front.

Mike was to enter the Order. He hadn't really done his part to earn it all, as he'd promised. He hadn't done what he was hired to do, or at least what he thought he was hired to do.

But he figured Jud and Earl knew him well enough to know he'd get myself mixed up in LaRue's scheme, and that he would be there to pull anyone he found in trouble out it. Except Fidel. They knew what McCaul's opinion of him would be.

Maybe LaRue - or Cienfuegos as he was now known - would be able to guide a peaceful transition to a new Caribbean democracy. Maybe he would fulfill a destiny his father never got to do. Or maybe he'd get knocked off by a drug cartel hit squad or by some of the Castro's pissed-off cronies.

Mike didn't have a load of confidence in the happy outcome that he hoped would come for all his friends on his favourite communist island. He'd gotten over his initial anger, and he wasn't unhappy about how it worked out. He wasn't even unhappy with his part in it, and would never be, if it worked out.

They exited the Chateau roundabout and the driver maneuvered them through one-way streets and narrow alleys back along the Ottawa River and onto Rideau Drive. They were at Rideau Hall in about ten minutes.

They followed the long driveway, not really noticing very much of the country's finest building and gardens. Kate and he had held hands all the way but not talked: neither of them felt easy with the pomp and circumstance. They came to the front door and entered. Six aides de camp, army, air and navy, greeted them with snappy salutes.

Normally a hundred new members are inducted at a time in the Ballroom. For a one-off, they use the anteroom for the ceremony and the Gallery-Veranda for lunch.

They were preceded by their personal guard who marched perfectly in half second, thirty inch strides.

As they entered, their friends and the big boys were standing. Mike's old and new boss, Ed Cormier was there, also in his scarlet serge. The Prime Minister looking out of place, awkward as always, but with a nice smile. Earl Inglewood was next to them, his folded arms showing off his Cartier. Josh was beside him. Mepham looked uncomfortable being off-the-record and suffered standing between his wife Carol and the Chief Justice of the Supreme Court. McCaul's Globalair colleagues were there; Mrs. Hollis was next to their air service crew chief, Ellen Fontaine, more than fetching in a Princess Di veiled hat. Felix almost smiled as Mike walked by him.

Mike broke into a grin when he saw Joel and his wife, new Canadians thanks to the PM, alongside Ronaldo in the front row next to Earl, Webster and Emmanuel Gant. They shuffled aside and Kate joined them.

As there were no other Orders to be presented McCaul stepped forward on his own and stopped at the front of the room. The Governor General was to his left. The moment came.

The Chancellor of the Order of Canada spoke: "To Mike Anthony McCaul, candidate for the Order of Canada for protecting the well-being and security of Canada and its friends and allies.

"Mr. McCaul, a veteran of the Canadian Armed Forces and a member of the Royal Canadian Mounted Police has significantly contributed to the safety and security of Canada. His record of exemplary service is notable. As a private citizen, Mr. McCaul has protected the security of Canadians during their travel overseas. And, as a private citizen and volunteer, Mr. McCaul intervened to protect the security of friendly nations to a level of bravery that warrants the highest degree of honour from a grateful nation.

"Mr. McCaul, you are to be inducted as a Member of The Order of Canada."

McCaul's colleagues in The Force who had avoided him would now know that his demotion had been bollocks.

He properly marched to the left then turned to confront the Governor General, removed his Stetson, and bowed. The G.G. reached up, Mike shrugged a little lower and he hooked Mike's order medallion onto his left top pocket, shook his hand, and smiled with Mike to the photographer on their right. Mike replaced his hat, saluted the G.G. and very correctly marched to his left to sign the Register and pick up his scroll amidst applause. McCaul was for once nonplussed and speechless. He wandered toward the veranda amid and amongst his closest friends.

If they only knew.

Gordon Lightfoot, who had been a fairly regular chartreuse drinking pal of Jud's back in the day and who McCaul had known from the neighbourhood, played a special favourite for Mike, "If You Could Read My Mind." McCaul hoped nobody could.

At lunch an hour later, the Governor General introduced Chef Olivier Bartesh. The GG's wife made sure they were well provided with Canadian white wines from British Columbia and brave little reds from Niagara and a sparkling Trius that wasn't Krug but wasn't Baby Duck either.

When coffee came it was Jamaican Blue Mountain and the liquor was vintage Havana Club.

That's almost the end; except a small collection of members from the Afro Cuban All Stars started to play, led by Juan de Marco Gonzalez, courtesy of a Cuban big-shot. Not even the Governor General could resist. He showed a very presentable Samba.

The End

ABOUT THE AUTHOR

Brian Lloyd French was born in Eastern Canada and lives as a writer with his family in Toronto Beaches. He was taught to write at TRHS in Sackville, NB and at UNB Fredericton. He was previously a columnist with the Toronto Sun.

He has been travelling to Cuba for many years; from Pinar del Rio to Santiago de Cuba and in between and has friends from one end of the "Caribbean Crocodile" to the other. Most of these Cubanos are just ordinary people striving to do better, a few are athletes, a few more are musicians and some, well, some are a little frightening to people they don't like.

His novel: "Tintamarre!", is an epic that follows a French Acadian family from Nova Scotia to Louisiana and back in the mid-eighteenth century.

William Marshall, O.C., of Toronto International Film Festival fame and author of "Dreadlock" was of great help to the author in his work.

www.mojitonovel.com
www.tintamarrenovel.com
www.brianlloydfrench.com

PHOTO GALLERY

all photographs copyright Brian Lloyd French

(c) 2016

La Gran Teatro de La Habana

La Catedral

Paseo de Prado

v4

Hotel Telegrapho

Grupo de Damian Marrero

Maestro Osvaldo "Pipo" Perigo

The Author and El Supremo Mojito Man: Lafitta

La Malecon

La Prado

www.ingramcontent.com/pod-product-compliance
Lightning Source LLC
Chambersburg PA
CBHW031155050726
47495CB00019B/1743